PRAISE FOR *THREE*

"Martha Anne Toll's *Three Muses* is so surprisingly soulful. The surprise doesn't lie in the existence of textured prose that explores dance, music, love, and time in wholly different ways; it lies in how that textured prose actually creates a new time signature wholly dependent on practice and discipline. This is phenomenal writing. It just is."

–Kiese Makeba Laymon, bestselling author of *Heavy, How to Slowly Kill Yourself and Others in America: Essays*, and *Long Division*

"Martha Anne Toll's three muses are those of song, discipline, and memory. In this beautiful, dark novel, she has choreographed the mysterious ways these forces push and pull and shape the lives of her characters—lives of terrible loss and precious if dismaying survival—through their dissonances, harmonies, deprivations, and recoveries. A meditation on history, music, the catastrophic inheritances of the Holocaust, and the so common, painful hiddenness of hope itself, *Three Muses* captivates the reader from the first page to the last."

–Paul Harding, Pulitzer Prize winning author of *Tinkers* and *Enon*

"*Three Muses* is a tender, well-told story about how tragedies reverberate through the years and shape the course of two intersecting lives. This is a wonderful meditation on trauma and loss—and a love story in its own right."

–Lydia Kiesling, author of *The Golden State* and former editor (now contributing editor) at The Millions

"*Three Muses* is a hauntingly beautiful testament to the power of art and love. With exquisite craft, Toll writes about dance and music in sentences that sing. She is a writer to watch."

–Lara Prescott, *New York Times* bestselling author of *The Secrets We Kept*

"A grand generosity of spirit pervades this book, which weaves together threads of love, loss, memory, and art. Martha Anne Toll's *Three Muses* takes art seriously, delves deeply into the discipline and sacrifice it requires, and connects its transcendent power to the messy, quotidian world not just of artists and performers, but the audience as well... This is the rare book that looks behind the curtain with genuine empathy, insight, and love."

–Philip Kennicott, Pulitzer Prize winning art and architecture critic for the *Washington Post*, and author of *Counterpoint: A Memoir of Bach and Mourning*

"Delving deep into the heart of the human experience, Toll has given us a capacious and deeply felt novel about trauma and ambition, art, passion, and the vagaries of memory. *Three Muses* is a love story that isn't afraid to contend with difficult questions, a wise and compassionate meditation on beauty, loss, and the many invisible lives we might have lived."

–Michael David Lukas, author and winner of the National Jewish Book Award for the *Last Watchman of Old Cairo: A Novel*

"*Three Muses* is a beautiful story about art, love, and the generational traumas that lead to both for its central characters. Martha Anne Toll's prose jumps off the page and kept me engrossed from start to finish."

–Sopan Deb, New York Times writer, author of *Missed Translations: Meeting the Parents Who Raised Me* and *The Elm Tree*

"Martha Anne Toll's *Three Muses* follows two characters for whom, as children on opposite sides of the Atlantic Ocean, art functions as both a means to salvation, and as a burden that can come close to feeling like a curse. Beautifully written, and vivid with detail and insight, this novel is brimming with moments of kindness and light that thread through tapestries of loss and pain."

–Moriel Rothman-Zecher, author of *Sadness is a White Bird*, Finalist, National Jewish Book Award & Dayton Literary Peace Prize

"*Three Muses* is a beautifully written, lyrical novel, a meditation on the way the past haunts and shapes us. Following Katya and John across decades and continents, Martha Anne Toll weaves a gorgeous story of love and survival."

–Jillian Cantor, *USA Today* bestselling author of *Half Life*

"*Three Muses* is a love story with a deep heart—powerful, resonant, and ultimately affirming—a dance of memory, grief and healing, and the saving grace of art."

–Sari Wilson, author of *Girl Through Glass*

"Martha Anne Toll's *Three Muses* makes song out of the toughest things: the inevitability of grief, the difficult work of remembrance, the hard-won belief that our abandoners release us to ourselves… This is a wonder of a novel, intricate, involving, soulful, and full of awe at all the ways human beings manage to keep their love intact."

–Paul Lisicky, author of *Later: My Life at the Edge of the World*

"In *Three Muses*, Martha Anne Toll's magnetic storytelling pushes past the limits of longing, memory, and identity to bring us into the fully realized world of her characters. Where the ravages of Nazi concentration camps through a child's eyes are brought to life with as much vividness as the flowers and ballet of modern-day Paris, at its heart *Three Muses* is a dance through time. Fates intersect and love somehow finds a way…so too does a woman find her way back to herself."

–Morowa Yejide, author of *Creatures of Passage* and *The Time of the Locust*

"Martha Anne Toll's moving and accomplished debut is transporting, lyrical, and deeply provocative. With a nod to the legendary work of George Balanchine, *Three Muses* excavates the legacy of trauma, the cost of secrecy, and the complex entanglements of art and survival."

–Amy Gottlieb, author of *The Beautiful Possible*

"What a lyrical, exquisite novel! Two people seeking love and not daring to give in to it: a Holocaust survivor, now a wistful young psychiatrist in search of his identity, and a prima ballerina who has given up her own to reach perfect beauty. From the public wards of the mentally troubled to the world of ballet barres and a Seder where the ghosts of the dead speak louder than the living, *Three Muses* is a haunting story of who we love and why."

–Stephanie Cowell, author of *Claude and Camille: A Novel of Monet* and *The Boy in the Rain*

"This gripping story renders humankind at its worst and most tender. *Three Muses* is so deeply engrossing that readers won't want to emerge from the dream Toll has created."

–Michelle Brafman, author of *Bertrand Court* and *Washing the Dead*

"Martha Anne Toll has written a beautiful, gripping novel, *Three Muses*. It is a story that explores grief and sacrifice, longing and ambition, in the years and decades that follow World War II, at once a complex love story and a modern dance."

–Devi S. Laskar, author of *The Atlas of Reds and Blues*, winner of The Crook's Corner Book Prize and the Asian/Pacific American Award in Literature

"If one had to choose, would it be art or would it be love? In an ambitious novel that travels from the Holocaust to the Paris *Opéra*, from the intimacy of a psychiatric session to the intimacy of a love affair between a renowned choreographer and his principal dancer, *Three Muses* wrestles not only with the weight of memory and trauma, but also with the nature of creativity, the value of art, and the power of desire to bruise and heal."

–Laura McBride, author of *We are Called to Rise* and *In the Midnight Room*

THREE MUSES

Martha Anne Toll

Regal House Publishing

Published by
Regal House Publishing, LLC
Raleigh, NC 27587
All rights reserved

ISBN -13 (paperback): 9781646032563
ISBN -13 (epub): 9781646032570
Library of Congress Control Number: 2021949156

Interior by Lafayette & Greene
Cover design © by C. B. Royal

Regal House Publishing, LLC
https://regalhousepublishing.com

The following is a work of fiction created by the author. All names, individuals, characters, places, items, brands, events, etc. were either the product of the author or were used fictitiously. Any name, place, event, person, brand, or item, current or past, is entirely coincidental.

Printed in the United States of America

In memory of my parents

Jean Barth Toll (1925-1999)

Seymour ("Spence") Irving Toll (1925-2018)

Who gave me reading and writing and infinitely more

Muse of Song:	*Music's primal form.*
Muse of Discipline:	*Rigor, practice, and preparation for prayer.*
Muse of Memory:	*Transforming forgotten to feral quicker than an asp's sting.*

PARIS

1963

He had no bearings in Paris. But the first morning, John awoke early, astonished to have left his dread on the other side of the Atlantic. He pictured it a sticky, lumpy mass sitting on Dr. Roth's floor. Finally, something useful from Dr. Roth.

John felt calm, bathed in a pleasant sense of mystery. With only three days in Paris, he knew not to tether himself to the World Congress on Psychiatry and Mental Health. At dawn he started toward the Seine, righted by balanced, elegant architecture and the singsong of blue-coated shopkeepers splashing water to ensure a clean start to the day. Whatever he had expected, the city held not the faintest echo of his German past.

And yet. Ricocheting bursts from small cars rushing through narrow streets and spent diesel mixed with the buttery scents of freshly baked pastries were familiar from his Mainz childhood. There were rows of honey-colored buildings, darkened by soot and age, punctuated by great wooden doors that opened onto flats where families lived—not in suburban houses separated by picket fences and clipped lawns, but around a courtyard in the city's heart. He remembered Mutti's wash hanging across the balcony, the whites flapping in tandem with those from the upstairs flats. (In America, they used clothes dryers.) And the *Portiersfrau*, taking a pause from sweeping to reach into her apron pocket for a hard candy when he came home from school. His name was Janko then, and Janko knew to keep the candy secret from Mutti.

Sweet memories blowing back. A cool spring had wafted into Paris, chestnut trees shimmering in fresh green leaves, the air crisp with possibility. Lovers scuffed the Seine's sandy path, walking languidly home from trysts. The river thwack-thwacked against its banks; pigeons cooed in gratitude at breadcrumbs scattered by old women. John surprised himself by naming the city's medley Music.

Dr. Leventhal was presenting at eleven, with John at his side to help with questions. It was a rare privilege that, as the senior psychiatric resident, John had been invited on the trip. "A boondoggle," Dr. Leventhal called it. Wending his way back through neighborhood streets, John stopped at a café, seduced by the tinkle of silverware and clattering china. Over café crème, he recalled Ann as if she were a gauzy film image—lovely, naked—her smooth skin, her sumptuous breasts, black garters striping her thighs, exotic zebra markings to which he alone was privy. He wondered what it would be like to squire her to medical conferences, his arm around her waist, just as Leventhal did with his wife. Ann could awake next to him with that same smile she gave when offering coffee to medical residents in New York's Beaumont Hospital Office of Psychiatry. She could sit across from John at dinner, lips gleaming with fresh red lipstick, her life joined with his in a brick colonial and a wide inviting bed to dissipate the memory of the awkward, narrow, closed davenport in her cramped apartment.

John arrived at the hotel, where Mrs. Leventhal—chic in lemon yellow—was holding forth to a knot of psychiatrists' wives. "…If Jackie Kennedy can storm Paris in a yellow suit, why can't I? My husband should take a page from the president: 'I'm the man who accompanied Lillian Leventhal to Paris, and I have enjoyed it.'" She looked up. "John!" she said, opening her black patent leather purse. "Dr. Leventhal said to give this to you." She smiled and handed John a ticket. "We've been invited to dinner with the head of the French psychiatric society tonight, and we can't turn him down. The New York State Ballet is dancing *Three Muses*—Boris Yanakov's breakout work. I'm heartbroken, but duty calls."

"Come all the way to Paris for the New York State Ballet?" John asked, before he could think. He had eagerly anticipated his evening perambulations around the city. Confined to a theater? He wondered how to refuse.

"There's nothing like taking in a major cultural event with an audience full of Frenchmen," Mrs. Leventhal said, snapping shut her purse.

"Most generous of you," he remembered to say as he put the ticket in his breast pocket.

John settled into a bench at the edge of the plaza. Dusk was gray-pink, backlighting the *Opéra*. Balletomanes were arriving—tuxedoed men with stylish women on their arms. It wasn't just the evening gowns, or the way women draped their shawls. Their pacing and carriage were glamorous too. Each with a distinctive walk; together, a pageant. If he weren't answerable to Dr. Leventhal, John would have disposed of Mrs. Leventhal's ticket. He'd much rather spend the evening out here.

Inevitably, he went inside. He picked up a program and made his way to the first balcony. The orchestra warmed up as a chorus took their places in the side boxes.

The music began: slow, plangent tones paced to the speed of a man's forward tread. The chorus entered—deep and serious and sad—as if their voices had taken the measure of John's memory. The curtain lifted on a snow-covered mountain against an aqua sea, a scene to conjure myth. Dancers in blue and green leapt in unison, legs like arrows, arms overhead. They fell into lines fracturing like kaleidoscope patterns, or forms in opposing mirrors.

Overcome by jet lag, John dozed off. He was in his family's Mainz living room: Mutti darning socks, Papa with his pipe—left thumb over the bowl, right poised to cock his silver lighter. Lopsided smoke rings meandered toward the ceiling. A few more puffs before the pipe hung limply from Papa's mouth as he grew increasingly absorbed in the evening paper.

Rubbing his eyes, John slowly woke up. He knew the music. After dinner, when Janko's schoolwork was finished and he was getting drowsy, Papa had played it on the gramophone. If Janko was lucky, he'd be permitted a few minutes to sit with the grown-ups before Mutti declared bedtime.

The chorus sang with veneration, permeating the hall the way the smell of Mutti's bubbling apple strudel filled her kitchen, or the first peaty drafts of Papa's pipe suffused the living room. John was flooded with grief, the music a piercing shorthand for what was gone: all of them. Mutti, Papa, even little Max, who hadn't been born until later. John had not thought about this music in decades, if ever. He recalled Papa starting the gramophone as Mutti settled into the horsehair sofa with her sewing kit. Janko was growing so fast, Mutti had to let out the hems of his trousers. The sewing kit was black walnut, the varnish on the edges smoothed from use. (It was from Janko's grandmother.)

The orchestra moved with gravity and purpose, music as familiar as childhood. Now it was named. Mozart's *Requiem*. Not only the people and the place, but this, too, had been stolen. John didn't need to stay. Dr. and Mrs. Leventhal would understand. Searching for the quickest exit, John struggled to call up something—anything—to stanch his anguish. What value were his sessions with his training psychiatrist? Dr. Roth was useless.

None of the patrons around John budged; he would be imprisoned here until the end of the act. Making another effort, he took a deep breath to marshal his defenses.

And then.

A lone ballerina sheathed in white floated toward center stage. The audience greeted her with shouts of *"Brava!"* She was the Muse of Discipline. She cut through the whirling dancers with precision and exactitude. John had never seen anyone so exquisite. She was a reverie, an evocation of grace. Each fluttering arm motion dissipated his pain. Her dancing ordered the music, rendered it alluring. He strained left as she exited, as if by craning his neck he could follow her.

She spun in duo with the Muse of Song, summoning peace and beauty. Together, the two made harmony. Their playfulness lightened John's mood. He glowed like a man feeling desire for the first time.

Intermission. What was her name? John riffled through his program. Katya Symanova, written in bold beneath a glossy headshot; her black hair parted down the middle, pulled back to accentuate an oval face. Her eyes were downcast.

She must be Russian.

He would stay.

Again, the hall grew dark and the curtain rose. John sat forward, heart pounding. Song and Discipline braided together, arms and legs intertwined, diving and floating like wind and water.

Lightning flashed. A third muse appeared, luminous in silver, her face masked. Muse of Memory: she was clearly the most powerful. The ballet was a psychological caprice, a revelatory dreamscape. Clever, John thought, the psychiatrist in him aroused. We can't see Memory's face. It's my job to make her visible.

Memory billowed her silver cape and cast a spell. Song was hurt. The music turned funereal.

Memory waved her cape and cast a second spell. An old faun galloped out and captured Discipline. The two danced glued together, as if they would never separate.

The stage was shrouded in fog.

A third time, Memory waved her cape. Song and Discipline danced backward on their toes (how did they do that?), lost, passing each other without seeing.

John was entranced.

At the end, the audience rose in unison as if choreographed, cheering and raving. John opened his program and found Katya Symanova once more. She was magnificent, her long fingers supporting her chin. He imagined a story of struggle behind her dark eyes. Slowly, he stood to watch her curtsies. She stepped before the curtain and knelt—exquisite, transporting.

At last, the hall lights rose.

Knocked flat by a sylph, undone by mirage, John followed the crowd into the Parisian night. This onrush, for a woman who danced out of a storybook. She was polish. She was splendor.

John knew better. He was about to become a full-fledged psychiatrist. Wasn't the crux of his profession to learn how to live in the present, to create reality from reality?

As he left the theater, he saw an old man standing sentry over a bucket with cut flowers. With a round of miming absent a common language, John purchased a bouquet of white roses, bound in crimson ribbon. He went in search of the *Opéra*'s stage door—blissful, expectant—offering up an entreaty that he was not crazy, that Katya Symanova would let him present flowers. He strained for the right phrase, a sentence to express a hint of what he felt.

The air was cool. John pulled up his collar, adjusted his scarf, and waited for the stage door to open. Clumps of dancers emerged, laughing and talking. What if she spoke only Russian, or her English was too poor to understand him? A few stragglers came out. What if he was at the wrong door? He was afraid to move, even given the dubious wisdom of his mission.

The door opened once again. Katya Symanova—John was sure it was she. Her black hair was up, covered in a blue chiffon scarf. She wore a black coat and black boots that extended her height. She stopped and adjusted the edges of the blue chiffon over each shoulder, then paused and turned behind her. When she looked forward again, she seemed distracted, as if she were looking for someone.

John approached, afraid to disrupt her reverie. "For you," he said slowly, handing her the bouquet like a celebrant presenting an offering.

She was startled.

"How lovely," she said after a moment.

"For the gift you have given me," John said, bowing with his hands to his heart. "Dr. John Curtin."

"Thank you," she said. She closed her eyes—the lissome arc of her neck—and lifted the bouquet toward her. Behind her, the stage door opened again. A compact man in a tuxedo looked out. His graying hair was slicked down. He scanned the area, stopping to consider Katya Symanova, now bringing the white bouquet to her face with the gentleness of a kiss. He stepped forward, then seemed to think better of it, and retreated into the theater.

"White roses are my favorite," Katya said, raising her head. She had total ease with English; she spoke like a native. "Thank you."

John made another deep bow and—enraptured—turned to go.

She had been there the whole time; a ballerina living in New York.

The room at the Hôtel Neuvième was empty, and it was hers. Katya Symanova pulled open the drapes, mauve like the bedspread. Sunlight poured in, illuminating the pale pink walls. She stepped onto the balcony, where the smell of pain au chocolat floated up from the street, accompanied by fumes from a little blue truck, idling as it provisioned the café across the way. Women with baskets of baguettes and fresh vegetables conversed below: French, eliding like a stream smoothing stones.

Two hours until rehearsal. Exhausted from the long, sleepless flight, Katya drew back the duvet and lay down. She had rehearsed *Three Muses* so many times, it was written on her body. Something still eluded her, however—something she had withheld from her choreographer, Boris Yanakov, and therefore from herself. A kernel—the essence of Katya Symanova—or was it the girl she once was—Katherine Sillman? No matter Mr. Yanakov's captivating life force, she had kept part of herself in reserve, maybe even hoarded it. Perhaps it was a nugget for her future.

Pulling up the duvet, she sank into the pillow and let her body go slack. Rest was critical; tomorrow was opening night.

Lars, playing the Old Faun, stood with Katya, readying their entrance. Adjusting his horns, he whispered ballet's favorite good luck term: "*Merde*, Muse of Discipline."

"Thanks, Lars. You too."

Mr. Yanakov paced the opposite wing, scowling. Head down, he gave the impression that his company had just suffered appalling notices, and not that they were, instead, poised for opening night before the cream of Paris. Katya felt it imperative to gather her forces and ignore him. She fingered her tutu netting and shook out first her right leg, then her left. *Three Muses* in Paris. Katya was relieved for the vast physical expanse separating her from her choreographer.

And the expanse between her and Mama? Mama had never even seen Katya dance. Her absence was enveloping, a reminder that despite being embedded in the company and despite Mr. Yanakov—who had willed Katya the stage, conferred on her this feast—Katya danced through life alone. Her memories had grown hazy with time; a few: Mama's toothy grin when she handed her daughter her school lunchbox; Mama's throaty laugh, her butterscotch housedress with the white rickrack. For years, Katya kept up an ongoing monologue addressed heavenward, as if her soliloquies could coat the void that was Mama.

"Places!" the stage manager called.

Katya made a last adjustment to the ribbon on her right *pointe* shoe and felt the house, feverish with anticipation.

Act One began.

Katya leapt onstage, parting the dancers as if her luminous heat would grill them alive. To dance was to live. To till motion; to impart the joy that welled up every time she took to the stage, her body the vehicle for her art. The lights were blinding. As the music intensified, she skimmed the energy from the audience to breach another dimension. Transcending reason, she danced through raw emotion and spun toward a new center.

Katya returned to her hotel room flushed with pride. She had done it; her performance had come off. She ran steaming water into the immense claw-footed tub and tossed in bath crystals, watching the bubbles form. Something had changed tonight. She wondered if it was her choreographer's distance. Mr.

Yanakov had been in the wings pacing with his usual anxious deliberation. But he had not proffered that final piercing look that was meant to catapult her onstage, to fire her with energy and conviction. He was that nervous. Tonight, she had summoned those things alone.

She thought about her bouquet of white roses. That man had soulful eyes and wavy brown hair. Tall, but not imposing. Good-looking, in fact. He radiated kindness. There was something foreign about him, though not French. There were always hangers-on at the stage door. They requested autographs or shoved scraps of paper at her with phone numbers. They were creeps and cads, or irresponsible dreamers, or married, or lost. This man was different. He wore an oatmeal-colored scarf and offered the flowers as if he were finishing *reverence*. Katya sighed, stirred by the memory.

The water was hot and soothing on her aching muscles; she leaned back and stretched first one leg and then the other. She sank lower into the froth and allowed that she just might have earned the Parisians' generous welcome. She had experienced a shaft of wonder and immediacy—a direct back-and-forth with the audience. Her legs were steel, her poses anchored. Her partner had been reliable but not interfering. He'd stayed with her—so had the conductor—as she pushed beyond herself to inhabit the music. She had an eerie sense that someone out there had understood her, that she had spoken directly and been heard. That her endless labors had been worth it—the blisters, the pain, the exhaustion, the interminable practice. To dance the Muse of Discipline, to feel what she felt.

She stepped out of the tub, wrapping herself in a thick mauve towel. Pointing her right foot across the tiled floor, she made a slow *ronde de jambe*, one final sweep before the night was out.

There was a knock at the door. Boris Yanakov rushed in, still in his tuxedo.

Katya was surprised. Where was his carefully manicured privacy? He never came to her; she went to him. It was part of their unspoken agreement.

"We had them eating out of our hands with my ballet," he said triumphantly. "Tonight you were a lightning bolt! *Three Muses*…"

The reviews had better be sensational, or tomorrow he would descend into a morbid gloom.

"We've conquered Paris! This evening," he said, glancing at the table where she had set her white bouquet, "we let them know what we could do."

"We?"

"They love my ballerina," he said, momentarily transfixed by the table. Apparently, he wasn't worrying about the critics.

His ballerina? Where did Katya fit in? It was true he had made her what she was. She had been with him five years—no, a lifetime—student, protégée, lover, collaborator; earning his delight solving choreographic dilemmas; and his passion, naked in his bed, molten and spent from a performance. Her outsized extension, her technique—sweated over day and night—her interpretive skills, polished under his guiding hand. The window into her sexuality, thrust open by his insatiable hunger. He had formed her like a sculptor chiseling marble. Nevertheless, tonight was different. Tonight she'd danced somewhere new.

He turned and opened her towel, scrutinizing her naked body. "You're a wonder, Miss Symanova," he said, fumbling to unfasten his cummerbund. He edged her onto the bed and kicked off his shoes to wriggle out of his pants. Licking her face, he pulled her toward him like a gravitational force, then lunged into her, a taut muscle overtaken by mania.

He was a man of blistering intensity, but this was unusual. Loosened from her bath, Katya burned in his fever.

When he had worn himself out, he hoisted himself up and swung his legs around to get dressed. He adjusted his tuxedo jacket and walked over to the table with her white roses. "Beautiful flowers," he said.

"Some loony Parisian threw them at me as I was leaving the theater," she said, bringing the duvet to her chin.

Mr. Yanakov looked at her. "Really?"

"Ran off like his tail was on fire," Katya said. It was easy, re-counting her evening this way. The words just slipped out. She had already pressed a white petal into her passport, a souvenir of Paris. There was something special about that man.

"Boris!" she said. "Stay the night?" For years there had been rumors that Mr. Yanakov had a wife in Paris, maybe two. But it wasn't the wives, if they actually existed. It was Mr. Y. How many hours had she spent in his bed, his body muscled and firm though he was a generation older? Yet he never asked her to spend the night. He guarded his privacy as he guarded the great roles, doling them out like scarce nutrients in a famine. On the other hand, he had bestowed those roles on her.

He gave Katya an indulgent smile and shook his head. "Not tonight. We need to save you for the rest of the run."

CREATION STORIES

I wrote, What is more beautiful than the hopeless singing?
Dear finder, listen.

    —Allison Benis White, "In a letter found buried near a
            gas chamber:"

Dance is the hidden language of the soul, of the body.
And I believe in discipline, I believe in a very definite technique.

  —Martha Graham

1

1944

Mutti jumped off the train holding little Max. She landed a meter away, her skin showing through the elbows of her coat, a remaining button hanging by a thread.

In place of air, a smoky stench. In place of sound, shouting soldiers. The ground was scuffed with ice.

Mutti, Max, and Janko clustered with the women and children. Men were ordered into single file next to them, even Herr Professor Goldstein, who taught at Gymnasium, and Herr Doktor Kornblum, who used to grind eyeglasses.

Janko tilted toward Max and tried his regular tricks. He stuck out his tongue and crossed his eyes. Max didn't giggle; he ogled Janko through tears.

An SS man pushed through the women and children and thrust his thumb at Janko. "Into the men's line."

"He's ten," Mutti said.

Janko opened his mouth to correct her. Actually, he was eleven. But Mutti didn't notice; she was glaring at the SS man.

"He's only ten," Mutti said again.

The soldier jabbed the butt of his rifle in the small of Janko's back and began angling him away.

Mutti raised her voice. "He can sing." With her free hand, the one that wasn't holding Max, she gripped Janko's shoulder and called him by his German name. "Johann, sing for the officer."

The first thing Janko thought of was the Four Questions from Passover, *Ma nishtanah.* "Why is this night different from all other nights?" Papa had rehearsed them with Janko—stern and man-to-man—even though Janko was hardly old enough to sit through Seder. "Singing and memory are members of the same family," Papa said. "We are a people scattered around the world. Songs help us hold our common memories."

"Janko!" Mutti's whisper sounded impatient. "Sing something different."

Janko tried to recall the songs from the schoolyard where he went before he wasn't allowed to. Before Aunt Ella's dress shop had the windows kicked in and everything stolen from inside, before Herr Goldman jumped out the window. When the synagogues were whole. When Papa… Mutti widened her eyes, hemmed by black circles, begging Janko to remember.

Janko struggled to summon tunes from Papa's gramophone. It was forever ago. Before the *Aktion*. That was when the police gathered the Jewish people who hadn't been shot or jumped out of windows yet. "You're the man of the family now," Mutti had said, handing Janko a valise with clothes and jewelry and photographs. It was heavy, but Janko did his best to drag it along. Mutti had to carry Max.

Mutti and Max and Janko were squeezed into the back of a truck and taken to a nearby town. They lived in a school with their neighbors and a lot of other people too, crushed together with straw mats for beds and not much food, and no toilets to speak of either.

After a few weeks, other people needed the school. (Janko never did find out where the students were.) Janko and Mutti and Max were pushed onto a train that had to fit everyone from the school plus more. They were supposed to settle east, in the *Protektorat*. Janko had once learned that the sun rose in the east, but this east was different. Janko's family were going there to make the *Altreich Judenfrei*.

Except Janko and Mutti and Max didn't stay there, a ghetto overflowing with people from far-flung places, smelling of onions and sick and sewage. Instead, they were stuffed into another cold, filthy train that ended here. Janko was still in charge of the valise, which he left in a pile near the train tracks with everyone else's. Mutti's jewelry was long gone—sold for stale bread and milk, the rest stolen.

Janko looked at Mutti again. He fixed his gaze beyond the slate sky and cupped Max's head against Mutti's breast.

Nothing came to him.

"Goes with the men," the SS man repeated. He pressed the butt of his rifle harder against Janko's back.

Mutti leaned over, Max squirming in her arms, and hummed in Janko's ear.

"Get away from him!"

But Janko had heard something; Mutti had unloosed a song.

Janko opened his mouth. "*Vor der Kaserne/ Vor dem Grossen Tor.*" Melody, soothing and relaxed, thawed the cold. "*Stand eine Lantern/ Und steht sie noch davor,*" the tune as familiar as breathing. Everyone knew the lantern by the barracks gate where Lili Marleen's soldier last kissed her. The SS man put down his rifle and dropped his shoulders. Women around Mutti and Max shifted their gaze from the front of the line to Janko. Men stopped muttering and shuffling and faced the singing. For the briefest moment, it felt less lonely.

The SS man poked Janko's shoulder. "Come!"

Janko looked at Mutti. She pressed her lips to his forehead, warm against his skin. Her eyes were closed.

The SS man shoved Janko through the line of women and children. Janko tried not to stumble as he was prodded along the frozen ground. Once, he twisted around. He could see Mutti, but he couldn't get her attention. She was staring in front of her, advancing in her line, clutching Max to her bosom.

The SS man walked Janko between the rows of short concrete buildings, past the smokestacks, past the truck convoys, toward the forest beyond the barbed wire. Just inside the fence was a yellow house with black shutters. Colorful and regular, it looked out of place behind the brick and cinder block.

The SS man led Janko to the back of the house and pulled open the door. "Frau Koch," he shouted, startling the woman at the sink. "This one sings. Name is Johann," and he handed Janko over.

"As if I didn't have enough to do." Frau Koch wiped her hands, chapped and red, on a soiled white apron. She looked Janko up and down and grimaced. "Johann," she said, more to herself than to him. She was a big woman with a few top teeth missing.

Mutti would never call him Johann unless she was talking to a grown-up. She rarely even called him Janko. "Jankele," she usually said—in homage to her Polish parents—her lips making a smile as she drew out the y sound at the beginning of Janko's name. She acted the same way with Max, calling him "baby-kins" or "cookie."

Frau Koch wiped her forehead with the back of her hand. "Over here," she said, limping toward the end of the kitchen. "These hips," she muttered. "The damp is bad for these old hips." She opened a narrow door to a closet with two huge burlap sacks, one for potatoes, the other for onions. Between the slats in the far wall, Janko could see gray light from outside and feel the wind leaching through.

"Your room," Frau Koch said. "You're a damn lucky boy I'm giving it to you." She looked Janko up and down again. "Another mouth to feed. The devil himself must think I need more work," she said, shaking her head and pressing her tongue against the space between her top teeth.

Frau Koch took a few potatoes from the sack and returned to the stove, flinging her hand toward the stool under the kitchen table. "Don't just stand there." The stool was so wobbly, Janko had to catch himself from falling off.

Frau Koch scraped the potato peels into a frying pan. She slid the potatoes into a bowl that she covered with a plate. She stirred and jiggled the pan over the flame a few times, then scooped up the peels, speckles of brown fat dripping from them. Looking anxiously toward the door, she threw the peels on a saucer and said, "Finish up quick. They don't like you to have our food."

Even though his insides were laddered by hunger, Janko could hardly eat. At home, Mutti would fry the potatoes, not the peels. Frau Koch washed her hands over a metal sink that was wide and deep, big enough for her pots to soak on one side. Her stubby fingernails were black even after she dried them on her apron. Mutti's fingernails were long and tapered. Janko closed his eyes to smell Mutti's lotion. She used to rub it on her hands when she finished filing her nails after dinner.

In the afternoon, the small window above Frau Koch's back door went from mushroom-colored to black. She pulled the chain for the light and furiously accelerated her activity. She sliced potatoes from the bowl and dumped them in a cauldron of boiling water. "Soup," she said, removing a slab of meat—all gristle and bone—from a piece of brown paper. She took out a cleaver and hacked at the meat, tossing it into a pan with onions. "He doesn't like waiting for his supper," she mumbled.

Mutti would never cook meat like that, nothing but sinew. Mutti knew the names of Herr Rosenberg's—the butcher—five daughters and his grandchildren too. There were so many, Janko could never keep track. It took a long time for Mutti to ask after everyone, but she wouldn't be hurried. She told Janko to be patient, that family was everything.

Herr Rosenberg died after his shop burnt down. Mutti said he had died of a broken heart.

"You're not going to sit there all day, are you?" Frau Koch wiped her hands on her apron. "Follow me." She pushed open the swing door to the dining room, where there was a long, shiny table with high-backed chairs around it. Three leather boxes of silver were on the sideboard. Mutti and Aunt Ella had a box like that for the holidays, but they had to sell it after Papa... "The big fork and the little fork go here, the knife on the other side," Frau Koch said. "The kommandant sits on the end." She waved a soupspoon at Janko. "Put it across the top. Make it straight." Janko looked down the table's expanse. Only one place was set.

Frau Koch tugged open the drawer to the sideboard and re- moved a linen napkin. "It has to be folded just so," Frau Koch said, turning up the corners of the napkin. "To keep me in washing and ironing."

A man cleared his throat outside the front door. Frau Koch jerked her head up from folding. "Get out," she hissed, as if it had been Janko's idea to come into the dining room in the first place. From the kitchen, Janko heard the man scraping his boots in the hall. Frau Koch grabbed a beer stein and admonished Janko, "Don't move. Herr Kommandant is here." She hurried in and out again. "Take the top off the soup, boy! Can't you see it's boiling over? Me with my hands full, doing the work of three slaves."

Breathless, Frau Koch trundled back and forth with a tray, talking to herself and sweating. She kicked open the swing door with a load of dirty dishes and put them by the sink, then arrived with more. Janko couldn't imagine what that man did with those dishes and silverware all by himself. He felt weak from the smell of Herr Kommandant's dinner.

Frau Koch settled back into the kitchen. "Finally," she sighed. "The rest of them will come now and have their cigars in the sitting room, before they do other things." Janko heard the front door opening and closing; he could smell the smoke. He was past exhaustion, but he was ravenous.

Frau Koch considered him. "Johann, was it?" She tipped the soup pot and peered in. "We have to save it for later." Moving the dirty dishes aside, she picked up a heel of brown bread. She motioned Janko back to his stool and sent a nugget of cheese and a clay pot filled with jam skidding toward him. "No one's going to eat this."

While Frau Koch finished up the dishes, the back door opened and a few women in ragged coats and bare legs filed through the kitchen. They had blond hair and spoke a language that wasn't German. Frau Koch shook her head and followed them with her eyes, then folded her soiled apron and laid it on the table. She clapped her hands diagonally as if she were beating the cymbals in a marching band. "Time to lay me down," she said. "Say your prayers, boy." But she didn't wait for his prayers. Instead, she looked past him. "It doesn't do those men any good, the ones out there. It doesn't do anyone any good," she said.

Janko didn't know what she meant by "it," but he didn't ask. Nor did he mention that the only people with whom he would ever pray would be Papa and Mutti and Max. A long time ago they prayed on Friday nights when Mutti lit the candles, and at *shul* too, when they used to go. Janko was a big boy, so he got to sit with Papa and the other men. Papa was important at *shul*.

"Remember your room?" Frau Koch asked. She escorted Janko to the back of the kitchen. "Lucky we have a toilet too," she said, pointing toward the other corner. She shook out a burlap bag emptied of its potatoes and handed it to him. "You can have this for a blanket. A luxury," she whispered, and went on whispering to herself. Janko couldn't make out what she was saying, but through the dark he saw her shoulders hunch as she closed the door behind her.

It wasn't a room. It was a closet. Even after Aunt Ella and all the cousins moved in, Janko's room wasn't this small.

First, Janko tried lying on his back. He heard men trudging up and down the steps to the second story, grunting and clearing their throats. The floor above creaked and groaned. Next, Janko tried turning over on his stomach, his arms splayed around the vegetable sacks. Even though he was the man of the family now, Janko squeezed his eyes shut so he could pretend he was between Mutti and Papa, as if he had crawled into their bed after a nightmare.

Maybe Mutti would come for him tomorrow.

In the morning, Frau Koch told Janko it was time to practice his singing; there was going to be a party tonight. "The kommandant must have heard some good news," she said, shaking her head. "I wonder how that can be."

"I'll have to teach you some songs," Frau Koch said. She must not have realized that Janko already knew some songs. Frau Koch leaned her ample bottom against the kitchen sink, slapping her red palms on her apron. She belted it out so that her missing teeth showed.

Janko wanted to cover his ears. Frau Koch had a way of spitting when she sang that didn't sound too different from the guards outside. Janko didn't like imitating her, but Frau Koch insisted on it. She rocked back and forth and started into "*Oh du Lieber Augustin*," then interrupted herself. "You know the story, don't you?" She chuckled to herself. "They find Augustin drunk in the street and figure he's dead, so they pile him in the pit along with his bagpipes. He wakes up at the bottom—people dead from the plague thrown on top of him—and plays his song. They hear him and he's rescued."

Frau Koch could hardly contain her laughter as she kicked open the swing door and trudged upstairs whistling. She returned with the kommandant's boots, thigh-high and black. Stuffing them between her legs, she began furiously polishing them.

Today they had to set the table for twelve. "The kommandant at this end, but no one at the other," Frau Koch scolded. "He doesn't like facing anyone."

In the afternoon, Frau Koch scrubbed Janko's hair in the icy water under the kitchen faucet. She snipped around the edges with a pair of scissors and combed it out. "Almost like new, Johann," she said, slapping his cheeks to get the color to rise.

At dinner, it was the same as the night before, except at fever pitch. Frau Koch sweated and limped in and out of the swing door. The voices in the dining room got louder and louder. Every time Frau Koch came through the kitchen, she said, "Make sure to remember our songs."

Janko was so hungry, he was afraid he wouldn't remember anything. When Frau Koch went into the dining room with another round of beer, Janko grabbed a few filmy onion scraps off the plates by the sink and tried chewing some leftover gristle.

Frau Koch grabbed Janko by the scruff of his shirt and headed for the dining room. The men were moving noisily into the room across the hall, balancing their chairs and beer steins.

"Bring him in!" the kommandant yelled over his shoulder.

Frau Koch pushed Janko into the sitting room. Without the men and the chairs, the room would be an empty wooden box.

The kommandant passed out cigars. He was so tall, he had to stoop as he went around the room lighting them. "Our kommandant is a gentleman!" the officers cheered.

Janko trembled in the dusky smoke.

When the kommandant sat down, he looked worn out. It seemed like it might be an effort to stand up again. He stroked the sides of his ginger mustache and said, "Sing for us, boy."

"Hear, hear," said the other men, sitting straight at the edge of their chairs.

It was too scary to look at the semicircle of men in their gray-green uniforms, their jackets buttoned and their boots tall and shiny, so Janko stared at a cobweb in the corner of the ceiling. He began with the *"Erika"* song—just like Frau Koch had told him to—about a little flower named Erika, or maybe it was about a girl named Erika, who was crying for her man. Every time Janko paused for breath, the officers stomped their feet. "C'mon, boys, let's march!" *Stomp, stomp, stomp.*

Janko's head was splitting. He needed to run to the kitchen and use the toilet. The cracking boots sounded the same as they had outside the flat in Mainz, only now Janko was in the room with them. Janko was the man of the family, but it was hard to be brave.

Mutti had told him to sing, and now he was singing. If only she would come.

Herr Kommandant didn't stomp. There was something wrong with him. When Janko finished, the kommandant sighed and asked, "What's next?" He looked at Janko as if Janko had the answer to a question that puzzled him or possessed something that might help him feel better.

Janko was getting hoarse. He couldn't figure out how to leave the room.

By some miracle, the kommandant yawned and said wearily,

"We'll finish up with one more, boy." Janko was so relieved, he went right into "*Hänschen Klein*," about little Hans who leaves to go out into the world, *tra la la la la*, but his mama misses him so much, *tra la la la la*, that he comes back to stay with her, *tra la la la la*.

The kommandant's feet were stretched in front of him and his eyes were closed. When the men clapped and shouted, he jerked awake. "Frau Koch!" he bellowed. "Take him away."

Frau Koch limped in—she must have been in the hall listening the whole time—and put her arm over Janko's shoulder to bring him to the kitchen, where soon the women in the ragged coats would start walking through. Frau Koch peered into her pot and put the remnants from the bottom in a bowl for Janko. "Thank me, boy. This is a feast."

She started cleaning up. "Only one of me and an army of them to dirty every pot in the house," she said. When she finished, she went through her ritual—folding her greasy white apron and clapping her hands. She ushered Janko to his closet. "Bedtime, boy." Janko clutched his burlap potato sack, wishing he could fall asleep and keep his eyes closed until Mutti returned.

But Frau Koch didn't allow him to stay still. Every day, in the dull light of morning, she threw open the closet door and started in. "You're a growing boy, and you can't stay in bed all day. Boys your age need to move."

The problem was, Frau Koch didn't want him out of her sight. "It's for your own good I don't let you have the run of the place," she said. "There is a badness and an evil out there," she whispered. Janko knew she was referring to the smoke and stench. She only let him out to walk around the house. He couldn't get past the barbed wire anyway.

Outside, Janko strolled the perimeter of the yellow house, poking the frozen ground with a stick, watching skeletal men in striped uniforms make their way through the gate and up the hill into the forest, prodded by SS men with rifles. Janko was pretty sure there were no women in that procession, but in case they changed the rules, he always looked for Mutti. He couldn't understand why she didn't try to come by, why she wasn't putting up a fight to get past the entrance guards. It wasn't like her. She must have been too busy taking care of Max. Maybe Max was sick.

Inside, Frau Koch told Janko to make himself useful. She taught him to peel potatoes, putting her chapped red hand over his to show how to avoid getting cut. "I wouldn't want you losing a finger," she said, though the knife was too dull for that.

At home, Janko used to help grate potatoes for Hanukkah latkes. Invariably he scraped his knuckles, trying not to cry when Mutti cleaned his hands in warm water under the kitchen faucet. When she was done, she put a bandage on and kissed him on the forehead, saying, "You grate like a big strong boy!"

As the latkes crackled and sizzled, Mutti spread a cloth for them to drain. Little Max wanted to eat them right away, but Mutti said, "You'll burn yourself, and besides we have to wait for Papa." When Papa came home, they each got a plate of latkes with a dollop of applesauce and sour cream. Mutti lit the candles on the first night of Hanukkah, and Papa told Janko to lead them in the *shehecheyanu* prayer, the one that thanks God for supporting us and protecting us and bringing us to this day. Janko felt like a grown-up.

Maybe there were seasons, but at the kommandant's, outside was always the same shade of bleak. The place reeked regardless of temperature or hour. Still, it was hard to avoid noticing that it was getting warmer. It could even have been spring. The ground was covered with slush that was the same color as the burlap bags in Janko's closet.

"You could polish the kommandant's boots," Frau Koch said. Janko used to watch Papa shine his shoes. Papa's quick, even brush strokes made the toes glow. "Someday you'll do this too," Papa said.

At Herr Kommandant's, the smell of shoe polish made

Janko's head throb. But anything was preferable to whatever was strangling the air outside. Even though Frau Koch mumbled about the heat, she didn't open the windows. "Too many flies," she said.

Next to the sink, there was a mop that was half bald. Frau Koch had Janko scrub the floor. There was no hot water for cleaning, so she filled the bucket with cold water and a concoction she put together from the dirt outside. "Use your muscles, boy," she said. "Your arms look like twigs. You're almost a man; you need biceps." When the floor dried, she had Janko sweep up the dirt and put it back in the pile outside for the next time.

At home, Mutti did the mopping. And Aunt Ella too, once she and all the cousins moved in. Mutti said the real cleaning was for Passover, when there was too much to do by herself. "And how can I do it with you underfoot?" she said, picking Max up and kissing his pudgy cheek. Mutti held Max on her hip and told Janko to wrap up the bread and crackers; then she had him climb on a chair and wipe down the shelves to make sure there wasn't a single bread crumb left. Janko was big enough to carry in the Passover dishes; he never dropped or broke them.

It was so hot that Herr Kommandant's house felt as if the air had turned to wool. "*Volkslieder for the Volk!*" the men in the kommandant's sitting room demanded, standing and pressing in on Janko like an iron scorching a shirt. The men stank of sweat and beer.

"In summer, we wander the hills," the kommandant said. He walked through them in a trance—swinging his arms, causing the men to disperse—circling them like a sleepwalker. "Let us swim in the streams," he mumbled with his eyes closed.

Janko knew what song Herr Kommandant was requesting. He tried to negotiate a space where he could stand without someone mashed against him. Each of the officers was massive. If any one of them came closer, Janko would be crushed.

"Sit," the kommandant ordered, suddenly snapping to. The men took their seats, noisier than usual. *Clomp clomp.* "In the center, boy!" They moved their chairs toward Janko, just as they had tightened around him a few minutes before when they were standing. They were rowdier tonight. Janko couldn't see how he would get past them to leave. If he forgot the words, they would throw him over the barbed wire into the forest.

He glanced at Herr Kommandant, who looked like he expected Janko to cure him of a terrible disease. Janko couldn't stand that look; it seemed to ask for pity.

Struggling to pretend the thuggish men enclosing him would fade away, Janko started in. He tried to remember that Mutti had wanted him to sing. "*Das Wandern ist des Müllers Lust.*" The officers slapped their thighs and banged their chairs. "How the miller loves to wander…learned it from the stream." *Beat, beat.* Their slapping sounded like bullets. "The millstones wander too…They dance, and would dance faster if they weren't so heavy."

Janko was running out of breath. "Wandering is my greatest joy."

"*Ja,*" the men grunted, shuffling their feet.

"Leave me free to go in peace," Janko sang.

A few rotten apples made their way into Frau Koch's kitchen. "They're a delicacy," she said, cutting them up for applesauce.

Janko's family ate apples and honey on Rosh Hashanah. Papa would dress with extra care for services, standing in front of the little hall mirror to get the crimp in his tie right. At synagogue, Herr Barth put a *tallit* over his head so you couldn't see his face, only the end of the *shofar*. Rabbi Kohn chanted and Herr Barth blew out sound that was piercing and ancient, straight from the Bible. Janko would hold his breath to see if he could outlast the *shofar*'s final cry, but he never came close.

Janko got to sit up front with Papa. At regular services, there was only one Torah, but on Rosh Hashanah there were two— one with a blue velvet cover, the other in faded burgundy. Papa and Herr Feldman were important, so they each carried a Torah down the aisle for the men to touch with their *tallit*.

Mutti's singing joined Janko's, her harmonies soaring flute-like from the balcony.

After the parade of Torahs, Papa sat next to Rabbi Kohn on the *bimah*. Looking solemn and dignified, Papa clasped the burgundy Torah to his heart, as if he knew that with one careless move it would unravel in a calamity of tangles.

"I can't let you freeze," Frau Koch said as she came in with a pair of wool trousers and two shirts. "Soon enough you'll need the warmth."

It was true, Janko was too tall for his clothes. The cuffs of his pants were at his calves; his shirt was hardly more than threads.

"Don't ask where these are from," Frau Koch muttered.

She wouldn't give them to Janko until she had scrubbed them in the sink. Her hands looked even redder than usual. "These trousers weren't meant for water," she said. "But what can I do? The boy needs clothes."

Now that she mentioned it, Janko realized it was getting colder. And darker too.

Herr Kommandant stopped waiting for parties. "Bring him in," he called after dinner, alone at the head of the table.

"What do you have for me?" he asked, drawing lines with his fork across the hardened bit of white cake Frau Koch had brought in for dessert. He paused to consider Janko. His face was wrinkled; there were black circles under his eyes. "It's getting to be Christmas," he said.

Janko started in on "*Lasst Uns Froh und Munter Sein*." He had always known this song; at school, his teacher used to line the girls up on one side of the stage and the boys on the other, each group taking a verse for the Christmas pageant. "Let us be happy and cheerful," Janko sang as Herr Kommandant moved crumbs from one side of the plate to the other. The cake was nothing like Mutti's *gugelhupf*, with its elastic, stretchy dough. Mutti sprinkled almonds and sugar on top before she baked it.

The kommandant leaned back, swaying back and forth. It wouldn't dawn on him to harmonize with Janko.

No one in Janko's family ate by themselves.

There was less and less food. Herr Kommandant talked on his radio at all hours of the day and night. Doors slammed; officers shouted. It was cold.

One night after dinner, Frau Koch tiptoed into the dining room with a piece of stale cake and suggested she bring in Janko. "Not now," the kommandant mumbled. "They're coming. Russians. Americans. It'll be bad for us."

Frau Koch returned to the kitchen. "The hell!" Herr Kommandant called after her. "Send him in!"

"What do you have for me tonight?" the kommandant demanded. But before Janko could answer, the kommandant said, "You know what to sing."

"*Oh du Lieber Augustin.*" For some reason, Herr Kommandant especially loved that one. Janko tried to ignore the picture of people piled in a pit, dead from the plague. Putting his arms across his chest, Herr Kommandant rocked back and forth. The tune seemed to take him somewhere he wanted to be; the wrinkles left his face and his mouth sagged. He fell asleep.

2

1945

When they came, Janko was crouched in his closet, juddering in fear. A cluster of soldiers surrounding her, Frau Koch pointed toward Janko's hiding place, talking too quickly to be coherent.

A soldier threw open the door. Janko glanced up in dread, shaking like paper before wind. There was a Black man, the first Janko had ever seen. Equally baffled by the boy in the closet, the soldier brought Janko to the center of the kitchen. All of the soldiers were Black men. Frau Koch was screaming now, gesturing outside. "He's not one of us. He's one of them!" The soldier raised his hands to silence Frau Koch. "Please," she whimpered, her hands clasped together as if she were praying.

The soldier nodded slowly, then put his arm around Janko's shoulder.

Frau Koch, spent as a dry leaf falling from a tree, said, "I kept you away from there." She flopped her hand toward the door. "Your people went in there and…didn't come out."

The soldier nudged Janko forward.

"They'll take care of you," Frau Koch whispered.

Janko couldn't bring himself to look at her.

His arm still around Janko, the other Black men following behind, the soldier walked Janko away from Herr Kommandant's fenced-in yellow house with the black shutters, along the barbed wire that bordered the forest. Daylight was blinding. Janko made out a large patch of burnt ground at the edge of the forest, charred and smoldering, a bonfire breathing its last. The soldier brought Janko's hand to cover his eyes in a protective gesture. But Janko did not cover his eyes. He stopped and stared. Those weren't logs, those were human remains. Leg

bones sticking out, feet and toes unconsumed by fire, skulls
poking beneath the ash. Wisps of smoke rose above the ground
as if some monster had abandoned a human feast.

Shaking his head with an expression of stunned disbelief,
the soldier said a few things—quietly, in English—that Janko
couldn't understand. Janko turned toward the barbed wire and
vomited, retching with a violence that suggested if he emptied
his body, he could dispel not only the horror that was before
him, but also his year of captivity, his year of willful ignorance.
Finally, he understood the stench and the burning and the smell
that never went away and what Frau Koch's clicking tongue had
been saying. She had been trying to tell him the whole time.
Mutti was dead, and Max too. Dead a long time ago.

The soldier waited until Janko had finished retching, then
handed Janko his canteen. Janko put his throbbing head back
and drank. The water was cool.

Again the soldier wrapped his arm around Janko and gently
urged him on, past the truck convoys, toward the smokestacks
and the brick and cinder block buildings at the entrance to the
camp. Dazed men and women—dozens and dozens—wan-
dered aimlessly toward them. Men wearing nothing but shirts,
their knees skeletal, their faces vacant and hollow. Women with
shaved heads, so gaunt it seemed they had no bodies in their
striped pants. There were more ashes, more fire pits. Smokestacks, smoldering.

Janko and the soldier stopped in front of a shed, empty
and rank, bunks stacked inside like an oversized chicken coop.
Janko leaned into the soldier and sobbed as if he had always
known him. The soldier tightened his embrace as a man in a
striped uniform shuffled over. "They must have fed you." He
came closer and kissed each of Janko's cheeks. "At least one of
us will survive. Be good to that young man," the man said to
the soldier.

He tried to smile. His teeth were gone. "A blessing on your
keppele."

3

1944

Aunt Mary hurried across the blacktop at school, motioning Katherine down from the jungle gym. Katherine knew something was wrong because Aunt Mary worked as a secretary for an attorney-at-law and would never be at school during the day. Aunt Mary earned enough money to get her hair done every week. But today her hair was every which way, and her blue eye shadow was smudged.

"Something terrible's happened, Katherine Sillman." Aunt Mary held her niece's arms and sucked in her breath. "Can't stand to say it." She shook her head. "Your mother's gone. Crossing Astoria Boulevard. It was instant," she said. "No pain or suffering, thank sweet Jesus."

Katherine was seven.

She remembered Tommy Wilkes punching her in the belly in kindergarten. That's what it felt like now, that twisty, suffocating feeling. (When Katherine came home from school that day, her mama called Tommy's mother and said she'd send her husband, Patrick Sillman, to clean Tommy's clock if he ever laid a finger on Katherine again. He never did.)

The children on the playground stared when Katherine left with Aunt Mary, as if she'd had an accident and hadn't reached the girls' room in time.

Mama's wake was in the living room, closed casket because according to Aunt Mary, Katherine's poor mother was a sight to be seen. Daddy moped around and forgot to give Katherine breakfast and didn't go to work even though he was an accountant and usually went to work every day including some Saturdays. Mama hadn't liked the Saturday part. She complained:

How could they have a family life when he worked all hours of the day and night?

For the funeral, Katherine wore her lavender-and-white-flowered party dress that was a hand-me-down from Alice next door, and her Mary Janes. Mama lay in that box and didn't magically come out of it even though Katherine prayed that she would.

Katherine had gone to church with Mama on Sundays. If Father Paul gave too bossy a sermon, Mama would mutter, "Does he think we were born yesterday and three days old tomorrow?" Mama's funeral mass was longer than regular church. It was frightening, watching the adults cry. Father Paul looked at Katherine as if he had never felt so sorry for anybody in his life. He kept saying Jesus would watch over her, but if that were true, why hadn't Jesus stopped that truck from running over Mama?

When Katherine returned to school, everyone avoided her except Mrs. Slattery, who let her be teacher's pet. Vicky Murphy sat behind Katherine and jabbed her pencil eraser between Katherine's shoulder blades and hissed, "You're only getting to hand out papers and wash blackboards because your mom croaked." Vicky made Katherine want to cry, but Katherine tried not to because it would only make Vicky meaner.

Dinner with Daddy was quiet, just the sound of forks going *clink, clink* on the plates. Daddy was getting pretty good at making cube steaks, but he didn't know how to get Katherine to tell him things that were going on at school, like about Vicky. One night, all of a sudden, he got up from his chair, reached under the kitchen counter, took out the bottle of bourbon, and poured it down the sink. "This stuff is poison," he said. "Without bourbon, Mama would still be here." Then he went into the living room without finishing dinner. Katherine didn't know what to do, so she washed the dishes as usual.

Daddy gave Katherine a key to the house. She made her own milk and cookies now when she got home and didn't turn on the radio, because she wasn't supposed to, although no one was there to find out. Mama had liked having the radio on while she was cooking. When the Andrews Sisters came on, she spun Katherine around and said how much she loved dancing and how she and Daddy used to go dancing when they were courting. Mama looked sad when she said that, as if she were thinking back to something better than right now. On Sunday nights, Mama put the radio on loud and made Daddy dance with her around the living room. Daddy said, "Not now, dear." But then he got up, looking like he didn't want anyone to see him and Mama dancing, which never made any sense because Katherine was the only one there.

Now it was Daddy who tucked Katherine in. If she asked, he read her a story. She didn't have a lot of books, so he kept rereading Rapunzel and Cinderella and Rumpelstiltskin. Finally, Katherine reminded him that Mama took her to the library on Saturdays, and he started doing that too. Katherine loved Saturdays, not only because she got a big bag of books, but also because Daddy brought her to the office, where she got to sharpen pencils and crayons at his secretary's desk while he worked.

Daddy went with Katherine to church on Sundays. That was new. Mama used to say it was his business if he couldn't bestir himself to go to church, but no daughter of hers was going down the road to ruin. Father Paul brought ladies over to meet Daddy, but he said, "I have my girl right here!" and patted Katherine's head.

For Katherine's eighth birthday, Aunt Mary showed up in a green tweed suit and black patent leather pumps. "Happy birthday!" she said, handing Katherine an envelope. "This'll give you something to think about besides your mother's empty chair at the kitchen table."

Katherine felt that same twisty feeling in her stomach she'd had when Aunt Mary found her on the playground that day at school.

A card. Katherine had been hoping for a piece of jewelry or maybe a new doll, but she was supposed to be polite. "Thank you," she said. She rubbed the silver glitter on the front of the card against her cheek. It was scratchy.

"C'mon, open it up," Aunt Mary said. Inside was folded onionskin. Katherine felt the thin paper between her fingers. "Don't tear it," Aunt Mary said, winking.

Katherine studied the note. She could tell Aunt Mary had typed it at work. *For Katherine, I.O.U. one year of ballet lessons.* Katherine didn't know what I.O.U. meant, but she could read "ballet lessons." Slowly, it dawned on her. She'd read stories about ballets and seen pictures of ballerinas in library books. They wore tutus and satiny toe shoes. "Really?" She jumped up and hugged Aunt Mary.

"Aunt Mary and I are splitting the cost," Daddy said, and gave her a kiss.

The next Saturday, Aunt Mary took Katherine shopping. They rode the subway from the Sillmans' house in Queens to the Lower East Side. Dallingers was the smallest store Katherine had ever seen, not much bigger than her dining room, which was not much bigger than the dining room table. The walls were lined with shoeboxes. Pink and white and lavender tutus hung on a stand in the corner.

An old woman squeezed around the edge of the counter.

"Would you be Mrs. Dallinger?" Aunt Mary asked.

"Last time I checked."

"We need ballet shoes for this little girl," Aunt Mary said, as if she were in charge.

"Not so little, are we? You must be eight," Mrs. Dallinger said. Katherine nodded. "Starting late. You'll have some catching up to do."

Katherine colored. No one had ever said she was too old before.

Katherine sat in one of the chairs with the cracked turquoise seats, and Mrs. Dallinger pulled up a stool. "Let me see." She stretched her palm along the length of Katherine's foot, then hoisted herself up and looked at the back wall.

"I think we have them." She yanked a box from the middle of one of the stacks. Katherine ducked, certain the rest would come tumbling down.

Sitting back on her stool, Mrs. Dallinger lifted the cardboard top and unfolded white tissue.

A brand-new pair of pink ballet slippers! "They're so pretty," Katherine said.

"You're going to have to sew elastic straps on them, Mama," Mrs. Dallinger said, looking up at Aunt Mary.

Katherine was relieved Aunt Mary didn't correct her. She didn't want Mrs. Dallinger to ask about Mama because then she would give Katherine that you're-a-poor-poor-thing look. Katherine didn't want to be a poor-poor-thing; she just wanted to be a regular girl.

"Point your toes, dear. Ah, a nice arch."

That sounded good.

Mrs. Dallinger glided the shoe onto Katherine's foot, then pulled the two pink ties in the satin band to tighten the sides. "Narrow feet. A fine thing in a ballerina."

Katherine reached down to stroke the soft pale leather, curling her foot to examine the stitching on the suede sole—gray framed in pink. They were too beautiful!

"Are they the right size?" Aunt Mary asked.

"Yes, ma'am. Not for long though; she's a growing girl. If she doesn't wear them out first, which she will if she bothers to exert herself."

"Oh, don't worry," Aunt Mary said. "She'll exert herself."

"I guess we'll need some elastic too," Aunt Mary said, snapping open her pocketbook and pulling out her billfold. Turning to Katherine: "We'll have a lesson in sewing on the straps."

"Aren't you lucky?" Mrs. Dallinger said.

"Yes'm," Katherine said.

4

1945

It was weeks before the barbed wire was removed from the camp's perimeter, now a camp for Displaced Persons. Food was gray soup and stale bread with tins of pinkish-brown paste unrecognizable as nourishment. There was never enough.

At night, lying in a wooden bunk that was more incarceration than liberation, Janko tried creating replacement memories, a different story. Papa was alive and took them sightseeing in the German countryside in his shiny new car. They lived in their flat, and food was plentiful: Aunt Ella hurrying from the kitchen with trays of meatballs and potato kugel; Mutti pulling warm challah and sugar cookies from the oven. At school, Janko furiously copied the blackboard, kicked a soccer ball with friends. On the way home he strained to look up girls' skirts as they climbed onto the streetcar. His worst experience was cramming for exams. Home in Mainz.

That's what he could do—return to Mainz. This was not living. He could go back and find someone, something familiar. Anything but languish here.

Joining packs of other children, Janko traveled with little expectation beyond the immediate—that a soldier might drive him a few kilometers or offer a corner of chocolate. Death and destruction were omnipresent, with skeletons shot last year or dead two weeks ago from fatigue. Whole villages were obliterated, replaced by wandering families seeking food, shelter, and purpose.

Was it weeks? Months? Janko entered the Mainz city limits. There were no shopkeepers in doorways, no well-groomed, resolute men conducting business. Buildings were ravaged, stoves and sinks bared to wind and rain, pipes swung like branches cleaved from dead trees.

Janko picked his way over brick mounds that were bombs' offspring and struggled to remember where home was. In alleys, he passed people clumped around fires: men who had forgotten when they had last shaved, women who had ceased washing their clothing. Babies, too tired to cry.

Finally, he knew where he was—*Die Hauptsynagogue*, where Janko got to sit with the men and Papa carried the Torah. Where Mutti joined Janko in harmony. From somewhere in his bruised, disordered memory, Janko recalled a massive building with two separate domes, one higher than the other. On a cold night in 1938 it was torched by brownshirts and their friends, its windows shattered. A few days later the police blew it up. Mutti wept. Papa too.

There was nothing left beyond a few broken columns that resembled a forgotten Greek ruin. Once, Janko had seen pictures of things like that in school. In fact, his school was up the block. He stared at the imposing entrance, now opening onto a roofless shell.

Their flat was not far. Janko could peek into his room, find the plaid blanket on his bed; see Mutti's soup ladle hanging on the kitchen wall; Papa's coat and scarf, draped neatly over a hanger in the closet; Max's blocks, stacked in the corner of his tiny room.

Janko rounded the corner. Their building stood intact, a lone tooth in a mouth full of gums. There were neighbors in those collapsed buildings down the block. The Kramers and the Lowensteins—big families. Frank Kramer was Janko's age. He had four younger brothers and sisters; the brothers were twins. Karl Lowenstein had an older sister—her name was Hannah. Hannah was pretty. Mutti waved to their mothers in the park.

Janko stepped up to the wooden door and rang the bell. He had long since lost his key. Frail and shrunk almost beyond recognition, the *Portiersfrau* cracked the door. Her hair was snow white. "*Ich bin* Janko," he said. "Janko Stein."

She put her hand to her ear. "I don't hear so well."

"Janko!" he shouted.

A glimmer of fear spread on her face. She opened the door a little wider and looked up at him. "Much taller. The baby must be a big boy by now. What's he called?"

Janko's stomach seized up. "Max," he said.

"No candy left," she said, tapping the pocket of her apron.

"May I come in?" Janko asked, trying to step over the threshold.

The *Portiersfrau* looked anxiously behind and shook her head. "Not allowed," she said.

"What about our flat?"

She wrinkled her forehead as if his question was absurd. "We're full up," she said. "Occupied." She smoothed down her apron. "Which one was yours?"

He stared past her into the courtyard. Lines of laundry hung over the balcony. Their home was on the left, two floors up. "Two C," he said.

"Hoffmeisters," she said. "Been there for months. Took the place after you moved."

But Janko's family hadn't moved. They had been forced out, Max in Mutti's arms, Janko dragging that leaden valise—all loaded onto trucks like so many bales of hay. "They won't mind if I drop by," he said, raising his voice. "Just a look around."

"*Verboten.* You'd best be going," she added, glancing behind again. "There are camps for you people. No one will bother you there." She closed the door. Janko pressed his hands against it. What had the Hoffmeisters done with Mutti's plates and Papa's books? With the things that hadn't fit into the valise?

Janko stared at the rubble around him. He had trudged here for nothing, for worse than nothing. He was delusional. He knew where the Kramers and the Lowensteins had gone. They had been murdered—Frank and Karl and their sisters and brothers (including the twins) and Hannah with her long blond braid and their parents too. Janko slumped against the *Portiersfrau's* door, bitter at his own inefficacy.

Why had he, of all of them, survived?

An American soldier picked him up and took him to a Displaced Persons camp west of Frankfurt. In the office, it was a shock to be greeted kindly by someone who spoke German.

The camp had a certain energy. Grown-ups started a theater company and a sports club. There were improvised schools. A relief worker encouraged Janko to learn English, though the idea struck him as senseless.

He prepared for the road to nowhere, his mind embroiled in furies. The Hoffmeisters—whoever they were—had invaded his home as surely as the brownshirts burned down *Die Haupt-synagogue*. Where was Papa's gramophone? The *Portiersfrau* had aided the Hoffmeisters. Of course. Helped herself to Janko's family's things, then given them the key. She, who had once been the kind old lady who gave him candy after school.

Janko went to the makeshift synagogue a few times. But Papa no longer sat next to him, and Mutti and baby Max were absent from the women's section. Prayers tolled an agony of loss. Singing had been destroyed at Herr Kommandant's.

5

1948

Katherine pressed her face against the small window in the door to the studio, watching Boris Yanakov, his legs wrapped around the back of a chair, tell his dancers to repeat the same few steps.

"Zee great Yanakov." Maya Bichette came from behind. She spoke in a fake low voice, imitating a radio announcer.

Why did Maya have to make fun of him? Mr. Yanakov knew everything there was to know about ballet.

"Shut up or he'll hear you," Katherine said.

"Wears a denim jacket to prove he's a cowboy," Maya hissed.

"Maya, seriously, be quiet." Mr. Y stood up and moved the dancers around. Katherine could see muscles under his blue tee. He slicked down his black hair—streaks of gray through it—and stepped back, stiff with concentration. With his eyes closed, he gestured to himself. The pianist sipped muddy coffee and read a dime-store paperback. She was a Chinese woman named Lydia.

"I'll leave you to your hero worship," Maya said. Katherine watched Maya go down the hall. Mrs. Bichette had plaited Maya's French braids and pinned them up. Mrs. Bichette came to parent visiting days with red fingernails and red lipstick and shiny high heels, her hair in a French twist. She chatted with the other mothers and smiled at Maya, even if Maya tripped. Sometimes she filed her nails or dozed off and didn't seem interested in watching how the girls learned new steps.

When Katherine first started lessons, she prayed to Mama in heaven to come by surprise for parents' day. Each time it didn't happen, Katherine felt a little sting of disappointment. But Katherine continued to invite her. She imagined Mama in one of the empty chairs up front. Mama wouldn't be fancy like Mrs. Bichette, but she would sit at the edge of her chair and watch everything. She wouldn't doze off; she would grin if the teacher put Katherine front row center.

Katherine didn't tell Daddy about parent visiting days because it would be embarrassing if he came. Aunt Mary was at work then, but once in a while she came after work, peeked in the studio window, and said, "I'm pleased my investment is being put to good use."

Mrs. Bichette invited Katherine out to Mr. Hansen's Ice Cream Parlor on a Saturday after class. It was a rainy November afternoon. Mr. Bichette came too, along with Maya's little brother Chris.

"How was ballet school?" Mr. Bichette asked.

"We learned a new combination. We could show you," Katherine said, pushing back her chair.

"I hear it's your eleven-and-a-half birthdays!" Mr. Bichette said, without any interest in seeing them demonstrate their new combination. "What a coincidence you girls are two weeks apart. Ever celebrated your half birthday?"

"Nope," Katherine said, wondering why he had no interest in dance class. Every year, when the school asked Katherine to take more classes, Daddy and Aunt Mary said yes, "because you love it, even though we'll have to pinch to make it work." Maya's parents complained a lot but eventually agreed. Now that they were in sixth grade, Maya and Katherine went to three classes a week—Wednesdays after school, and Saturdays for a regular class and beginning *pointe*. Katherine showed Daddy her new combinations when she got home, and Aunt Mary too if she was over. Maybe Maya didn't do that with Mr. Bichette.

At the moment, Katherine felt she was missing something she was supposed to know. She hadn't heard of going out for half-birthdays, or having ice cream in November. Mr. Bichette was wearing a bow tie even though it was Saturday. Mrs. Bichette was in a herringbone suit with a white blouse and pearls.

ThreeMuses

They wore matching wedding rings and their faces looked kind of alike.

"What about my half birthday?" Chris said, squirming next to Mrs. Bichette in the booth. "Do I get ice cream?"

"Not if you don't behave yourself," Mr. Bichette said.

"Do you have plans for Thanksgiving, Katherine?" Mrs. Bichette asked.

Thanksgiving was for people whose mothers made turkeys. Katherine was tired of cutting turkeys and pilgrims out of construction paper at school. She was too old for that this year, but they would still have the "feast" at lunch when mothers came with trays of turkey and stuffing and cranberry sauce and sweet potatoes and then stood behind their children at the long tables in the cafeteria. Mama was the only one who wasn't there. Mrs. O'Connell or Mrs. Creswell patted Katherine's head, making pity faces as if she were a kindergartner.

"We go to my aunt's," Katherine said to Mrs. Bichette, which wasn't exactly true, but she couldn't figure out what else to say. She and Daddy and Aunt Mary went to Howard Johnson's, where there wasn't a whole turkey but just a slice on each plate slathered in gravy. Katherine felt a little miserable thinking about it, even though she liked Howard Johnson's. It was just that no one did that on Thanksgiving.

"Are we going to Grandma's?" Chris said.

"Of course," Mrs. Bichette said.

"Maybe you can try not to throw up on me on the way to New Jersey this year," Maya said.

"Shut up," Chris said.

"Children!" Mrs. Bichette said.

"Tried my hot fudge?" Mr. Hansen approached the edge of their booth. Katherine shook her head. His straw hat had a black band around it, and he wore a red-and-white-striped jacket.

"You're in for a treat," Mr. Bichette said, with a ho-ho-ho kind of laugh.

"Daddy gives me money for the Good Humor man when

he comes around," Katherine said. "But that's only in summer." She vaguely remembered Mama putting a scoop of vanilla in a glass of root beer on special occasions. Was it for New Year's or Easter?

Katherine and Maya shared a banana split in a crystal bowl shaped like a boat. Whipped cream twirled up in a tower. Mr. Hansen had put two cherries on top, one for each girl. The hot fudge was thick and creamy and delicious. "Yum," Katherine said, licking the end of her long spoon.

"Bet mine's better," Chris said, his face covered with chocolate ice cream.

Katherine focused on Mr. Yanakov, wandering among his dancers, dragging around arms and legs, fixing ballerinas' arabesques, their partners' hands spread across their torsos. If only Katherine could join the company, perspiring in an old leotard cut haphazardly down the front, leg warmers drooping at the ankles, *pointe* shoes scuffed from rehearsing. Imagine Mr. Yanakov holding her like that—looking like a movie star—pushing her leg higher, positioning her arms over her head! He would take care of her; he knew what she was supposed to do.

Time for class. Katherine tore herself away and walked down the hall.

Katherine took her place with Maya near the piano, faced the wall, and put her heels in first position. Save for the wooden barre snaking the room, three walls were bare. The fourth was mirrored.

Lydia arrived with a stack of music. Adjusting the bench, she sank into the slow, measured harmonies of Chopin. The music silenced the chaotic hallways in Katherine's school and the noisy cafeteria, as well as the smelly subway ride she would have to take to get home.

"Derrières tucked in!" Focused and stern, Madame Swoboda strolled the room.

Pliés. Slowly up and slowly down. To dance. Katherine straightened her shoulders and sucked in her tummy, immersing herself in all her different parts. She quieted her upper body and summoned a rainbow of muscles; you were meant to grow taller as you went down.

Everything mattered here.

Katherine pretended she was like those other, mothered girls, who were watched and pampered. They didn't know that Mama watched from heaven. Mama was glad Katherine was taking ballet, and she was proud of her. Besides, when Katherine told Daddy that Maya's mother took Maya to get her ears pierced and bought her a purple velvet ribbon to weave through her bun, he'd agreed to both. (Katherine chose aqua.)

Tendus, feet sliding to a point. Katherine worked through the arch to the ball of each foot, her toes extending, her body waking up. "*En croix.*" To the front, to the side, to the back, to the side. The same routine every class. Nothing was simple. "In discipline is art," Madame Swoboda reminded them, adjusting elbows, moving feet, slapping thighs. Each step demanded effort and precision; that was how you improved.

"Remember the head!" Madame Swoboda was once the star of the Moscow stage. Now her orthopedic shoes displayed a splendid arch when she demonstrated. Even when she was pleased, she was never satisfied.

Katherine's exertions made her warm and limber, a particular pleasure. "*Grands battements*. Eight times *en croix*." Madame Swoboda counted over the piano's accented beat. Katherine focused on her kicks. It was harder to bring your leg down than up.

"Time for center." Madame Swoboda placed the girls one at a time in rows. They started over, without the barre. *Pliés, tendus, jetés, frappés*. "Steady! Do not tense the shoulders. Do not look down." Katherine extended her neck and tried to infuse her arms with lightness. The mirror never lied. Long before Madame Swoboda shouted it out, Katherine would notice if her line was off or her stomach hung out.

Slow to vigorous; rooted and stationary to jumps across the room. In the last twenty minutes, they began to dance. More music, more combinations, more complexity. From the back corner, they leapt and turned to the opposite corner. Katherine imagined herself bursting from the wings of a giant stage, performing *grands jetés* before a crowd. Mama would be proud of her for that too.

"Katherine! Don't bite your lip! Relax your face, no sign of effort."

Katherine was mortified. She lined up in the back corner again. In pairs, they launched themselves equidistant from one another. Maya and Fiona crashed into each other and ran to the side to prevent a pileup. "Girls! No giggling."

Madame Swoboda called them to the front.

"Reverence."

They placed their hands across their hearts. To the right, to the left, and curtsy. Thanks to Lydia, who played the music. Thanks to the music beneath their motion. Thanks to the discipline that made it ballet.

Katherine felt sad; the lesson was over.

6

1948

Then one day Janko was on a ship bound for America; he didn't know how. All he knew was that he'd better do something; he'd better be somebody.

He slept with the men in an open space two stories below deck, canvas bunks stacked in threes. The place was rife with seasickness and damp, but Janko liked the engines' purposeful grind, noise that signaled retreat from chaos and misery. There was no one left for him back there.

In the morning he climbed the crowded steps to the dining room. Passengers had poured from Displaced Persons camps—women with scarves overhanging craggy faces and wiry young men who had survived on guile alone, adults and children shorn of relatives and country. Families, too, formed in the years between the war's end and the start of a future. They spoke a cacophony of languages, or not at all. For some, it was too much to drag one word after another; silence was mourning's raiment.

The Americans were a mixture of white people and Black people. Sailors were white, the mess staff Black. And across the dining room were several tables of Black GIs, returning home from service in occupied Germany.

Janko waited in the breakfast line, eyeing the baskets on the long tables. Those must be oranges. He wasn't sure because he had never seen one. He was famished. People jostled him on all sides—mothers running after toddlers, old men trying to get to the front. It was so busy. No one would notice. Quick as he could, he darted to the table and shoved one in his pocket.

"Hey, big boy!" one of the GIs across the room called out.

Janko froze. Storm troopers kicked in people's sides for less.

He pulled out the orange, shaking, frantic to undo his crime.

The GI turned to his buddies and started laughing. "Nobody cares. We won't get scurvy before we get home, will we, boys?" His grin displayed two rows of bright white teeth. It didn't matter that Janko couldn't decipher the words. The man's face overflowed with good cheer. This wasn't a shadowy street patrolled by brownshirts, or the last stop on the train. This was a ship bound for America.

Janko looked at the orange, covered in a thick skin, and rotated it in his palm. He bent forward and smelled it.

"Holy moly, you don't know what to do with it, do you?" The GI strode over and removed a penknife from his pocket, carving the orange. Janko offered him a wedge. He watched the GI take a bite and followed suit, the orange dripping in his hand. What a dazzling burst of flavor! As he sucked the rind, he noticed the family next to him gawking. Sheepishly, he offered them the remaining wedges. "Nice kid," the GI said. He reached into the basket and tossed Janko another orange before returning to his seat.

Janko was sailing in a dream. If this was America, he had nothing to fear. He filled his breakfast tray with warm oatmeal, eggs, toast, and another orange. The supply of milk was infinite. He had no reason to hoard his rations because there were none; it was incredible.

After breakfast, he took the blue blanket from his bunk and climbed up to the railing at the bow, watching the ship slice whitecaps. The air was brisk, the ocean vast and gray, daylight a metallic sheen punctured by slivers of sun.

Someone tapped his shoulder. "Hello," said an old man with hollow cheeks and a scrim of gray stubble. The man's black coat was shiny with age. "What's your name?" He spoke a heavily accented German.

"Janko Stein. Johann, really."

"Ach, you're from the Fatherland." The man spat over the side. "Where?"

"Mainz."

"My name is Chaim, and I'm from hell." He sounded Polish. "How old are you?"

"Almost sixteen."

Chaim put his hands on Janko's shoulders. His fingernails were long and his arms shook. "I bet I'm younger than your father." Janko didn't know how old his father would be if he had lived. "What do years mean in this worthless life?" Chaim turned back toward the railing. "I'm older than God."

They watched the water. "Been on a boat before?" Chaim asked.

Janko shook his head.

"Me neither," Chaim said. "Who you got in New York?"

Janko shrugged. "A family."

"You know them?"

"Nope."

"They found me a second cousin," Chaim said. "I never heard of him before. Though I knew Great-Aunt Fanny's family had gone over around 1904."

Janko cleared his throat. "The family in New York isn't my family," he said.

"Ach." Chaim looked at him. "They're taking you in."

"I guess that's it," Janko said.

Chaim looked over the side. "Know any English?"

"Some." Janko had learned some numbers, and what he had thought was passing English. But he couldn't understand much on board. The Americans were friendly, but no one slowed down or stopped to explain things. There was so much Janko didn't know—everything, really. He could drown in worry, but what good was that? The ocean was generously lengthening the distance between there and here. Maybe his past would dissipate like a fading siren.

Dinner, too, was a marvel. There were great trays of piping hot meat. You could help yourself to potatoes and gravy. The quieting hum at the end of the meal was an ode to abundance, the other passengers as sated and awestruck as Janko. He left his tray at the mess station and noticed a small group gathering at the far end of the dining room. At the sound of an accordion, his stomach turned over. There would be singing, he was sure. Across the room a group locked arms. Wheezing melodies and a thumping beat were making Janko seasick. The group raised their voices, boisterous and loud.

Janko pawed his way through the crowd, quaking in the suffocating cigar smoke at Herr Kommandant's, surrounded by jackbooted officers who grew more threatening the longer Janko sang. He would forget the words; they would put him outside in the stench and the cold.

He stumbled up on deck, his hand at his throat. The door to below-decks shut. A steady wind replaced the singing. Janko groaned in relief. "Feeling queasy, are we?" Chaim had come up without Janko noticing. "A little green around the gills?"

"Kind of." Janko held his stomach. "It's just that…" He stopped himself. There was no one he could tell. He was supposed to be the man of the family; instead, he had sung for their killer. Papa would shake his head in disbelief.

Chaim wrapped his arm around Janko. Off the bow, the sun dipped beneath the ocean, flecks of pink and orange on the water. "They say in America you can reinvent yourself."

"Really?"

"You can choose a new name." Janko found that astonishing. "But it has to sound American."

The sky turned cobalt. One by one the stars came out.

"I wouldn't know how to do that," Janko said.

"Maybe I can help," Chaim said. "Ever see anything like this?"

"Never." The sky was aflame; the Milky Way seared a blazing white arc around the world.

"If there's any music left in this punishing life, it's out here," Chaim said.

Janko listened to the engines' rhythmic drone and nodded.

The next morning, Chaim sidled up to Janko at the railing. "I brought us something." He reached into his pocket. "A Yank left me his German-English dictionary," he said, covering his face to guard against the wind whipping over the bow. "Let's find a bench...What did you say your name is? Johann?"

Janko nodded.

"You know what that is in English?" Chaim asked.

"John," Janko said confidently.

"Good. How about a surname?"

"I thought about that," Janko said. "What about 'Curtain'?" Mutti used to draw the drapes to keep darkness from their flat. "Curtain" could stanch regret. "How do you spell that in English?"

"Hmm..." Chaim thumbed through the little book, then stopped and held it at arm's length. "These old eyes don't see too well," he said, considering the dictionary for a few moments. "This is the size of the *siddur* my *zaide* carried in his breast pocket to *daven* when he was traveling on business. He prayed after every meal no matter where he was. Very religious..." Chaim teared up. "Awfully windy today, don't you think?" He rubbed his eyes. "*Tateh* carried one too," he said, leaning back. "*Davened* every day of his life. At least so far as I know." He sat up with a jerk. "But I don't, do I?" He raised his voice. "I don't know a goddamn thing." He was shouting. "I don't know about any of them at the end." He collapsed like a piece of worn-out clothing fallen from a hanger.

Janko put his arm around him. Poor man. You could sink from sadness or try to swim forward. The main thing was not to think.

"Catch me if you can," a little boy said, racing past, chased by his older brother. Janko watched them run up and down the deck. The little boy was the same age as Max.

Then again, there were times when swimming forward was impossible.

Chaim sat up and shook himself. "Where were we?" he asked, as if he had just woken from a nap rather than vanquished an encounter with memory. "Oh yes," Chaim said. "Damn the dictionary." He took a scrap of paper and a pencil from his pocket and wrote *Curtin*. "When you get to America, tell them who you are."

FEAST AND FAMINE

7

1948

John sat between men and women who smelled of sweat and soiled garments, watching the chirpy aid worker up front. She wore red, her hair up in a fancy knot. Her teeth were very straight.

"Curtin." He jumped up. "John Curtin," he whispered, formulating the words to himself as he hurried to the desk. He was fifteen—almost sixteen—years old. He wanted never to hear Johann or Janko or Jankele again. Everyone in America was named John.

Clutching a cardboard case that contained a change of clothes provided by the Hebrew Immigrant Aid Society, he approached the woman in red. She was speaking in torrents. John made out a few words: "…your new father and mother, Barney and Selma Katz."

They were shorter than Mutti and Papa. Barney had thick black glasses and Selma, a crown of silver braids. "Welcome," Barney said, extending his right hand and squeezing John's hand with his left. Selma spoke so quickly that John could only catch a few words. "I see I have to slow down," she said, laughing and embracing him as if she had known him all her life.

"We'll catch the train to Yonkers," Barney said.

They stopped at a brick row house with a patch of grass out front. In Mainz, everyone had apartments. Inside, the brown carpet was plush and deep and wall to wall; not like Mutti and Papa's Oriental rugs. John looked around. A photo above the couch showed a boy in uniform, his hat centered over his forehead.

"Buddy," Barney said. "Killed in Sicily." His glasses fogged.

John understood. He set down his case and walked to the picture. The boy looked tall and proud. John turned to Selma and Barney and put his hands over his heart. "I'm sorry." One day he might have more and better words.

"We'll eat soon enough," Selma said, breaking the silence. "Barney, take John upstairs."

"This was Buddy's room," Barney said, over the clatter of pots and pans downstairs.

John bowed.

Barney took John into the bathroom and handed him a towel that was bright white and as thick as a blanket. He turned on the water, saying, "Come down when you're ready. Selma's outdone herself, I'm sure."

The white tiled floor was spotless, the sink gleaming. John undressed and lay in the tub, water as warm as sunlight. Two more towels hung on a rack. There was a bar of pink soap and a bottle of something else. John opened the top. It smelled sweet. "Shampoo," he said aloud, sounding out the label. He lay back and closed his eyes, the motion of the ship replaced by the gentle splash of bathwater. He could have spent the night here listening to the silence, but he was expected at dinner.

He tiptoed downstairs to a burst of smells. Selma had set the table in the dining room, a lace runner down the middle. For a split second, John trembled in front of it—Frau Koch chiding him—wondering how one man could eat so much by himself. "Stuffed cabbage," Selma said, setting down a steaming pot. "Here's brisket," she added, hurrying back to the kitchen for potatoes. "Coffee too," Selma said, pointing to the sideboard. It was so small compared to Herr Kommandant's. "I'm never sure what people want to drink."

"We won't be in here normally," Selma said. "But today's special. The dining room's for holidays. We're usually cozied up in the kitchen."

John peeked in. The kitchen was barely big enough for a little table and an oven and—what was that big white box? Selma opened the door and pulled out a tray of greens. She turned around and laughed. "Refrigerator," she said. "Keeps things cold." She edged past as if John were a wall fixture. What had she done to get this much food? This wasn't a ship; it was a house where two people lived. Well, three now.

Selma returned with a pitcher of juice, wiping her forehead with her apron. She turned to John. "Please, you must be hungry. Don't be shy, you live here." She handed him a plate. "C'mon, Barney. Set a good example."

Several neighbors trooped in. Barney and Selma talked at the same time, introducing John. No one noticed that he was lost in cascades of words.

"Selma always makes a great meal," one of the men said, sitting next to John.

"It's delicious," John managed.

"Moe, Moe Horwitz," the man said, extending his hand. He was older, and bald. "*Ich habe ein bissele Deutsch.*" He thumbed his chest, looking pleased. "Selma told me to get my tail over here and *kvell* over you. Make you feel all *gemütlich. Sehr gut*, eh?" he said. "I'm here to help. Me and my wife, Gertie, live right next door. Happy to *kibitz* any time."

John smiled. It was funny to hear German and Yiddish mixed with English.

"Good," Selma said, returning with a large bowl and a plate of cake. "I told Moe to make you feel at home." She scanned the table. "Dessert. Rice pudding and honey cake," she announced.

More food! John couldn't figure out how it had all fit in the kitchen. The rice pudding tasted like warm milk and sugar. He could have as many slices of honey cake as he liked. Everything tasted better than on the ship. He had never been so full.

While the neighbors laughed and talked, John's eyes began to droop.

"Barney, dear," Selma said, breaking into the conversation. "Put John to bed."

John bowed. A chorus of neighbors started chattering again.

"Don't act like a guest." Selma stood on tiptoe to kiss his cheek. "We're so glad you've joined our family."

John felt a wave of panic. He already had a family. He couldn't lose the flakes of memory he'd managed to extract, nor the sounds from his childhood: Mutti humming, darning socks; Max giggling; Papa's whistle as he unlocked the door after work, Janko's cue to run down the hall and jump in his arms.

Selma took John's hands in hers. "Honey, I mean we're your second family. Your new home."

"Thank you," John said, relieved.

"Make sure he knows to sleep in," Selma called up the steps to Barney. "Just because you leave for your pharmacy at dawn doesn't mean he has to wake up."

"Yup." Barney pointed to a switch by the door to Buddy's room and turned the light on and off. He went to the lamp next to the bed and did the same thing.

A whole bed to himself, a room even, and unlimited quantities of food. John lay down without taking off his clothes, as he had done ever since boarding a truck with Mutti and Max, a lifetime ago. Maybe he had never lain in a bed before. Certainly not between such clean sheets, or under such soft blankets. No longer ocean borne, he was still floating. Drifting atop Papa and Mutti and Max, buoyed by the dreams of a boy who had lived in this room and died in war. You could have what you needed—like Barney and Selma—and still lose everything.

He closed his eyes. Maybe he had never slept before. Or maybe he had, but along with his family, the memory had gone up in smoke.

8

1952

Just after her fifteenth birthday, Katherine was accepted into Variations Class. "Mr. Yanakov teaches it!" she told Daddy. "It's where you learn how to partner—like in a real ballet."

"What time does it meet?"

"Seven to nine, Thursday nights."

"On top of Mondays and Wednesdays? How're you going to get home?" Daddy had that same anxious expression he had whenever he asked Katherine about taking the subway at night. Honestly, she didn't like it either. There were hoboes who rode through until morning just to have a warm place to sleep.

"Same as always," she said. There were boys in the class now. They weren't as good as the girls—they had lower extensions and flatter feet—but they jumped higher. Two of the boys took the subway home. Katherine dressed quickly after class so she could leave with them.

"Who's that girl you're friendly with—Maya? You still walk to the subway with her?"

"Yeah, Dad." Katherine hadn't walked with Maya in a year. Maya had had a big fight with her parents just to try out for Variations. Mrs. Bichette sent Mr. Bichette from Riverdale to pick Maya up, and Mr. Bichette was getting tired of it. He didn't want to add another night, but somehow Maya had won.

Why explain? Daddy would only worry. Or stop her lessons.

Mr. Yanakov strode in, trademark denim jacket dangling from an index finger. "The studio knows one time—time to work," he announced, throwing the jacket on his chair. He may have left forty behind, but he was ready to spring. "There is no day or night here," he said, tucking in the T-shirt that covered his burly chest and biceps. "No too tired or too sore; no seasons other than the season for excellence."

He snapped his fingers at Lydia and scanned the class. "Music is your medium." In the soft leather shoes that costumed male dance teachers from Broadway to Moscow, he paced the room. "Look pleased, put out some effort. *Tendu* to second." He pulled himself up to his full height—rather short—and placed a palm across his torso. "Your feet are your paintbrushes. Caress the floor."

"*Grands battements* up front. New girls come forward." He took them by the arms and measured them against the boys, matching them into couples. Katherine was assigned to Fernando Sanchez, whom Mr. Yanakov had discovered on a talent-scouting trip to south Florida. Fernando had long, graceful legs and a head full of black curls. Maya said he would join the company before he was eighteen. (Maya found these things out; Katherine never knew how.)

"Ballet, my friends, is about Woman. It's the man's job to make that clear." Katherine felt as if he were urging her to grow up and be a woman right now. She was too embarrassed to look at Maya. Mr. Y was foxy. Maya didn't think so, so Katherine tried not to show how she felt. But then Mr. Y moved Fernando aside, came behind her and spread his hands around her, and she felt herself turn red. As he held her in his firm, reassuring grip, Mr. Yanakov's index fingers grazed the bottom of her breasts. Katherine had never felt anything like that.

"Stand tall, Miss Sillman." Mr. Y turned to Lydia. "Music, please. Boys, watch me steady her. Right leg, Miss Sillman." Katherine kicked higher than she ever had.

"Girls, find your center. Boys, don't get in her way." (At the ballet they would always be boys and girls.) He snapped his fingers for the music to begin.

Katherine was trying so hard that she tipped and stumbled. How humiliating. She wanted to please Mr. Yanakov; she wanted to be the best.

"Miss Sillman." Mr. Yanakov sounded solicitous, not angry.

"Choose a place to spot or you're bound to fall." Katherine lifted from her core, pulled up her supporting foot, and spun slowly around to land in a clean fifth position. The left side of Mr. Y's mouth turned up. "Not bad. But let's go around twice next time."

Katherine knew it was a compliment. She bobbed her head. Fernando was superfluous; Katherine just had to keep her balance.

9

1949

"I hate to interrupt the young scholar here," Barney said, dragging a stepstool into John's bedroom. "But Selma's started her annual assault on the kitchen cabinets. Woe to every last bread crumb." He angled the stool inside Buddy's closet and disappeared up it. "Passover dishes," he said, straining under the weight of a quilted plastic container. He handed the stack to John.

"They should call *Pesach* the housewives' full employment act," Selma said as Barney and John arrived downstairs. "Put the plates in the dining room. Where was I? Oh yes, stock for the matzo balls." She lifted the lid off a pot of simmering chicken soup.

The smell was Mutti's embrace. Janko woke up to it and walked sleepily down the dark corridor lined with family photographs to the kitchen. Mutti was in a whirl of activity. Papa, too, shining the Seder plate and the silver carving set. Instead of "good morning," Mutti said, "You're not to play in the dining room." Janko wouldn't dare. He turned around to the newly laid table, covered in white damask with a stack of Haggadahs at Papa's end, a crystal goblet at each place setting. Long white candles, smooth as swans' necks, were mounted in the silver candlesticks.

Papa dressed for Seder, a gold watch chain tucked into his gray flannel vest, a black yarmulke on his head. When it was time to start, Oma hobbled over from her rocker in the corner of the living room. She wore a lacy white shawl; for once, something light over her dark clothing. The relatives pinched Janko's cheeks. Max wasn't born yet.

It took forever. The reading and the singing; everyone

reciting. Janko was starving by the time Papa put down his Haggadah. China clinked behind the kitchen door—Mutti ladling soup. It tasted so good! Pieces of onions floated translucent in broth; bits of carrots too. The matzo balls were a special kind of squishy. Papa gave Janko a look that meant "don't slurp." But Janko couldn't help it; he had to be careful not to burn his tongue.

"Is that okay, John?" Selma sounded exasperated.

John shook himself. "Sorry?"

"You and Barney empty the dishes from the kitchen. Pots too. Then bring the folding table and chairs in from the garage."

"Of course." Each resuscitated morsel of memory was a tiny, hard-earned victory.

The Seder table extended through Barney and Selma's narrow living room to the front door. Rachel arrived early. She was a short, big-breasted girl of eighteen. "This is my niece," Selma said to John, who put his heels together and bowed. Rachel blushed furiously under her black curls. Had he done something inappropriate?

Barney's pharmacy assistant and his wife came with two little boys, then Moe and Gertie Horwitz from next door. "Careful, it's still warm," Gertie said, handing Selma a steaming casserole of *tsimmes*. "I hope I didn't overcook the carrots." John was struck by the informality; everyone was on top of each other.

"Barney, call people to table," Selma said. "Put John and Rachel together." Clasping the *tsimmes* to her bosom, Selma negotiated her way through the crowd.

"Kind of her to seat a seventy-year-old bald guy with the young people," Moe said, lining up behind them. John pulled out Rachel's chair and helped angle her in. "I see they taught you some nice European manners over there," Moe said, slapping John on the back.

"Go ahead and start, Barney," Selma said, opening the oven door to remove tin foil from the capon. "I'll just be a minute."

Barney passed out Haggadahs and tapped a glass. "A special

chag sameach to John, who joins us for his first American Seder."

John nodded, bewildered. What happened to his early Seders? Where had Janko gone? He had a glimmer of Papa at the head of the table, dressed more formally than anyone in Yonkers. The Mainz dining room was grand. Even with all the relatives seated, there was plenty of space to walk around the table. Oma dozed next to Papa. For the life of him, John couldn't come up with the name of Aunt Ella's mother-in-law, the one who sat on the other side of Oma. No one was left to help him remember.

"And let us remember those who cannot be with us tonight." Barney looked toward the living room wall, Buddy brash and confident in his army uniform. The guests around the table hummed in agreement. Buddy had Selma's easy smile, as if he might enjoy a good laugh.

"First, we light the candles and say a prayer for *Yom Tov*," Barney said, removing his fogged glasses. "Selma, are you coming?"

"Let Rachel do it," Selma said from the kitchen.

Barney handed Rachel a box of matches. "*Baruch Atah Adonoi*," she sang in a quavering voice. The Seder guests joined in chorus. The prayer was identical to the one in Mainz. John opened his mouth. "*Eloheinu melech ha'olam*." To sing was to grind corroded gears, blow dirt off jagged shards of memory.

Selma squeezed into a folding chair next to Barney.

"John, the *shehecheyanu*?" Barney said.

John gripped his palms under the table until he cut off circulation. Papa had them sing the *shehecheyanu* at Hanukkah. Papa was a man of impeccable integrity. He would never have sung for Herr Kommandant.

Selma elbowed Barney. "I'll do it," she whispered, catching John's eye.

Holding up his silver Kiddush cup, Barney intoned the blessing over the wine. Every time Papa said Kiddush, he reminded them that this was his great-grandfather's cup. "*L'dor vador*," he said. "From generation to generation." What happened to

Papa's cup? The Hoffmeisters probably had it melted it down to make a bracelet for Frau Hoffmeister, or the *Portiersfrau* stole it. John blinked and sat up straighter. There was no place for bitterness here.

Barney started around the table, assigning a Haggadah reading to each guest. The Passover story unfolded—Moses left in the bulrushes by his mother, escaping Pharaoh's edict to slaughter the firstborn. Saved by Pharaoh's daughter, he was raised in royal splendor. His people enslaved. His God inciting him to the grueling, thankless task of leadership.

"Time for the Four Questions," Barney said. "We call on our youngest member."

"*Mah nishtanah halailah hazeh mikol haleilot,*" the little boy at the end of the table sang in a high-pitched voice.

Finally, John found Janko. He was sitting with Papa, practicing for Seder. They had been working together for weeks, Papa's Haggadah open on the dining room table, annotated in his slanting script. "Singing is embedded in our tradition," Papa instructed. "It's a way to keep our memory." Papa moved his index finger right to left, tracing the Hebrew words, but Janko was too young to read. "Memory holds us together," Papa said. Janko imitated Papa, memorizing the tune phrase by phrase. "One day you'll teach the Four Questions to your son, just like I'm teaching them to you," Papa said. Bertha Weiss. That was the name of Aunt Ella's mother-in-law. She sat next to Oma at Seder. Oma lifted her head when Janko sang, her face animated.

"On all other nights we eat all vegetables, and on this night only bitter herbs," sang the little boy. John's ears pounded. Max was born after Janko, so Max became the youngest. Papa would have expected Janko to teach Max the Four Questions, but Janko hadn't done so.

"Great job!" The guests erupted in applause.

"Did you know Moses was a stutterer?" Moe called down the table.

Several people started talking at once.

Selma whispered to Barney, "The capon's drying out."

"It's like hiring a Yankees coach who doesn't know a bat from a football," Moe said.

"Yes, God picked an ordinary guy to lead the Israelites. Remember," Barney said, scanning the table. "Moses never reached the Promised Land. It's about the struggle and the effort, not the result."

John was trying to concentrate but a riot of memory fragments were clamoring for attention. What happened to Papa's three dark suits, pressed and lined up in the wardrobe? And Papa's gold watch that he wore at Seder? (He wore it to work, too, and to *shul*.) Papa used to tease Janko that he could gauge how full Papa was from Mutti's cooking by how the chain tightened across his midriff. Mutti's challah was silken, but you weren't supposed to think about bread during *Pesach*.

Barney pulled his Kiddush cup toward him. "Time for the plagues. Blood, frogs, lice." They dipped their pinkies into their wine glasses for each affliction. "We remember the suffering of the Egyptians too," Barney said. "We remember suffering the world over."

John hoped little Max hadn't understood what was coming to him when he sagged in Mutti's arms. Mutti must have known. She told Janko to sing and he had survived.

"Pass up your books," Barney said, closing his Haggadah. "And now, if you'll excuse me, I have a bird to carve."

"What did you think of your first American Seder?" Moe asked while Selma and Gertie distributed bowls of matzo ball soup.

"It was over so quickly," John said vaguely, his memory like an eleventh plague—chains of hammering jackboots extending to forever.

Moe laughed. "My kids never thought Barney conducted a short Seder. They used to dread it! Maybe you're just older."

John looked at Moe. Dread sounded right.

"We're not a religious family," Moe said. "But we thought the kids should have a little something at the holidays. There are different ways to be Jewish, right?"

"Right." John wondered what his was. He was trying to fit into Barney and Selma's version—a feast at the holidays, brisket on Friday nights. Beyond that, what did it mean to be a Jew? A branded member of a herd, wrenched from home, shorn of family, driven in trucks and hauled to the slaughter; the past desecrated by a stinking, smoky stench. Strangers commandeering your home. Was that a way of life, or a belief system? Belief was beside the point. The "chosen" were skeptics and zealots alike, equally condemned to die.

"Aunt Selma says she's helping you," Rachel said.

"She's very patient," John said, fighting to stay present. "She tutors me at the dining room table." Selma wore a faint touch of rouge on her peach-fuzz cheeks and smelled of face powder. "I've just learned a new word for English," John said. "'Inscrutable.'"

"Ha, that's a good one," Moe guffawed.

What was the difference between "there" and "their"? How come no two *gh*'s were pronounced the same? "It's hard not to trip over the silent endings," John said. "I don't like all those past tenses," he added. There were too many nuanced forms of time. "Fortunately, Selma gets me to laugh. She thinks I can start CCNY in a year or so." Would he be ready? He was trying as hard as he could.

"What are you kids going to study?" Moe asked, pushing his empty soup bowl toward the center of the table.

"I'm going to be a teacher," Rachel said.

"Nice profession for a woman," Moe said. "And you?"

"Barney and Selma want me to study medicine." Barney had not had that chance; his family was too poor. The Katzes had saved for Buddy's education and wanted John to have it. He needed to prove himself worthy.

"I wanted to be a doctor," Moe said. "But I only got as far as chemistry. Ran out of money. I made out okay though. What kind of doctor you want to be?"

"I didn't know there were different kinds," John said.

Moe leaned in. "If I were you, I'd look into psychiatry."

"What's that?"

"Take it from me, kid." Moe put his palm over his chest and tapped up and down. "You got a heart full of *tsuris* and a *keppe* full of nasty memories. It's scrawled on your forehead like a headline in the *New York Post*." He bent closer. "Be a brain doctor. Unleash your dreams."

10

1954

"And again." Mr. Yanakov snapped his fingers. Katherine spun a double pirouette with Fernando's hands around her waist. "Are you bored, Mr. Sanchez? You're playing Don Quixote! He's a dreamer and an adventurer." Mr. Yanakov pushed Fernando aside and clasped Katherine's waist. His hands were a glistening flare.

Katherine pulled taller and spun again, this time a triple. "Now *penché*." Mr. Yanakov tilted her forward, his palms on her sides, her leg extended behind.

"Very nice, Miss Sillman," he said, righting her. "Mr. Sanchez." Mr. Y pushed closer to Katherine. "This is the grand *pas de deux* from *Don Quixote*, to be performed for your graduation at the Peter Stuyvesant Theater, not some two-bit twirl at a high school sock hop. This may be a student show, but the critics will be there, ready to pounce.

"Don Quixote, you'll recall, is a lover of women," Mr. Yanakov continued, his hands still gripping Katherine's waist. Mr. Y had assigned her the part—lover of a lover. Just the word gave her shivers. "Give us your passion!" He squeezed Katherine against Fernando until they were soaked in each other's sweat.

The great choreographer touched where he wanted, inclining Katherine's pelvis and pressing Fernando against her chest. There was no personal space. Time held no limits. Mr. Yanakov worked them until they got it right. He stood back and latched on with his gaze—exacting, demanding, imperious—then repositioned them, sliding his palm down Katherine's derrière and not always to correct her pose.

When Katherine got home at night, she lay in bed and touched where Mr. Yanakov's fingers had burned into her.

Whatever he wanted, she would do. Let him bear down, scrutinizing every part of her, his body firm and directive. Let him shape her, his fingers kneading signals into her muscles.

"Tall enough, I guess," Mr. Yanakov said, as Katherine drank from the water fountain after rehearsal. "It's fine to part your hair down the middle." Instinctively, she checked that her bun was secure. "Remind me how old you are?"

"Seventeen." She felt herself blushing.

"The brown eyes and long nose suggest Modigliani," he said, tilting his head.

Was that a compliment? "It's the oval face," he said, gazing down the rest of her. Yes, she thought it might be. He smoothed his hand over his salt-and-pepper hair. "We're going to give you a new name."

She had never considered her name.

"For the stage. You can't use your name."

"I didn't realize that."

"What do you think of Katya Symanova?"

"Wow," she said. "That's nice. It sounds like a Russian ballerina. Okay!"

Mr. Yanakov smiled. She could see the pulse in his neck. "Okay," he murmured.

"What was that about?" Maya asked, sidling up to Katherine as Mr. Yanakov headed down the hall.

Katherine stared as if Maya were a stranger.

"Katherine! What is wrong with you?"

"I have a new name," she said dreamily. It didn't matter that the muscles spreading from her spine screamed in distress. Or that her hair was pinned too tightly and her toes bandaged. Why fixate on pain? She would dance through the blisters; she would become Katya Symanova.

"You have a new name," Maya said, "and I'm a clown."

"No, really."

"Pray tell. What shall I call you?"

"Katya Symanova."

A look of realization crossed Maya's face. "So it's true."

"What?"

"He means business. He's grooming you for prima."

"Stop it!" But Katherine couldn't help wondering the same thing—whether Mr. Yanakov's hands around her rib cage meant something more, whether the press of his body, the demands he placed on her portended something bigger. Prima ballerina was unimaginably distant; Katherine hadn't even taken company auditions. But the name; Boris Yanakov had chosen her name. It was as if some legendary tutued ballerina, fresh garlands in her hair, had risen from a sepia-tinted photograph to summon Katherine to the stage. She felt as though Mr. Yanakov had given her a priestly blessing.

"It's not like he gave me a new name," Maya said.

"You don't need one—Maya Bichette is perfect."

"I'm worried about tripping during my *Swan Lake pas de quatre*," Maya said, taking a drink from the fountain. "Fiona says if I hold her hand any tighter during our *emboîtés*, I'll bring down all four of us in the line."

"I wish I had your sense of balance," Katherine said. "No way you'll pull that line down—you're the anchor. They depend on you."

"Tell Fiona that."

"You'll be great. Aunt Mary is making such a fuss over this performance that she has reservations at three different restaurants," Katherine said. "She can't decide which is the most festive. Fortunately, she and my dad seem to have forgotten about my graduation from high school."

"You're lucky."

"For once, I'm not arguing," Katherine said. Still, she wished Mama could see her *Don Quixote* excerpt. She wanted to save Mama a seat. Just in case.

"My mother's taking me to the beauty parlor," Maya said. "So I'll look swish in my cap and gown."

"Cute." Katherine smiled. She was a child tonguing a new tooth: Katya Symanova.

11

1952

"You got a date this weekend?"

Morty Klein's goggles were in John's face. Every Friday in chemistry lab he asked the same question and got the same answer. "I have to work in my father's pharmacy," John said. The blue flame of the Bunsen burner was making him sweat. He was almost twenty-one, running to keep up with Morty and the other boys at City College. They may have grown up dirt poor and Jewish, but they had grown up in New York. Baseball and politics consumed them in equal measure; they were thoroughly American.

John hated that his language remained slightly off-kilter. When he wasn't studying, he glued himself to the radio to try to adapt to the fast-paced clip. Every vowel was a minefield. If he wasn't attentive, he slipped on some unpronounceable diphthong or failed to grasp the myriad alien cultural references—the in-jokes, the puns, the ads that flew past despite his efforts.

More than once, he had to repeat himself until Morty understood what he was trying to say, then suffer Morty's riotous laughter as he offered some pithy substitute: "Oh, you mean…" John skirted questions about where he came from. He never mentioned Mainz, or Germany, or disclosed that once he'd had a different father and mother, even a little brother and an extended family. It was easier to say he was from Yonkers. Morty knew better than to inquire further.

"Betty wants me to take her to Coney Island this weekend," Morty said, adjusting his safety glasses. "But I don't have the dough. She'll have to settle for dinner with the folks. Maybe an ice cream afterward." Betty was his soon-to-be fiancée; they would be married once he completed his degree. She and Morty went to the same temple. John marveled at the ease with which Morty navigated the school and the girl. Most of all, he marveled at Morty's certainty that all would go according to plan.

What would it take to become American? John's clothing never felt right. Buddy's pants were too big, even though John had filled out with Selma's lovingly prepared meals. He continued to be awestruck by the cornucopia. Fresh fruit and sweets whenever he wanted. Three square meals; every day a feast. Selma wouldn't let him leave the house without eggs and oatmeal. She packed him two sandwiches every morning, in addition to an apple and homemade cookies.

Saturdays he spent with Barney at the pharmacy. A little spending money, Barney said, to take out the girls. But John didn't know whom to ask, or how.

Still, he noticed them everywhere. Striding purposefully around campus, their hips in A-line skirts, their buttocks round and pleasing. Walking their dogs in Yonkers, laughing over the sodas John served at Barney's pharmacy. Clumps of office girls rode the train to work in the morning—breasts showing through close-fitting sweaters, groves of shapely legs, black lines sliding down their stockings.

12

1954

Katya was invited to join the company, and so was Maya. They rented an apartment together on the far West Side. "I have an old grip," Daddy said, as Katya lugged a box from her bedroom to move out of Queens. He disappeared into the basement. "Your grandfather gave this to me before your mother and I got married," he said, coming up the steps. "We took it on our honeymoon to the Poconos." He wiped the dust off his initials, stamped in gold.

Daddy kept a wedding photo on his dresser: Mama in a satin dress spilling around her feet, Daddy gazing at her. They looked young and hopeful. "Your mother thought we should share luggage." He chuckled. "When we got to the hotel, I found two of her dresses on top." Katya knew which they were; she had smelled them for years, looking for a trace of Mama. One was black crepe—cinched at the waist with a cowl neck. The other was robin's-egg blue, patterned with small white swans. It had a keyhole neck and a twirly skirt.

Mama loved to dance—not Katya's kind, but nevertheless, a connection. Katya vaguely remembered Mama spinning her around the kitchen to the Andrews Sisters. The two dresses in the closet would have been good for a swing. Katya pictured her parents while they were courting, dancing at a club, the band suited up in light-blue dinner jackets with black piping, tapping their feet to the music.

"We had five heavenly days on our honeymoon," Daddy said.

Mama and Daddy were married at seventeen. Imagine having a husband at Katya's age, right after high school! It was alarming, even though girls did it all the time.

"Daddy?"

"Mmm?"

"Never mind."

"What?"

It was lodged beneath the surface of her memory like skin grown over a splinter—Daddy pouring out a bottle of bourbon, draining the remnants.

"A long time ago…" Katya said. Had he been angry? Distracted by grief? "Did Mama…?" Had he been trying to erase something? "What about the bourbon?"

Daddy looked surprised. "What bourbon?"

"You poured it down the sink one night; you said something about Mama." Katya had heard whispers: Aunt Mary and Daddy, and occasionally people at church. She hadn't had the courage to ask.

"You remember?"

She nodded, afraid to upset him.

"Too bad," Daddy said. "I wanted to keep you from it. You want to run time backward. To undo that day. You wish she hadn't been so desperate for a drink that she didn't notice oncoming traffic." His words spilled out, fermented wine from a broken bottle. "I tried to get her to stop, but she wouldn't listen."

"You mean—"

"That's just what I mean." He choked up. "I guess you're old enough now," he said, wilting. "Can you use the grip, Katherine?"

"Sorry, Dad, it's just a tiny apartment. There's no place to store it."

"Who said life was a barrel of laughs? What with joining the company and moving out, you're old enough," Daddy said again. He stared at the gold initials on the suitcase as if he had nothing else to offer. "We get educated in the school of hard knocks. The thing is, you've got to pay attention. If I have one lesson, that's it. I wasn't paying attention with Mama. Not enough, anyway."

"Oh, Daddy." Katya had breached a taboo and couldn't retreat fast enough. Was he blaming himself, or Mama?

"I'll come back as often as I can," Katya said, with the sense that she was shoving the contents of an overstuffed pillow back through a ripped seam. She didn't need Daddy to offer anything; she needed him to be less isolated. She hated thinking of him by himself in this forlorn, deserted house. She hated to think that Mama had been drunk that day, that she'd thrown away her life like that. That Mama had done that to her.

"Don't worry about me, Katherine," Daddy said.

Within the oppressive quiet, Mama's absence had become a palpable, shattered peace, Mama less a victim than a participant. Katya had imagined Mama smiling down from heaven, sad to have been taken from her child. But this was different; this was new.

"You have a big job ahead of you," Daddy added, taking a stab at good cheer.

Katya looked at him. "Thanks, Dad."

She couldn't wait to leave.

13

1954

Company rehearsals were hours filled with lines. "You have no identity, girls!" Mr. Yanakov barked as he sketched out *Seasonal Colors*. Lines that went sideways, that stacked from back to front, that formed diagonals. "I don't care who you are. Surrender to the whole!" Katya was assigned to *Spring Green*, *Autumn Red*, and *Winter Gray*.

"Bury yourselves in the collective!" Mr. Yanakov shouted. The *corps* fell like dominoes—boys on top of girls—dancing to a contemporary pastiche heavy on percussion. "*Spring Green* is about fertility. Leave your personalities home."

"Why hasn't Mr. Yanakov started rehearsing *Autumn Red*?" Katya asked Maya as they headed back to their dark little walk-up on Ninth Avenue. "It's so close to opening night."

"None of your business, bonehead," Maya said. "Or mine," she added as they climbed the four flights. "We're the lackeys. We do as we're told."

Katya put her ballet bag down on her bed. "What if Mr. Yanakov can't pull it off?"

"You don't trust him?"

The next Sunday, Katya visited Maya's family in Riverdale. Seeing Maya's mother, her face made up, eye shadow just right, her strawberry-blond hair—same color as Maya's—swept in her usual French twist, Katya felt stricken, as if Mama had not only fallen from grace, but from heaven. Katya's memory had been reordered. The puzzle pieces—which hadn't quite fit together in the first place—were now strewn around the floor. She thought of the hoboes on the subway, sleeping with their hands around a bottle in a paper bag, and women hidden under the eaves of buildings, dirty and afraid. Was that what Mama would be now?

"Bloody Marys, anyone?" Mrs. Bichette asked. Sunshine streamed through the windows. There was a set of blond furniture and books, artfully arranged on the coffee table.

"You mean me?" Chris said.

"Very funny, Chris."

"No, thank you," Katya said.

"Teetotaler, eh?" Mr. Bichette said. "Or just trying to keep your girlish figure?"

"Shut up, Dad. Leave her alone."

On the subway ride over, Maya had asked, "Why the hang-dog look?"

"You'll say I'm crazy," Katya said.

"Try me."

"My mother."

"You never talk about her."

"I don't remember much. But when I was packing up to move out, my dad said... Oh, never mind."

"C'mon."

"It's just that...he's going to be so lonely at the house." She couldn't bring herself to say more, couldn't talk about Mama as a drunk, couldn't say what had preoccupied her since that miserable conversation with Daddy, that Mama was in some way responsible for her own death, that there was intent in her absence.

"Your dad will be okay," Maya said. "He has his work, right?"

"Yeah." How could Daddy have let Mama go out like that? Why hadn't he stopped her? He told Katya to pay attention, when he was the one who hadn't been paying attention. "My dad knows I have to grow up," Katya said halfheartedly.

"Well, there you go," Maya said. "I'm jealous. My parents think I should do something more 'traditional.' Whatever that means."

"What's up first for the company?" Mrs. Bichette asked,

bringing a tray of scrambled eggs to the dining room table. She was wearing pearls.

"*Seasonal Colors*," Maya said. "The *corps* is in all four movements."

"I've never heard of that."

"Of course not, Mom. These things come full blown out of Yanakov's head." Maya buttered a piece of toast.

"Orange juice?" Mrs. Bichette asked.

"Over here," Chris said.

"He's so creative," Katya said.

"If you go for slave labor," Maya said.

Mr. Bichette looked up from the *Sunday Times* piled to the right side of his plate. "That's what you bargained for."

"Where's the bargaining when only one side's got the power?" Maya asked.

"Now you're objecting?"

"I don't think of it that way," Katya said.

"You better start," Maya said.

"You can always quit," Mr. Bichette said.

"Quit!" Katya was astonished. "Never."

Two weeks before opening, Mr. Yanakov began rehearsing *Autumn Red*. "You," he said, pointing to Katya. He motioned to Micheline Lafitte and Lars Andersson. "The rest go next door to rehearse the ensemble dances." Maya glared at Katya as she trooped from the room. "Back in a minute," Mr. Yanakov said.

Dancing with Micheline and Lars? Micheline was Mr. Yanakov's favorite. In company class, she worked out at the metal barre in the center, the first in line, the closest to the mirror. She opened in New York and London; it was she whom Mr. Yanakov escorted from the theater. She was a French beauty, auburn haired and long limbed, though not so lithe and graceful as some. What Micheline had was athletic assurance, no wavering turns, no quavering poses. Her partner could set her in an *arabesque en pointe* and run laps around her while she stayed fixed and steady.

Mr. Yanakov had brought her from Paris when he came to the New York State Ballet. It was said he had fled Leningrad for Paris as a teenager. His bursts of anger stoked rumors that one of his deserted French wives had resurfaced. But when he was sullen and distracted, the reverse circulated—that he was a lovesick man who failed to master his passions; that the women had abandoned him, and not he them; that he was possessed by a Sirens' chorus he was incapable of silencing.

Micheline pulled up her leg warmers and turned to Katya. "The great master has singled you out." She was on the far side of thirty, perilously old for a ballerina. She wasn't much of a talker, not because her first language was French, but due to a native aloofness that wasn't quite haughty but not quite modest either.

"I don't know," Katya said, shrugging her shoulders.

"You're here, aren't you?" Lars said. He was New York State Ballet's top male dancer, born in Minnesota, a strapping blond known for his jumps.

"I'm not sure what he's thinking," Katya said.

"No." Micheline looked at her. "Perhaps not." She glanced at the clock on the wall. "Time for a cigarette."

"Center," Mr. Yanakov ordered, as he swung open the door. "How many times do I have to tell you, Miss Lafitte? Put out that poison stick." Unperturbed, she tamped out her cigarette in the glass ashtray on the piano lid and ambled over.

"This trio is the pivot for *Autumn Red*," Mr. Yanakov said, smoothing down his hair. Katya adjusted a pin in her bun and tried to look confident. "The *corps* will come round when necessary," he continued, gesturing toward the room next door, "but you three are it. Micheline and Lars will show you how it's done," he said, wrapping his arm around Katya's waist and moving her forward. His strong, guiding embrace felt good.

Mr. Y put Lars between Micheline and Katya and pressed the women into him.

"No," Mr. Yanakov said, moving Lars aside.

He extended a hand for each woman. "Miss Lafitte, come

behind. Put your arms under mine and reach for Miss Symanova. Closer, Miss Symanova, right up against me." He pulled
Katya flush against his torso and had Micheline flatten her
palms over Katya's shoulder blades. Katya breathed against Mr.
Y's commanding chest. "Okay?" He slapped her buttocks and
pushed Lars between the two women.

"Autumn is a season of foreboding," Mr. Yanakov said,
squeezing them together. "You three form a monolith. Your
breakup heralds winter, the bringer of ice and snow, cold and
death. Look for that dark place where you stow the worst of
your past. Make them quake at what you discover there."

What did her past have to do with it? Katya needed concrete
instruction.

"Miss Symanova! Where are you?" Mr. Yanakov tapped her
cheeks as if he were trying to revive her. "Are you an individual
or not?" Hadn't she just been taken from the ensemble, where
she'd spent weeks being admonished to sink into the whole? "I
need to see inside!" he yelled, poking her abdomen. He clasped
her hips to reposition her, his hands on fire. He had Katya and
Micheline bend sideways on either side of Lars, then snapped
his fingers for Lydia. Over the music's rhythmic drone, Mr.
Yanakov split them one from another, flinging them to the far
corners of the studio.

In an instant, Katya got it. No more "fix your fifth position."
Mr. Yanakov had stirred her like a sorcerer creating a spell.

"Crouch," he shouted. "Crouch in fear of what is to come."

Katya somersaulted across the floor, arms tucked in, while
Mr. Yanakov stood with his chin in his palm, considering his
work.

"Better, Miss Symanova."

"I see where you're going," she said. She'd expected him
to assemble steps like a carpenter building furniture. But of
course, furniture was static. Instead he wove feeling with ingre-
dients plucked from air. He may as well be spinning breezes or
tracing a hummingbird's flight. Katya had not perceived this in
all her years peering through the studio window. Now, under

his exacting tutelage, she sensed the magic. "May I try again?"
"Certainly," he said, grinning.

Opening night at the Peter Stuyvesant Theater, Mr. Yanakov
crisscrossed the wings, insensible to anyone around him, pausing only to adjust his tuxedo jacket and straighten his bow tie,
his black cummerbund girdling an immaculately pressed shirt.
As the audience quieted, the volley of his pacing grew more
pronounced. *Click, click, click,* reverse. His patent leather shoes
flashed bright in the shadows backstage.

Katya's buzzing nerves were living, breathing obstacles to be
subjugated. To dance was not so much an artistic enterprise as
a call to battle. The critics were watching; the stakes were high.
Fanning out the emerald mesh on her skirt for *Spring Green,*
Katya moved to stage right. She was to stay in her line and
blend in. If her leg rose an inch higher than the girl ahead of
her, the critics would excoriate the company's ensemble, and
Mr. Yanakov would know who'd caused it.

The curtain lifted. Katya cantered forward. Troupe members tumbled one on top of another like dominoes—just as Mr.
Yanakov had ordered—before skittering away to make room
for the next tranche. Time to change for *Autumn Red.*

Katya stripped off her green leotard and threw on a red
one, swiftly pulling up a scarlet-colored skirt over her sweaty
legs. She fixated on the music—sinister and foreboding—and
pressed herself between Lars and Micheline. Was Mr. Yanakov
watching? She had to concentrate; she had to execute every step
meticulously. Breast to breast with Lars; Micheline on the far
side. They were a circular saw, carving up the stage.

The music accelerated. A sea of red-suited *corps* surrounded
them, diving and leaping. Time to suck the remaining life out
of *Autumn Red* and make way for *Winter Gray.* Katya could hear
Mr. Yanakov. "Take yourself to that dark place, make them
quake." She would show him she understood. She threw herself
sideways. Give it your all, that's what he wanted. In a final thrust
offstage, she jumped as high as she could, her thighs burning

with effort. Hurling forward, she caught her left foot and fell.

She heard a panicked inhalation ripple through the audience. Picking her head up from the floor, Katya crawled out of public view. Before she could get up, Mr. Yanakov towered over her, looming and ominous. "Lucky you didn't cause Micheline to land on you," he growled. Standing erect and flattening his abdomen, he sputtered, "Where I come from, this would earn you a place in the circus, Miss Symanova. Or a one-way trip to Siberia."

Katya was an impostor, with her manufactured Russian name. Why did he have to hover here? Some choreographers sat in the audience, or traveled to distant cities to coach other companies, or had a night out. Mr. Yanakov stationed himself in the wings every matinee and every night as if his furious stare alone were what propelled his dancers forward. Without waiting to see whether Katya was injured, he stormed off.

Blood leached through her tights. There was a hole over her right knee and no time to fix it. She ran to change for *Winter Gray*.

Clammy with sweat and contrition, Katya adjusted her leotard and positioned herself stage left. Through the shadows, she made out the hot tip of Micheline's cigarette. Micheline was dispassionate, imperturbable. While she, Katya, had recklessly thrown herself offstage.

Katya couldn't help but think of Mama, who in the last few weeks had transformed from a smiling, two-dimensional figure, mute as stone, into a pressing question. Mama was no longer in heaven, proudly ticking notches on the yardstick of Katya's life; she was a fallen angel. Now Katya had fallen too, before an audience of thousands.

Maya and Fiona crossed the stage in *Winter Gray*'s first line, crouching and rising with the rest of the *corps*, the music growing more ominous. Katya had to do as Mr. Y instructed. She tried to think about cold and ice, even as she blistered with humiliation. What if she had squandered the opportunity Mr. Yanakov had given her? Two more years in the *corps*, minimum.

Her line began to advance. From the orchestra pit came rumbling timpani and the rat-a-tat of snare drums. No more mistakes. She aligned herself with the girl in front; she couldn't stick out. As the strings emitted prolonged high-pitched squeals, Katya spread her legs and jumped through Mr. Yanakov's leap-frog formations, now withering on the floor, now throwing up her arms. Louder and louder the music, bursts of sound detonating with increasing frequency. She couldn't fall again, but she couldn't be too guarded either. Rhythms boomed and thumped throughout the theater.

The music stopped and the curtain fell. Katya lined up for curtain call. Dropping to a curtsy, she felt the newly formed scab on her knee split. The clapping intensified; the audience expressing its pity for her. Katya felt a piercing loneliness, along with the certainty that whatever happened from now on, Katya was on her own.

You weren't allowed to trip onstage.

14

1955

"This thing is perkier dead than Aunt Topsy alive," Alfred said. Along with two med school classmates, John hovered over his cadaver. Alfred had named her after his late great-aunt.

"She's not a thing," John said. "She has a name."

"There goes Curtin, keeping us on the up-and-up," Bill said.

"Topsy, you're my gal!" Alfred bellowed.

John was used to his raucous anatomy partners. Still, he went on. "It bothers me that no one took care of her," he said.

"How the hell would you know?" Alfred asked.

Her tag said she died at thirty, her body riddled with cancer. "No prior surgeries, nothing to alleviate her symptoms," John said. "No signs of minimal, exploratory incisions. She was too poor to see a doctor."

"Jesus, Curtin, there's a reason you're going to be a head-shrinker," Bill said. "Your imagination is way too active."

"What could a surgeon have done with her?" Alfred asked.

"If she'd seen a doctor, her cancer might not have advanced this far," John said.

"Doubtful, you sap. It was terminal."

"He could have eased her pain or given her some hope."

"Where's the hope when you've got a death sentence?"

"Everyone needs hope," John said.

Bill snickered. "Very scientific, Dr. Headshrinker."

John was tempted to lecture them on hope's fragility—nothing more oppressive than its absence, nothing more potent than its slim possibility. They wouldn't know.

"Aw shucks," Alfred said. "Isn't that sweet? Topsy's human."

"That's right," John said, studying the cadaver's waxen face and ignoring their jibes. She was so young. The worst part was that her uterus indicated a live birth. Somewhere in the world she had a child mourning her. Hope came and went like an electric current. Grief, on the other hand, was a reliable constant.

"Topsy and I are bosom buddies," Bill said.

In her leathery skin and stringy muscles, John read desperation. Too poor to seek medical help, too sick to protect her child, who had to fend for himself. How could her son survive New York? He must be sleeping in doorways and haunting restaurant garbage for food. In winter he would have to find a warm grate and pray that the thieves and murderers stayed away. Did his shoes have soles? Frozen and unprotected, every evening a nightmare, every day a terror. Within this teeming, crowded city, no one would notice a frightened orphan hiding in the shadows.

"Ta-ta, Topsy," Alfred said, replacing the sheet over her body at the end of class. "Don't do anything we wouldn't do."

John wished he could be more like Alfred and Bill—jokesters who kept things light. He was trying mightily to master the American way: Don't take anything too seriously, and if you do, for Pete's sake don't show it.

A father, John realized. The child might have a living father. He breathed a sigh of relief.

"*Au revoir*, Topsy," Bill said.

15

1956

"Aren't you tired of this hellhole?" Maya asked Katya, locking the door to their apartment and walking down the four flights on the way to a performance. "What're we doing squished into a place that's not big enough to fry an egg?"

"We're dancers, that's what," Katya said. "How're we going to afford another place?"

"*Danseurs*, madame?" Maya said, with an exaggerated slur. "We're stuck in the back row."

"I figured I'd get two more years there, and I have."

"You make it sound like a prison sentence."

"I earned it, tripping like that," Katya said. She had to ensure that it would never, ever happen again. She had to prove her mettle. She had—once more—to catch Mr. Yanakov's eye.

"My idiot brother just started at Columbia," Maya said as they rounded the corner to the theater. "I can't get over it. The little twerp is going to have more education in his pinky finger than I'll ever have."

Katya stopped and adjusted her bag. "You're really upset, aren't you? What about college? You could do it. You're plenty smart. But Mr. Yanakov wouldn't let you. You'd have to leave the company."

"He doesn't own me."

"I guess we made a different choice," Katya said. How many days had her conviction flagged, Mr. Yanakov zipping past her as if she were a blade of grass on an immaculate lawn? Still, she pushed forward, holding herself to a punishing standard, working through company class with precision and drive.

"Tell me about it," Maya said. "Don't you ever want a normal life?"

"No." Katya didn't like to think of what she had come from—Mama home drinking (was that true?), Daddy stuck in a boring job. "I just want to dance." Every night when she made the last adjustment to her foot position and heard the conductor's downbeat, she felt the rush of performance and the heat and glare of the lights. It didn't matter that she was in the back row.

Well, no. It mattered terribly. If only Mr. Yanakov would consider her again. "It's harder than anything, isn't it?" Katya said.

"I fantasize about taking a stenographer's course. Anything for something different."

"I'd hate it if you left. I'd miss you too much," Katya said, surprised to be tearing up. "I know it's selfish, but I can't imagine ballet without you." They'd been together since they were little girls, Maya poking Katherine as she peered through the studio window; next to each other at the barre, having ice cream with Maya's family, living in their cramped little hole-in-the-wall.

"Nice of you to miss me," Maya said.

"I mean it," Katherine said. Underneath Maya's bluster was Katya's closest friend.

"Don't worry, I can't give my parents the satisfaction. They'd be thrilled if I got my MRS as a stenographer, or in nursing school. I can see them jumping for joy."

"What about Jim the banker?" Maya had been dating him on and off for a year.

"What about you?"

"You know the answer to that. There's no one." Katya went out occasionally, a double date with Maya from time to time. But those men held no interest.

"You're fixated on Boris the Dictator."

Katya laughed but didn't deny it. Mr. Yanakov was a quest. She longed to recapture the sensation she'd had rehearsing *Autumn Colors*—fragments of his choreography crackling like sparks from a fire, his palm searing her diaphragm.

"Jim the banker is as nonconformist as we are in the back line of *Les Sylphides*," Maya said. "Not a hair out of place. Has to fit in just so. He's rocking the boat when he wears a blue shirt instead of a white one. If I don't ditch him, I'll die of boredom."

"You'll break his heart," Katya said.

"Let's hope so."

Little wings affixed to their bodices quivered when they began the *bourrées*, an infinity of swift, tiny steps. Their gossamer skirts fanned out as they sailed back and forth *en pointe*, lines of girl-women floating evanescent through *Les Sylphides*. The back row swung lengthwise and split into columns. Katya in the rear, drilling her blistered toes to anchor her pose, fighting to keep her arms steady.

A ballerina named Katya Symanova should execute her steps perfectly, but perfection was not enough. Nor were her long neck, black hair parted down the middle, and taut, erect back. Her most important job was to form a piece of a whole that would fail if she did anything to distinguish herself. She arched her eyebrows and tilted her head toward center stage. Arms clasped to her small bosom, she prayed—as she did every night—that her beatific expression would alight on Mr. Yanakov.

"I invited my dad tonight," she said to Maya as they walked to the dressing room after curtain calls. "I didn't exactly ask. I told him I was leaving him a ticket at the box office."

"Aren't you Little Miss Social Secretary," Maya said, brushing out hair spray.

"I'm just encouraging him to get out. He might like it."

"Meet us downtown afterward."

"Okay." Hoisting her ballet bag over her shoulder, Katya left the company dressing room, edging past Micheline.

"I see you understand, Miss Symanova," Mr. Yanakov said, emerging from the shadows. Out of the corner of her eye, Katya saw Micheline light a cigarette. "Dancing in the back requires the same attention as dancing solo." He gave a half smile and leaned closer. "I like that. Maybe you'll walk out with me after I finish up here."

"Mr. Y." Katya could feel her thumping heart. "I'm, I'm so sorry. My father's here."

"I couldn't tell which one was you," Daddy said when Katya met him outside the stage door. "But you girls sure make a pretty picture."

"Thanks, Dad." She turned around to try to catch a glimpse of Mr. Yanakov. Why tonight of all nights?

Afterward, she joined the company members at the Bee's Knees in the West Village, their favorite gathering spot. A mediocre band played through a haze of smoke and whiskey.

"Drinks?" Riccardo from the company asked, pushing his way through the crowd.

"No, thanks," Katya said. She was afraid of liquor.

"C'mon," said Fernando, pulling her into the mass of over-heated dancers. He wrapped his arm around her and tipped her backward. Along with the other boys, he would comb the shadows in the Village once the club closed. He pulled her in and out to the extent possible; there was barely room to move. Dancing with him felt comfortable, like putting on a frequent-ly worn cardigan. In fact, the whole place had a comfortable familiarity. Released from the rigors of *Les Sylphides*, company members' joints were loosened—arms flapping, hips gyrat-ing—unwinding after a hard night.

Maya came over as Katya sat down between numbers. "What's up with you? You're woolgathering."

"He asked me to leave the theater with him."

"Who?"

"You know who."

"Not Boris the Dictator?"

"Yeah. But I had to meet my dad." Katya wanted to cry in frustration. Two years in the back row, two years in which she'd worked harder than the years before. Mr. Yanakov had seen her! She was afraid she'd missed a one-time chance, that he'd move on to someone else, as company members said he did.

"Going out with your dad is a capital crime?"

"My dad could have come another time." He couldn't even pick her out of a line, although he did like chatting over a corned beef sandwich afterward.

Maya looked at her. "Good thing he came tonight."

16

1960

John's alarm was a hornet's buzz. Throbbing temples and cramped muscles preceded his awareness of anything else. He hoisted himself up and mashed his fists into his eyes. The residents' bunks were too narrow.

Four-thirty a.m. A new day on Beaumont Hospital's psychiatric ward. John still wasn't acclimated to residency. Dousing his face in cold water, he combed his hair and smoothed his mustache. Two hours before the first hint of daylight, three and a half before he could reward himself with coffee and a conversation—however brief—with the office secretary. Ann had such voluptuous hips.

John threw on his white coat and trudged up the concrete steps to the double glass door on Fifth Floor East. Ann had a white coat—not like his—with a belt at the waist. Every time she tied it, she tossed back her blond hair. Only Ann would wear white in New York, where soot was the city's calling card.

The night nurse buzzed John through; New York's refuse pile, given over to his care. Elton Miller was first, a large man whose mother had turned to doctors when she couldn't persuade him to come in from the street. John wondered whether the Pope had had time to telephone Elton last night. This morning, thankfully, Elton was asleep. Who wouldn't be? John scanned the chart at the end of his bed. No troubling matters of Catholic dogma during the night. Elton looked almost serene.

John followed the red stripe along the linoleum floor that led to the solarium. In a few hours, a couple of patients would be sitting in there, leafing through *Look or Life*. He tiptoed toward Candida Jackson's room. She was the choir director at her church in Harlem. Her family assured him she had a beautiful voice.

Mrs. Jackson was sitting up and sucking repetitively, her face a shriveled walnut shell. She had recently abandoned her false teeth, claiming they interfered with the singing—an allusion to the Metropolitan Opera, which had begun inhabiting her brain. Until his residency, John hadn't appreciated the human capacity for invention; there were endless permutations.

"How come you're not sleeping, Mrs. Jackson?"

"I have to keep time. Do you want to know what's going on, Doc?" She laid a bony finger on his forearm.

"Sure." John pulled up a chair beside her bed.

Mrs. Jackson looked from side to side, as if she were about to share a state secret. "Maria Callas is threatening to boycott tonight's performance," she said. "She had a fight with the conductor."

"And?" He perused the list of meds on her chart.

"There's no replacing the great Callas, Doc. The human voice is unique. Window to the soul," she commented as John shined a light into her pupils.

John paused and gazed at her crinkled face. "I think you're right, Mrs. Jackson."

She put an index finger to her lips. "I'll tell you another secret," she whispered.

"What's that?" He picked up her wrist to take her pulse.

"There was a fistfight in the orchestra." She laid her hand over her forehead. "Must be why it hurts so much, Doc."

Poor thing; she suffered from the singing. "Let's see if we can help with that."

"You'll have to take it up with the conductor."

"Okay," John said, going out to find a nurse to administer aspirin.

Louisa Matthews was screaming on the fourth floor. Running down the hall, John heard the commanding voice of an orderly. "Hold still, Mrs. Matthews!" Two men leaned on her shoulders while a nurse sedated her. Her screams devolved to moans. She was a living cadaver—all sinew and bone—finally breathing evenly. John picked up her chart. "No next of kin." That was the problem—outliving her family.

17

1957

Katya was assigned the Arabian Dance in *The Nutcracker*, paired with Paolo Ferraro.

"Biggest moneymaker of the year, and Yanakov can't be bothered," Maya said, as she and Katya walked home one night.

"Magical," Katya said.

"He can't even bother to direct."

It was true; Lars was directing. Having reached his mid-thirties, he was increasingly serving as the company's junior choreographer. But not for Katya's scene. Mr. Yanakov was in rehearsal every afternoon, hovering over her, positioning her leg, holding his arm out as she arched backward. "It's amazing," Katya said.

"Jesus, you're nuts," Maya said. "Wasting all that time on the winter warhorse? You're only saying that because you got a part. You wouldn't feel that way if you were me, one of the nameless snowflakes." She slapped her hand against a parking meter as they walked past the strip joints near Ninth Avenue. The drumbeat inside was so loud the sidewalk shook. "Who said no two snowflakes are the same?"

For the performance, Katya and Paolo were wheeled onstage in an oversized coffee cup. He rested her foot on his shoulder, then genuflected and leisurely turned her upside down. She wore a sequined bikini top and loose-fitting sapphire trousers. Pressing his palm across her bare belly, Paolo elevated her and spun like a waiter with a dessert tray.

The conductor had to rein in the orchestra to maximize the thrust and heft of the dancers' movements. Landing weightless *en pointe*, Katya bent backward toward the floor, Paolo's arm just above her buttocks, slower than they had rehearsed.

"We want to see more of Miss Symanova," The *New York Times* insisted. "Her technical confidence, combined with a lithe sensuality, suggests she needs more challenging roles. In contrast to the clichéd character dancing we dread in *The Nutcracker*, Miss Symanova's performance leaped out, calling attention to a promising young artist."

Emerging from her coffee cup backstage, Katya saw Mr. Yanakov. He extended a hand to help her down, and with the other, leisurely traced the muscles of her naked abdomen. "Maybe it's Paolo we needed for you," he said. "Come to dinner with me."

They crossed Fifty-Sixth Street toward a green awning with Luigi's Ristorante spelled in white cursive. Mr. Yanakov stopped underneath. He put two fingers under Katya's scarf and swept them in a semicircle around her neck. "Take that off inside, will you?" he said, swinging open the door to the restaurant. She felt incandescent.

Signor Luigi walked toward them, arms outstretched. "Signor Yanakov! In from the cold. I have your table ready." He took Mr. Y's coat. "I see you brought a pretty girl tonight. I don't think I've met this one."

What girls was Signor Luigi referring to? Katya didn't want to think about them.

Mr. Yanakov had his own table! Katya's heartbeats were a thousand jumps landing at once. Luigi's was hushed and grand, the walls lined with red velvet drapes, every table set with starched white linen and cut-glass goblets. Even the breadbaskets were silver.

She played with a crust of bread and watched Mr. Y wolf down a plate of pasta. "The maestro loves his baton too much," he said. "He ignores my dancers. He pushes the tempo when he should slow; he slows when he should speed up. Did you see him tonight?"

"I can't see anything from the stage." She danced to the black void, staying with the music's ebb and flow. The conductor was like a second set of *pointe* shoes, supporting her, even if he was a little fast sometimes, or slow. "Girls, let the music find you! A hesitant dancer is a poor dancer," Mr. Yanakov was fond of saying.

He leaned across the table. "I'd like to wring his neck. Violette couldn't finish her final *penché*."

"I must have been changing; I didn't see her."

"I did! That glorious arch in her back, the hesitancy in her drop forward. It's a crime to interfere with that kind of pacing."

"I'm sure the audience didn't notice," Katya offered.

"Don't!" Mr. Yanakov said, raising his hand and his voice simultaneously. A few diners turned around. "Don't ever judge anything by the audience. What do they know? You are the best judge."

"I only know that it's never enough," she said.

"That's a very good place to start." Mr. Yanakov looked at her. "You," he said quietly, "are a canvas awaiting a paintbrush. A piano in search of a sonata. We'll see what we can do with you." She inhaled the way he was eyeing her, the way his tone of voice pitched low when he spoke to her. She laid her hand on the table.

He moved his plate aside and squeezed her fingers. "Someday you'll accompany a lonely man home," he said.

Did that mean what it sounded like? She dared not think about it; it seemed presumptuous. She felt a renewed commitment to please him in the studio. To kick higher, to hold herself tighter, longer, taller. She could be better meshed with Paolo onstage; she could keep her poses a split second more. What would it feel like to put her palm over Mr. Yanakov's muscular shoulder—not the way she did in rehearsal—and run her hand across his taut midriff? He would bring her gently to him for their first kiss. He would embrace her with measured deliberateness, like sinking into a *plié* at the beginning of class. He would dance a slow dance with her.

At the entrance to the subway, he stopped and ran his fingers under her chin once more. "I'm not far from here, you know," he said, walking off.

Maya had her head wrapped in a towel and was buttoning the front of her light-blue satin pajamas when Katya got home; she was just out of the shower. "So?"

Katya didn't want to answer.

"Out with it!" Maya poured some wine into a chipped drinking glass. "Want one?"

"No, thanks," Katya said quietly. She didn't feel like talking about the muted elegance of Luigi's, or that Mr. Yanakov had asked her to take off her scarf when they got inside.

"Well?"

"He's irritated with the conductor. He thinks 'the maestro' doesn't follow us well enough."

"Is that all?" Maya took a sip of wine.

"He said Violette's final moves were constricted."

"What about you?"

Katya couldn't describe the way he had looked at her, or what they had talked about. It was different from before. "I have to try harder." For the first time, she felt his desire fixed on her alone. The memory of his fingers across her chin made her blush.

"Is that why he took you out?" Maya asked with an exasperated huff.

"No." Katya shook her head. "No, I think I was just supposed to figure that out from what he was saying. Something about the importance of being your own harshest critic. About an empty canvas waiting to be painted on."

Maya finished her wine with a gulp and set the glass in the sink. "You know something?" she said, brushing out her hair. "You can be extraordinarily dense."

18

1962

John's first impression of Ann's place was that she must have left in a hurry that morning. A stack of dirty dishes teetered precariously above the rim of the sink. Several lipstick-covered cups were on the small counter by the sink, along with a partially eaten slice of toast. It was a sharp contrast with Selma's kitchen, which, although cramped, was ordered and spotless. On the other hand, Ann's wasn't really a kitchen; it was just one side of a room.

Ann hung her white coat above a pink satin bathrobe on the coat stand and led him to a muddy-colored davenport. Next to it was a crate, with a scarf bunched on top that he had seen her wear last week. There were half-empty perfume bottles too.

"At night I pull this out for my bed," Ann said, sitting on the davenport. She leaned over to switch on the lamp, also balanced on a crate. Her rear was in a tight-fitting skirt, the stripes down the back of her stockings elongating her legs. John saw the penny-sized mole on her right calf and was seized by the same rush of desire he'd felt watching her bend over the coffee urn in the office. The shape of her buttocks, the curve of her hips. She walked to the door and turned off the ceiling light. "That's better," she said, tiptoeing toward him and sitting so near she was almost on top of him.

There was no mistaking her intention. "Why so sad, Dr. Curtin?" she whispered, running her index finger across his chin. "Or are you just quiet tonight?" She pressed her lips to his and searched for his tongue.

"Not sad," he said, pulling back a little. "Not at all."

She put her hand on his thigh. This wasn't the Ann who was the secretary for the psychiatry residents. Moving closer to kiss him again, she stretched her legs across his lap, inching up her skirt. He traced her garter with his index finger, afraid his hammering heart would split open his chest. So that was where those tantalizing black stripes ended. In the silky, warm skin of her thigh, in the lacy V of her panties. She kicked her heels over the edge of the couch and slid lower. His eyes roamed down her face to her creamy neck and her blouse opening. "May I?" he asked.

"I've never met anyone as polite as you," she said, bringing his trembling hand to her top button. One, two. It wasn't so easy to open them. Three, four. She held up her cuffs for him to finish—he felt so inept—then wriggled out of her blouse. "I don't want you to go to too much trouble," she said, unfastening her bra.

He gasped, speechless, and placed a hand on either side of her breasts. Alabaster skin, bosoms like ripe fruit. He felt besotted with the office secretary—with her open thighs, the warm pungent smells under her garter, the mole on her calf, the vein in her translucent cheek—and yearned to lie on top of this gorgeous woman and pump back and forth between her legs.

Then it was over. Come and gone in an instant, too fast and too soon. Depleted, John pulled himself up and searched for words. "That was nice, Ann," he said, stroking her blond hair back from her forehead. "Are you okay?"

"Stay overnight with me," she said, clutching him with unexpected force.

"I don't think I can, Ann."

"Please, just this once."

"I don't want to get you into trouble," he said. He didn't want to leave but was afraid to stay. "I don't want the neighbors bothering you," he added. Where was the joy he'd anticipated with such fervor? He was sinking. Maybe this was what happened the first time. After all, he was, according to Ann, a "greenhorn."

"If I don't mind the neighbors, why should you?" she asked.

"I'm thinking about tomorrow morning," he said, kissing her forehead before he sat up. "I don't want to jeopardize anything for you at work."

"Tomorrow's a long time away," she said. She looked forlorn. "Work's a job, John, that's all it is."

"Do you really feel that way?" He paused. He had staked his future to it, Barney and Selma's investment in him. "That's not what it feels like to me," he said. It wasn't just for Barney and Selma. What about Mutti and Papa? He had his patients, too, about whom he worried incessantly. He held their memories like prized possessions, afraid they would shatter if he let up for an instant. When would he know enough? He had to give his patients everything he had; he had to take away the hurt any way he could.

"You'll be wanting your jacket and scarf," Ann said, getting up. She walked leisurely across the room, naked from the waist up, still wearing her garter belt and stockings. He was shocked by her lack of modesty and overcome by hot, scorching desire. Tying the pink satin bathrobe around her waist, she returned with his suit jacket and scarf and stood over him as he zipped his pants. "It's okay to change your mind," she said, handing him his things.

He wanted to say something but was tongue-tied.

"See you in the office," she said, closing the door behind him.

He groped his way down three flights in the dark stairwell, remorse and euphoria sparking like the electricity administered in shock therapy. Is this what girls wanted? Maybe things shouldn't have gone so far. He pushed open the door to the sidewalk, careening through the emotional spectrum with the speed of one of his patients. How was he supposed to act?

19

1958

"We need her in white," Mr. Yanakov said to the wardrobe mistress. "I'd like to see the exact line of her breasts." Katya flushed at his words about her body. "The skirt should cling to the ankle." She stood in second position as he sculpted the length of her leg.

"And the boy in black," he said. "Maybe with red trim. No… more red than black. Sputnik and the damn Soviets." Tossing his head at Paolo and Katya, Mr. Yanakov continued, "Rockets inspire the fear of naked aggression. But the specter of the heavens as well. The endless universe, the skies above."

"Only in the US," he muttered to himself, snapping his fingers for Lydia to begin. "There's a special brand of American arrogance. The certainty of rightness and the refusal to be cowed by the threat of bombs." He moved Katya and Paolo around in his firm grip. "I love the sweep of an orchestra," he barked over the piano. "The Shostakovich Fifth Symphony. We'll call this one *Space Race.*"

He put Katya's hand in Paolo's and lifted their arms to an inverted V. "*Tendu* to second, and *plié*. Into first and again. Miss Symanova, hold your head high. Throw back your chest. Electricity in the fingers. Show the connection between you two." Her connection, she was certain, was with him.

"Bend over, Miss Symanova," he said, motioning for Lydia to stop. He placed one hand across Katya's chest, and the other at the small of her back. "From here," he said, sliding his hand down her buttocks; his charged fingers.

"Diaphragm parallel to the floor. Legs apart. Derrière to the *corps*. The slow stepping of danger. But sexed. In my ballets,

there is always sex between a man and a woman." Was he referring to her? With him?

Mr. Yanakov's voice orbited her head as Shostakovich blazed
from the orchestra pit—Russian music to underscore her Russian name. Pounding bass, melodies pulled one from another,
weaving plaintively through the strings. Tonight, please may
I deserve her name, Katya thought. Palm against palm with
Paolo, charting the nation's anxieties, burying innocence.

Katya faced the dark cavity beyond the stage and danced for
Mr. Yanakov. Her choreographer fueled her performance. He
was waiting for her in the wings; she sensed it—no, knew it. She
was lit. Her white dress, tight against her skin, was evanescent.
She arched her back and flung her arms from herself. From
the nape of her neck to her unfolding legs, she was a comet
streaking the sky.

"Now." Mr. Yanakov stepped in front of her as she came
offstage. "You are ready to come home with me."

Mr. Yanakov closed the door and turned on a light in the
vestibule. "Your coat." He lifted it off her and hung it in an
overstuffed closet, then turned and slowly smoothed his hands
down her sides, bending his knees as he went. Not a *plié*; he was
touching her body as if for the first time, she felt.

He took Katya's hand and led her into his living room. She
was trembling with anticipation. From the dim light at the front
door and the city lights coming through the window, she could
see the outlines of a room crammed with records. She made
out a stereo system and an armchair.

He pulled her into him and pressed his lips against hers. She
could have choked for the shock of his tongue, probing her
core. Whatever she had expected, it was not this.

"Relax," he whispered. "It's not so different from the studio.
Mr. Y knows what to do."

Could it be?

He had the same intent look he had while choreographing.

"You've come straight from a performance," he said, nibbling her ear. "Do you want to freshen up?"

"Yes, please."

He pointed to the bathroom next to his bedroom. "You'll find a clean towel in there." He held her chin for a moment and gazed at her. "Just wrap yourself up in it, let's not bother with clothes."

"Oh." She had never been so nervous. Was that a kiss? She climbed into the bathtub and turned on the spigots. Her virginity dragged beside her, an alarming and intimidating appendage.

Knotting the towel around her chest, she opened the door cautiously.

He was lying sideways on the bed in his underwear, his chest covered in gray hair. He got up and walked toward her. "Let me see you," he said, brushing his palm over her hair. He was so close. "We'll have a good time together." He laid his hand on her breast. "Would you like to take off your towel?"

She looked at him, unable to speak the word "yes" or even nod. She struggled to unknot the towel, wondering if her thumping heart was visible.

"Stand and be proud," he said firmly. "Just like I see you do in class. I know what you're capable of." He stepped back and stared her up and down, then, with the towel cloaked over her, put one arm around her. This was not like rehearsal; it was deliberate, intentional, intimate, with one hand on her shoulders, the other on her crotch. He walked her to his bed as if she needed his assistance. What was an audition, or even a performance, compared with this? She was suspended from a precipice. Naked in front of Mr. Yanakov.

He took off his underwear. Now he was naked too.

"Katya Symanova," he said.

Named anew. "Mr. Yanakov," she managed, sitting on the edge of his bed.

"Please, it's Boris," he said. "I've waited so long."

"You have?" she blurted out before she had time to think. It was she who had waited, for forever it seemed.

Tentatively, she lay down.

"Nice. Beautiful," he said. He bent over and sucked her nipple. His lips pinched, and his encircling tongue sent a rush through her. "Patience is a virtue, especially at my age," he said, pausing. "Before you know it, I'll be fifty…well, really only forty-eight on my next birthday." He looked almost sad to acknowledge it. "The sight of you coming out of that coffee cup."

"The Arabian Dance," she said, feeling like she was melting.

He stroked her abdomen the way he had at *The Nutcracker.* "So sexy. *Les Sylphides* too. You made me want to devour you." His words were unrecognizable. He studied her body, tracing her shape with his palm. "But I was right to wait for *Space Race.* You're electric."

She was in an alternate universe. "I couldn't tell if you ever noticed."

"I notice everything," he said. He kissed her again, his searching tongue expanding her mouth. "We'll warm you up, just like in class." He took his index finger and dipped it inside her. She could feel his fingernail. It took all her courage to put her arm around his back.

"That's it," he said. "Hold me."

"Okay." Reassured, she held him tighter.

"So new." He pressed his lips over hers again, his kiss a mix of curiosity and drive. "Now see what you've done." He took her hand and placed it on his groin. She was nowhere familiar. His hardness scared her—its strangeness, and his attributing it to her. There were no steps, no music, no rhythm she recognized. She had never felt so exposed, not in class or rehearsal. Not in the dressing room where she changed with the other dancers.

He pulled her legs apart and bent his head in that direction.

"Slow is beautiful; remember that, Katya?" He looked up and grinned. She couldn't stop shaking. He was sparking jets of lightning. Licking her—there? Unimaginable, yet it was happening.

"Relax," he whispered. "Mr. Y promised to take care of you, didn't he?"

She nodded.

He reached next to the bed and opened the drawer to his night table. "You don't have a body that's meant to make babies," he said, sliding on a condom. "We have much more interesting things to do with it."

Condoms in the drawer. Did he do this all the time? Had he planned it?

He climbed on top of her.

She wanted to scream with pain. And with the bulk of him, thrusting and heaving. And with the occasion, which was momentous. He closed his eyes, his body a force field. It was different and more than what she had imagined—the strength of him, the fervor with which he plunged into her. With a final panting snort, he released himself, his weight crushing her. Is this what people did behind closed doors? It was difficult to breathe.

Why was he so quiet? Had he fallen asleep?

She had to make it right for him—whatever that meant; she had to make him happy.

"You're precious," he said at last, propping himself on his hands and opening his eyes. "With a big talent." He looked at her—longingly?—then rolled off her and sighed. "If you work hard enough. Let's not forget that."

"I won't forget," she said. He wanted her. It was a new ordering. Maybe she would not be left splayed on his bed like a rug made from a skinned animal.

He hovered over her like a chef sampling his favorite sauce and for the second time tonight, said, "We'll have a good time together, you'll see."

She was stunned by his sexual intensity. She had suspected it, but she had not understood. "Boris," she said, in part to prove that she could say it in front of him.

"That's the spirit," he said gently. It almost felt like love. "Do whatever you need to."

"I'll be right back," she said, picking up the towel and heading for the bathroom. It hurt to bend over and turn on the faucets. Warily, she stepped into the shower and let the water wipe her tears. She couldn't tell if she was crying from pain, from relief, from astonishment, or from joy. Maybe all of them.

Katya put on her clothes and opened the bathroom door. She wanted to be his. Still, more than ever. She wanted him to love her.

Everything felt consequential.

"I don't do well with sleepovers," he said, running his finger under her chin. "But if you're agreeable, perhaps we'll do this again?"

She had a fleeting thought that naked, he looked smaller, more diminished than in the studio. "I think I'm agreeable," she said, smiling weakly and wondering how there could be a second time.

He reached for his bathrobe, draped across the back of the wicker chair next to his bed, and walked her to the vestibule. "You'll come to enjoy yourself," he whispered, putting her coat around her shoulders. "Think what a good teacher you've got." He took a long look at her, the way he sometimes did during rehearsals, especially recently.

"Yes," she said.

He smiled. "Here's cab fare," he said. He picked up some change from a bowl by the front door. "I don't want my girls walking the streets at this hour." Then he patted her bottom and sent her out into the night.

NEW YORK

20

1963

"Coffee, Dr. Curtin?" Ann handed him his cup.

"Thanks, Ann."

"Nice trip?" John nodded, foggy from jet lag. He reminded himself that Ann had a gorgeous vein tumbling down her left cheek. She must be wearing garters. She had a penny-sized mole on her right calf that before Paris had sent him into paroxysms of desire. Her left cheek was smooth as spun sugar, but he didn't care anymore. He wasn't going to marry her, and she wasn't an antidote to anything.

"How're things here?" he asked. He had returned to a city nervous with possibility, where a ballerina of incomparable skill lived and danced, where he could make himself understood and therefore would have no trouble buying a ballet ticket, where the Peter Stuyvesant Theater presumably had a stage door, where there had to be legions of florists selling white roses and the florists must supply crimson ribbons that could be tied in a big bright bow (John could ask specially for them) and…

"Nothing's changed here," Ann said, rolling a fresh sheet of paper into her typewriter. He recalled his first date with her. They went to a coffee shop where she sang along with a jukebox playing, "The more we get together, the happier we'll be"—the same tune as *"Au du Lieber Augustin,"* for God's sake—"'cause your friends are my friends and my friends are your friends." John would never understand this country. Tunes leaked from the most unexpected places, drenching supermarket aisles (with prodigious quantities of food) and blaring in the five-and-dime. You couldn't avoid them.

"Hope you had a good time, Dr. Curtin." Ann only called him that at work; he had finally persuaded her to call him "John" when they were off the premises. Now that he thought about it, he didn't like the chaos in her apartment—dirty cups covered with lipstick and stale food lying around. The half-empty perfume bottles on the milk crate made him feel tawdry, as if he were sharing her with other men. Maybe he was.

John tried to collect himself. Had it been sex and nothing else? What an appalling indictment of everything he aimed to be. She seemed to sense he'd moved on. Their relationship—such as it was—was snapped like a wishbone, all because he had fallen for a ballerina. Even to himself he sounded ludicrous. An apology would be meaningless. He felt bad, and felt guilty for not feeling worse. He never wanted to hurt anyone.

"Tell us about Paris," Selma said as she seated everyone at the table.

"Dr. Leventhal's paper went well," John said. "He's been so helpful, getting me extra hours downtown at Mercy Hospital so I can pay the rent. It takes a while to build a private practice." John needed to find a place. Maybe he could look near the Peter Stuyvesant Theater; apartments were cheap on the far West Side.

"That's all you have to say?" Selma asked. "Barney, pass the beans around, will you?"

"Beautiful," John said. He was insane to think of moving near Katya Symanova's theater; he sounded as unhinged as his patients. "It's a beautiful city. Mrs. Leventhal gave me a ticket to see *Three Muses*. Katya Symanova was dancing." He felt his face getting hot. "The New York State Ballet. It turns out she's from here. I mean the whole company is." He had already bought a ticket for two months hence. The New York State Ballet was dancing a short two-week season toward the end of June. It was a restless eternity until then.

Selma cocked her head. "You have more to tell."

How did she know? "I'm thirsty," he said, picking up the empty water pitcher and heading into the kitchen.

Selma turned to her niece, Rachel, and her neice's new husband, David. "Have you chosen names?"

John ran the tap. Selma would have preferred that he marry Rachel—she hadn't been subtle about it—but it wasn't possible, not at this stage in his career. Besides, Rachel was too much like family. Then there was Ann.

"We have names for a girl," David said, cutting a piece of brisket. "The boys' names are the subject of intense negotiation."

"He'll see it my way before the baby comes," Rachel said.

David laughed. "Maybe. It's my job to take care of you, isn't it?" he said, putting his arm around her. "I'm the father."

John considered his. Papa's shoes squeaked as he paced the hall awaiting news of Max's delivery, his face creviced. The Oriental runner in the hall was long gone. Papa must have been worried about much more than Mutti's disquieting labor. Aunt Ella's whole family had moved in by then, including her in-laws. Mutti's gravy was thinner, and she had started serving stale bread. She wept when Papa left with the silver box that was her grandmother's wedding set. The paintings had been sold too. "For pennies," Papa said.

"How's our expectant father managing the shoe business?" Barney asked, spearing a potato.

How terrible for Papa, John thought, sitting back down at the table. Fathering a brand-new life, for entrance into *this* world.

"I'm not complaining," David said. "Kids always need them. The boys grow so fast; sometimes they come back every two months. Makes me think about taking over the lease next door when the tenant moves out."

"Excellent," Barney said, picking up the brisket and handing it to John, who was making an effort to return to the conversation. "Any good stories for us?"

John put down his fork. "The thing is," he said, "crazy becomes routine." He had lost the distinction between night and day, apparently between past and present as well.

"Residency's no picnic," Barney said, reaching across to pat John's forearm. "Fortunately, it won't last forever."

"True," John said. But everything else seemed to.

21

1963

Mr. Yanakov gazed at Katya. They were in his bed, just back from Paris. "The audience needs to know you better," he said, fingering her lips.

"Me? What about you?" Five years in, their relationship felt incomplete, part of him walled off. Part of her too, given his lack of interest in the personal. Other than the vague notion that he was born in Russia, which was received wisdom in the company, Katya knew little about his background.

"We did so well over there; we have more to do," Mr. Yanakov said, his evasiveness a rebuff. But truth was, there *was* more to do. There was a bouquet of possibility, ideas sparking between them like St. Elmo's fire. "We'll call this one *Present Tense*."

"Boris, do you ever get tired?"

"No time for tired! 'Present' has a lot of meanings," he said. "A gift, for example."

"The here and now," she added, forcing herself alert.

"You understand where I'm headed."

She did, and it felt like a benediction.

"Forget the past," he said. "We spend too much time there, burdened by memory. Best to leave memory out of this. And 'tense'—think of all those meanings." His energy did not abate, nor his appreciation of her body. He opened her legs and stroked her with his index finger. "Let yourself go, my dear. You make such an effort onstage. The more present you are in my bed, the easier it will be to convey spontaneity to an audience." Back and forth went his finger. "Your body is an instrument, Miss Symanova."

Was he being kind? Issuing veiled criticism? And what did he mean, for her to forget the past? Hadn't she surmounted her roots to become Katya Symanova, a dancer who deserved her name? A flawless technician (no one was flawless, she reminded herself), a new order of dance artist?

Boris Yanakov had already awarded her a succession of roles. She'd danced *Patina* in Kansas City, *Liquid Gel* in Denver. In Los Angeles, she premiered the role of Discipline in *Three Muses*, Mr. Y testing his creation in southern California before taking it to Paris. Flying west, Katya had been transfixed by America passing below, a patchwork of green and brown squares that looked deceptively orderly from thirty thousand feet. The earth grew craggy and wrinkled, then steep and mountainous. At age twenty-six, Katya had traveled farther than either of her parents in a lifetime.

She had endeavored to acclimate to the mantle of prima ballerina, pushing back her shoulders on the red carpet at opening-night parties, standing at Boris Yanakov's side balancing a flute of champagne from which she never sipped, honoring local dignitaries or major donors with the smile that only slightly widened her oval face. She recognized her role debuting Discipline in *Three Muses* for what it was: a milestone for her eight-year-old self, who had fallen in love with ballet because of a birthday present from Aunt Mary. And for her twenty-one-year-old self, who had, over pasta at Luigi's, heard Mr. Yanakov call her a canvas awaiting a paintbrush before she fully understood where he was headed: toward her.

He brushed his palm down her front. "Come, Katya." He sounded generous. His hand was assured, rhythmic. Her torso bent and flexed. Tap tap tap. He bore down; his muscular chest pressed into her. She flung her wrist over the side of his bed and lay still, heart thudding within her inert body.

"You're still trying to seduce me," she said lazily.

"Why not?" he said.

"I'm not objecting." She put her arm around him.

"That's fine then." He stood up and threw on his bathrobe. "Tomorrow, Miss Symanova, we'll begin *Present Tense*."

It was Sunday, the company's day off. The school was quiet. Katya and Mr. Y were alone in the studio. "We'll have a grand piano onstage, with the lid removed," Mr. Yanakov said.

She lay flat and began to stretch.

"I'm making a ballet for you and Paolo, and the pianist, naturally." He turned on the record player. A bass arpeggio hurried up the keyboard. He twirled around, knifing his hands through the air. "Scriabin's *Fifth Piano Sonata*. Scriabin was a mystic and a romantic," he said over the assertive chords. "An inventive, passionate Russian. The sonata has an epitaph from his *Poem of Ecstasy*. 'It's about longing and darkness!'" Mr. Yanakov exclaimed, reading the liner notes and waving the record jacket as if he were marshaling a rally. "'Summon Dance, Miss Symanova. Don't linger at the edge of the cliff, jump off it!'"

Mr. Y boiled with creative fervor as Katya pulled first her right leg to her ear, then her left.

The melody was interrupted by loud, urgent bursts. Mr. Yanakov spun around, tracing an invisible maze. "Shall we?"

"Take center stage," he commanded. "The curtain rises with Paolo on top of you." Mr. Yanakov lay on her. It felt so familiar; she almost reached around to hold him. He stood up. "Paolo rises when the music starts. Your arms are in fifth, legs doing *entrechats* over the floor." Katya circled her arms overhead and beat her feet quickly back and forth.

"Wake up—now! Paolo walks around you, like so," Mr. Yanakov said, extending his arms and stepping like a horse parading the edge of a circus ring. "Arch and contract." The music accelerated. "More! Throw yourself open. Show your excitement. Sit! Bend your knees," he said, increasingly stimulated—by her, apparently. "Toss your head back, and…your hair should be down, so it sweeps the floor. Take it out."

She dashed over to her bag and shook out her hair.

"Better," he said. He paused to gaze at her. "You're a marvel. Now, where were we?" he asked, stepping back. "Yes, on the floor, knees bent, head back. Chest up. Up up up! Arms above. Hold."

She arched her back and steadied her arms while Mr. Y stared at her in a creative swoon, unscrambling what came next. Her shoulders cramped and her hands trembled.

Slicing his fingers up and down, he walked slowly around her. "Paolo," Mr. Yanakov said. "Paolo needs to…" He stopped and scratched his head.

"Mr. Yanakov, may I?" He nodded. Katya got up and shook out her arms. "What about…?" She thought for a moment. "Let's say I'm Paolo," she said, looking at Mr. Yanakov. "Put the music back a little."

She strutted around the space where she had just lain, raising and lowering her head, accelerating from a canter to a gallop.

"Good," Mr. Yanakov said.

"Paolo moves on his own so he can establish a separate identity. Then we come together," she said.

"Such scorching chemistry between you two." Mr. Yanakov smiled hungrily.

She galloped around the room again, giddy and breathless. "He carries me likes this." She put one arm around Mr. Yana-kov's waist, gesticulating with the other.

"Good girl," he said.

"I'm glad you like it," she said, wiping sweat from her forehead and smiling with satisfaction. Her art lay beyond her technique; it lived between her stage persona and whatever fueled her partnership with Mr. Yanakov. Not their personal relationship—fraught and bewildering—but their joint cre-ation, language born in the studio, a secret tongue that was their means to reinvent movement. Katya's understanding of Boris Yanakov's choreography was shared more deeply than anything she had shared with anyone. She felt the hot potentiality of further collaborations and—though unspoken—knew he felt the same. "That expands your concept," she said.

"Does it?" He grinned.

"I believe so," she teased.

"Very nice, Miss Symanova." Mr. Yanakov looked as pleased as she had ever seen him.

❧

John finished his rounds and checked his watch. Seven a.m. Time for his training psychiatrist. A dentist's drill would be preferable.

"It's a curse to win sole survivorship," John said quietly. Dr. Roth's office was overheated, but John was shivering from cold.

Dr. Roth sighed. "Dr. Curtin, I'm hoping you'll detour from that road. Otherwise, you'll keep getting stuck at the same dead end."

John was chastened. He looked around the room, settling on the photo on the corner of Dr. Roth's sizable oak desk. This morning it was facing out. Two smiling daughters in striped bathing suits, their feet buried in sand, were sitting with Mrs. Roth under a beach umbrella. It must be an old photo. Somewhere along the way, John had learned that Dr. Roth had grandchildren.

"I hate Frau Koch," John said. "You know that means 'cook' in German. Mrs. Cook."

"Let's explore that," Dr. Roth said.

"I mean I hate her."

"Can you take it any further? Hate rarely stands alone."

John shook his head. The radiator clanked erratically.

"I wonder," Dr. Roth said at last, "whether it's possible you harbor any warm feelings toward Frau Koch. Let me hasten to add, I can see why you might find that hateful."

John hated Dr. Roth's making presumptions. Dr. Roth was oblivious to how awful this process was.

"She fed me, if that's what you mean," John said. He thought of Selma's tangy brisket and her chocolate rugelach. "In a manner of speaking. Sometimes she let me chew a piece of gristle or gave me a heel of stale bread. For Herr Kommandant, she prepared huge meals. I was always hungry."

"Did Frau Koch do any more than that?"

Where was Dr. Roth going with this line of questioning? "She made Janko practice his songs before Herr Kommandant came home," John said. It wasn't a home, not in the American sense of the word. "Before Herr Kommandant returned to the house."

"Ah."

"Janko had to memorize new songs," John said.

"Why was that?"

"Frau Koch wanted him to be prepared for Herr Kommandant's parties."

"Was that taking care of Janko?" Dr. Roth asked. "In a way?"

John felt checkmated. "Maybe." The space between Frau Koch's two front teeth was more prominent when she belted out songs. "She loved '*Oh du lieber Augustin.*'"

"May we pause for a moment?" Dr. Roth asked. "Perhaps you've noticed that you've been talking about Janko in the third person."

"No, I hadn't."

"What's the difference between you and Janko?"

"Janko sang for Herr Kommandant."

"What about John?"

"John was left to bear the consequences."

"Is that the only difference?"

John rubbed his eyes. How was it humane for Dr. Roth to be so unremitting? "I don't know. They both bear responsibility, but John more so. John survived."

"Is that all?"

"Isn't that enough?"

"For now."

"It's an endless maze, Dr. Roth."

"Yes," Dr. Roth said quietly. "I understand. Shall we explore that or continue with Frau Koch?"

There was no good choice except to get up and walk out. Or find a pill that killed memory. Where did Janko leave off and John start? These sessions were fruitless. After a long pause, he said, "Frau Koch never hesitated to remind me how lucky I was to live in a freezing closet."

"That must have been hard."

"The floor was hard. She thought she was generous to give

me a few burlap bags for blankets."

"Do you agree?"

"Maybe." John had never considered that. "If you're suggesting I see it from her point of view."

"I'm not suggesting anything," Dr. Roth said, straightening his bow tie. "Although it might help to consider Frau Koch's point of view. There are reasons we value empathy in our profession."

Frau Koch was standing in the kitchen, shouting hysterically at the Black soldiers. ("Negroes," they were called in America.) "He's not one of us! He's one of them!" If she hadn't shouted, the soldiers might have assumed Janko was her son, or that he belonged to the kommandant, although Janko's rags should have made things clear. Nevertheless, John hadn't recognized Frau Koch's protestations as an act of courage. She alone had spoken up. Herr Kommandant was nowhere to be seen; he must have escaped by then. "At the end, Frau Koch made sure Janko wasn't arrested," John said quietly to Dr. Roth.

"I guess that's something, isn't it?" Dr. Roth asked.

"I guess so," John said. He had failed to thank Frau Koch for keeping him alive. Even those greasy potato peels were some kind of effort. "I never said goodbye to her." He owed her a debt that would remain forever unpaid. This, a new shame. "I suppose I should have."

He recalled that the soldier who discovered him in the closet was incredulous, drained, incapable of processing the hellish crop of surrounding death. He recalled his own inescapable urge to retch. And the soldier handing Janko his canteen, embracing him as if he were his own son, while Janko crawled toward an awareness that led to an unending tunnel of torment: he had survived by singing for his family's killer.

He should have thanked the soldier. Of course. John sighed, despondent. Another unpaid debt. And the man with no teeth who blessed him outside his moldering bunk. And the soldier who picked him up after his deranged trip to Mainz and brought him to the Displaced Persons camp, and the anonymous paper pushers who miraculously put him on a boat to New York, and even Chaim, who had given him his misspelled name.

And what about Barney and Selma, to whom John had recounted a piece of his crippling history after one of their annual visits to Buddy's grave?

"Every year," Selma had said, collapsing at the kitchen table, next to John who was doing his homework. "We visit the same nineteen-year-old. Crazy with energy."

There was a pair of sneakers in Buddy's (John's) closet that Selma had forgotten to throw out. They were scuffed and dirty, as if Buddy had just come in from playing. "Next month he'll be thirty," Selma said. "He was a prankster; that boy loved a practical joke." Buddy's sneakers were too big for John. Selma didn't believe in hand-me-down shoes anyway. She turned to Barney. "Remember the time he switched the sugar and salt for April Fools'? He couldn't have been more than six. You were so mad!"

"Madder than a hornet brandishing a hot poker," Barney said, shaking his head. "You have to wonder why you got so angry. If you'd known then what you know now, you'd have let the boy have his fun." He took off his glasses and rubbed his eyes.

"We were constantly getting notes from school," Selma said. "'Buddy upended desks, Buddy stuck chalk in the erasers, Buddy had to stay for detention.' He was the class clown." John pictured a gregarious boy, the kind who punched you in the arm when he said hello. The opposite of serious; nothing like John.

"And the air raids!" Barney said. "He entertained the class by making make spitballs and getting the alarms going in tenth grade history. Mmmm, mmmm, mmmm." Barney whirred, imitating a fire siren.

"Their poor teacher," Selma said. "Mr. Henderson. He was practically deaf. The kids scared the living daylights out of him. Unfortunately," she added, in a tone that suggested she didn't find their behavior the least bit unfortunate, "he wasn't the student you are." John wondered what he had done to earn the right to Buddy's shirts. They were comfortably worn, washed and ironed by Selma.

"I swatted him more than once," Barney said. "To keep him in line. Pointless, wasn't it?" He looked sadder than John had ever seen him.

"He would troop in with his friends after a game of stickball," Selma said, smiling at the memory. "Hot and sweaty. Noisy as all get-out. You couldn't buy enough to keep them in food. One day I got home from the store and they plunged into the bags and ate every last morsel before I could say 'boo.' Apples, pretzels, cheese. A loaf of bread. You name it."

"He was a baby when he entered the service," she said wistfully.

Barney nodded in agreement.

Selma hadn't forgotten to throw away the pair of Buddy's sneakers in John's closet. She meant to keep them, a small essence of her son.

"They were all babies," she added.

"So young," John said.

"Too young," Selma said. She stood up abruptly. "I better pay attention to dinner. How's my stuffed cabbage?" she asked, lifting the lid.

"I kept it on a low flame like you asked," John said. He leaned back, remembering Papa coming home one cold night after work. *What do you think Mutti's made for us?* And Janko knew! He had watched Mutti cut meat and onions and toss them in sizzling oil. Janko sprinkled paprika into the pot before she closed the lid.

Barney looked at him. "What about you, John?"

"What about me?"

"All that math and chemistry. It's enough to curl your hair."

John patted his wavy hair and smiled. "I'm all right."

"Are you?" Selma eyed him. "I worry about you."

"You worry about everybody, Sel," Barney said.

"No, really," she said, with a probing look. "You have a few things to think about." Goulash—that's what Mutti had made that night. John could taste the smoky, piquant tomatoes. He gazed at Selma and Barney. Forming his own family with his own home seemed as remote as Mainz. He started to cry.

"What is it, dear?" Selma abandoned her stuffed cabbage and sat back down, putting her hands over John's.

Why now? He hadn't even felt it coming on. He was trying to be a good son and honor their grief, listen to their stories about Buddy.

"That's what we're here for," Barney said. "You can't keep everything inside."

"I went back to Mainz," John blurted out. "It took a long time to get there…I don't really know how long." It struck him as odd how segmented and ordered his days were now. Time for breakfast. Time for the train to school. Time for class. Food whenever you were hungry. He couldn't remember who had trudged beside him to Mainz, but they all wore that same vacant expression. The skeletons by the road he remembered more clearly. No, wait—there was a boy from Budapest. András. His parents had told him to jump from the train. Practically pushed him out. It was a miracle the shots had missed him as he fled. He had relatives in Sydney. John wondered if András had managed to reach Australia, and whether any one of those boys and girls had been cushioned with the kind of caring John had at Barney and Selma's. He cried harder.

"Mainz was destroyed," he said through tears. Why was he speaking? This was Barney and Selma's day for mourning. "Another family had taken our flat."

"Criminals, that's what they were," Selma said.

John looked up, his face streaked with tears. He was making it worse for Barney and Selma. "I'm here because I sang for him."

"Sang for who?" Barney asked.

"Herr Kommandant. Mutti told me to, so I did." He put his head in his hands and sobbed. "In his house. For the officers."

John recalled him grunting upstairs while Janko hid in his closet, trying to sleep away time.

"We're here, dear. We're listening," Selma said quietly. John wasn't being fair. They had enough heartache. He was sleeping in Buddy's bed, wearing Buddy's trousers. When they heard what he had to say they would lose all respect for him.

He needed them to know who he really was.

"I lived there," John said, thinking of the officers demanding more songs, closing in with their chairs. "Mutti and Max were already gone, but I didn't know it. I should have, but I didn't. While I sang for their killer." There! No taking it back. Now Barney and Selma knew.

"Oh my God," Barney said. "What a horror."

"You poor baby." Selma got up from the table and wrapped her arms around him. "You poor, poor thing. It's more than anyone should have to bear."

John picked up his head. He had to make sure they had heard. "Don't you understand?" He raised his voice, as if by doing so he could render his memory visible; then they would see. "I sang for their killer. That's how I survived," John said.

Selma nodded intently. "Yes, dear, we understand."

The kitchen fell silent.

"You had no choice. Never forget that," Selma said after a few moments. She leaned against the counter, her voice stern and resolute. "They made you do it." She looked at Barney, her face anguished. "Thank God you did. The evil of it. You were just a little boy. Thank God you're here."

John was astonished by Selma's conviction, as if she were reprimanding him for feeling otherwise. Her verdict was wholly unexpected, even a little miraculous. Their faces shone with love. He was overwhelmed to be at their kitchen table, to be the beneficiary of their kindness. He had done nothing to deserve it; quite the opposite—he had intruded on their day and tainted it with his wretched past. If he had said more, they would see how he'd let Papa down by not acting as the man of the family.

They shook their heads—blanched, concerned.

"Thank you both," John said, humbled, exhausted.

No one would ever understand.

Dr. Roth checked his watch. "I'm sorry, but we're up for today," he said, breaking the silence. "It's not a good place to stop; I see that." He stood. "I try never to insert myself into my patients' therapy. It's a basic tenet of treatment. I'm obliged to convey the same to you during your training. However, you present an unusually painful history." He walked toward the door. "We're diverging from the book in here. Quite unorthodox, but we're making progress."

Maybe Dr. Roth was making progress. John was in a miasma of regret and despair. The only thing that was keeping him going was the faint possibility that in two months (well, six weeks to be exact), he might deliver a bouquet of white roses to his ballerina, who was not his ballerina. "Who knows, you may take away a thing or two about novel treatment techniques," Dr. Roth said, sliding his tortoiseshell glasses up his nose.

It was 8:00 a.m., but it felt like the deepest part of the night. As he pushed the elevator button, John wondered whether every psychiatry resident was left this tortured and desolate by the process. Maybe he had drawn a bad card with Dr. Roth. It was supposed to be a healing profession, after all.

22

1963

Six weeks later, John took his seat ten rows from the stage. Breathless with excitement, he felt his future distilled to a single purpose: to present Katya Symanova the bouquet of white roses that lay in his lap like hope.

She was dancing *Present Tense* and *Charged Particles*. For *Present Tense*, there was no conductor and no set. Only Katya, wearing flowing violet, lying in the middle of the stage, her partner on top of her. Oh, to be that man.

In the back corner, a pianist dug into the keyboard; music pregnant with vigor, then contemplative and questioning. Katya rose and spun, gliding on puffs of music, truer than air, lighter than vapor. Bounding and turning, her movements tracing a circle of moods. Earthy coupling displaced the gauzy, fairytale quality of *Three Muses*.

John's heart beat to Katya's rhythms, accelerated with her jumps. He soared with optimism, certain her power flowed from something deeper than years of training. She was a splendid, stunning puzzle. He was awash in a mysterious sensation: she was a song being born.

Sheathed in gold, Katya rose *en pointe* to prepare her entrance. *Charged Particles* was choreographed to embody the threats of the atomic age. "Mankind was never meant to split atoms," Mr. Y had said. "It is grotesque to imperil the future of the species." Katya's job was to convey danger. "Fast!" Mr. Yanakov had insisted. "As if someone were prodding your torso with a hot poker."

With a surge of energy, she spread her legs and jumped,

arms overhead. More than anything, Mr. Yanakov wanted a shock wave of physicality. Katya bent over—her back to the audience—clasping her ankles. Her partner flipped her and set her down, legs thrust upward, her body a V. He grasped her midriff as dancers twisted around them in a tightening circle.

Katya felt sexual, menacing. "Set the stage on fire!" Mr. Yanakov had admonished. The music hammered and the *corps* stamped and thrust their rears. Lying flat, Katya put her hands by her ears and arched her body, then pulled up, opened and closed her legs, contracting and releasing, tracing a jagged ellipse. She seared lines through air, sharp as flame, molten as hot steel.

Someone was out there. To whomever it was, she sent a heat ray.

John waited anxiously as the curtain rose on *Charged Particles.* Against a huge screen of the periodic table, dancers in black and tangerine ran helter-skelter—bumping each other, somersaulting, and rolling offstage. Beating drums punctuated occasional bursts of angry music. John's fragile equanimity started to rupture, attacked by cigar-laced grunts in Herr Kommandant's sitting room, officers stomping to songs that had lost their music.

To see his ballerina defy physics and illuminate the wind, John marshaled the discipline he'd learned from hard-earned experience and—he conceded grudgingly—tortured sessions with Dr. Roth. He reminded himself he was safe in New York.

Katya Symanova danced like shaken sheet metal. Her performance was naked and personal. If it felt voyeuristic to watch, John refused to avert his eyes. To do so would degrade and ignore her art. He was hypnotized. Reality compressed to the four corners of the stage. No matter the torturing drumbeats, John had to listen *and* watch; he had to see every inch of her. Her writhing torso, her outstretched limbs, her elongated neck.

She danced on the cusp of music and coaxed the edge of sound. The angle of her head communicated something beyond words. However absurd, John wanted to rescue her and take her home.

The curtain fell. John gathered his bouquet and went in search of the stage door. He would meet her and try to ask her out. Nothing felt more compelling.

Katya decided to wait for Mr. Yanakov outside. He never left until the theater was cleared and the stagehands gone; he had to walk through the scenery, check that the boxes of rosin were set for tomorrow's matinee.

She opened the stage door. It was a warm night with a rare, clear Manhattan sky.

"For you." A man put forward a bouquet of white roses tied in crimson ribbon. His face looked meditative, prayerful—as if it were inscribed with wisdom. "For the gift you have given me."

Wait. She knew him. The dark brown eyes, the wavy hair. Kindness, radiating like melody from a ballad.

"I had the honor of seeing you dance in Paris," he said. "At *Three Muses.*"

That was it! "Yes," she said. "I remember." He was at that performance, where she'd breached a new dimension, woven an intense immediacy with the audience. "And now you're here?"

"Dr. John Curtin," he said, reintroducing himself. "I live in New York."

She couldn't place his accent.

"I was attending a psychiatrists' convention there. I'm just finishing my residency."

The stage door opened, and several dancers walked toward them, their feet turned out and shoulder bags slung behind them. "Hey, Katya, coming with us?" one of the men called out. His blond hair was stiff with hair spray.

"Not tonight," she said, pulling up her sleeve to check the face of a small silver watch. Her wrist was so thin.

"Ooh la la!" the blond man teased.

"Did you say psychiatrist?" she asked, turning her attention back to John.

"Yes."

"I don't think I've ever met one," she said.

"Well, now you have." He was aglow with friendliness. "May I take you to wherever you're going?"

She lowered the flowers and cradled them in her left arm. "That's kind of you." She turned around. Mr. Y was taking longer than usual tonight. "I don't think that's possible. But I appreciate your kindness."

He bowed. "I appreciate yours," he said, and walked away.

Katya set her roses on the steps to the stage door and went back to find Mr. Yanakov.

"Go ahead," he said. "I'm tied up here for a while. Sets."

She felt a whiff of disappointment. Not that Mr. Yanakov was staying. That wasn't unusual. His surveillance of the theater was total. It was the man with the white roses. Katya could have left with him. But of course she couldn't have, because who goes out with strangers? New York was a dangerous place.

She picked up her roses from the steps down to the back lot and hurried home; it wasn't safe to be out alone. Maya was down-town at the Bees Knees. Katya put the roses in water and set them on the tiny counter next to the sink, then sat down on her bed to look at them. They were a spray of beauty. The man was a psychiatrist called John Curtin. She'd had a good feeling about him in Paris, although she couldn't say why. She reached under her bed for her passport and found the rose petal inside, a gift from the same man. It was still white; she had pressed it before the edges turned brown. She waved it gently against her cheek, then tucked it back into her passport. He lived in New York.

"Who are they from?" Maya asked when Katya returned.

"I don't know," Katya said. "I mean I do. I mean I don't."

"Finally! Please say you're two-timing Boris the Dictator!"

"What? Some guy handed me roses at the stage door."

"You don't look like it was some guy."

"He gave me roses in Paris."

"Wait…this is New York." Maya leaned back and squinted

at Katya. "I didn't give you enough credit. You've been carrying on with him since then?"

"Stop it! He's just a stranger who likes ballet. Who happened to be in Paris…and then in New York."

23

1963

"We left off with Frau Koch."

Dr. Roth was leading John back into quicksand. "It's hard to forget that Mutti and Max were murdered less than a hundred meters from her oven," John said.

"I'm not asking you to forget, Dr. Curtin."

John glanced at the picture on Dr. Roth's desk. "I don't have any photographs of Mutti, or anyone else in my family."

"That's very sad, Dr. Curtin," Dr. Roth said, turning the picture around.

Dr. Roth didn't sound very sad. Was he supposed to reflect emotion commensurate with John's? Why would he? He wasn't the one presiding over this snarling, untamable mess.

"I have a feeling Mutti gave you to the SS man in hopes that someone like Frau Koch would turn up," Dr. Roth said.

John halted, paralyzed. Even though Janko had retrieved the song Mutti wanted him to sing, it was Max she kept; Janko she sent before the butt of the SS man's rifle. Something in John snapped. He bent over and placed his hands over his breaking heart. What was Dr. Roth doing, except removing the last vestiges of his defenses?

"Mutti couldn't have known about Frau Koch," John said into his sleeve. He rocked back and forth like a patient on Fifth Floor East. "You have no idea what it smelled like. Wake up to the stink. Fall asleep to it. And what did I do? Comforted the monster, because I was too much the fool to realize what was going on. Every hour—no, every minute—some family had their history erased, their loved ones murdered. While I entertained their killer."

"You're right," Dr. Roth said quietly. "I'm sure I don't have any idea. But that doesn't mean I don't care. I'm capable of caring deeply. So are others...so are you."

"I kept waiting," John said. "Expecting Mutti to knock on the kommandant's door. I couldn't understand why she never came for me." He was sobbing.

Mutti sat beside him in bed and held his good-night storybook the way his teachers used to, her thumb and pinky in front, the other three fingers supporting the book's spine. Her saliva gathered at the side of her lips when she came to a particularly exciting passage.

"All that time waiting," John said, clutching his stomach and raising his head, his face wet with tears. He was supposed to keep talking. "Frau Koch made it perfectly clear that Mutti and Max were gone; I just refused to hear." Max never got the hang of blocks. He threw a tantrum when he stacked the bigger ones on the smaller ones and they all toppled over.

Dr. Roth sighed. "Children who come from loving families instinctively place their faith in hope. Who among us, child or not, believed such mass killing was possible?" He sat forward and adjusted his bow tie. "Can you say a little more about leaving that line?"

John lowered his head.

Dr. Roth plowed on. "What were you feeling when Mutti kissed your forehead and gave you to the SS man? Desertion, fear, relief? Something else?"

No one was this brutal.

"What is the last thing you remember?"

John shoved his thumb and index finger into his eyes and listened to the sound of his breathing.

"The last thing," Dr. Roth repeated.

"I can barely walk," John began slowly. "The SS man's hand is digging into my shoulder. My feet are numb." John heard himself speaking German. "I have holes in my shoes and there are rocks sticking out of the ground. Sharp rocks." Was he talking to Dr. Roth or the SS man?

Or Mutti?

"And?"

"Why did she make me go with him?" John stopped and looked up, begging for a reprieve.

Dr. Roth twirled his pencil and waited. "Please, go on," he said.

"His rifle is so big. I want to go back." The burning stench that never went away. John was gasping, but Dr. Roth didn't care.

"How come she kept Max and sent me away?" John said.

Dr. Roth was still.

"This man is going to kill me."

Tears rained down John's face. "If I can get Mutti's attention, she'll change her mind." He wiped his eyes with the back of his sleeve. "So I turn around. The SS man squeezes my shoulder harder." The noxious combination of smoke and cold. "It hurts."

"And?" Dr. Roth would persist, no matter the effect.

"Mutti is holding Max and kissing his hair," John rasped.

"And?"

"I can't even get her to look at me," John said into the floor.

Dr. Roth shut the door behind him as if he were pulling up a drawbridge on a moat.

John headed upstairs to see his patients. He felt hopeless.

At least after his previous torturous session with Dr. Roth, John had had Katya Symanova to look forward to. Now all was lost. John had no one to tell; he would never confide in Dr. Roth—or anyone else—about his futile efforts at the ballet. He didn't want his sanity questioned.

Katya Symanova said she remembered John, but when he pressed further, she had pulled back as if she were afraid. Had he caused her to react that way?

And what did it matter? He was out of options. He couldn't show up again at the stage door. He didn't know how to see his ballerina again, his disappointment both nonsensical and crushing.

24

1963

Mr. Yanakov began talking about returning to Europe. Was he never tired? It must be two in the morning. "How about one called *Johnny Appleseed*?" He rolled off Katya and got out of bed. Throwing on his navy blue bathrobe, he said, "We'll celebrate Americana over there." He paced back and forth in the small area by the bed. "Milk-fed enthusiasm and Hollywood endings." He paused for a moment. "I'm going over for a few months," he said, looking wistfully at Katya. "To work with a few troupes in Europe." Something in his expression made it clear she wasn't invited. She felt a wave of disappointment, surprised at its intensity. He never went anywhere; he was joined at the hip with his company.

Draping herself in the sheet, she got out of bed. He wrapped his arms around her. "Why don't you take me along?" she said. "You know it's a good idea." She kissed him gently on the cheek.

"I hate it when you go," he whispered, ignoring her comment. "It's a little twist to the gut every time."

"Are you asking me to stay tonight, Mr. Yanakov?"

"Why don't you call me Boris?" His tone had changed. He held her face between his hands. "That is my name."

"Why don't you call me Katherine? That's my name." She saw his hesitation and it felt good. "It was a great choreographer who renamed me," she said. He gazed at her, but he wasn't asking her to stay. Or to travel with him.

"Shall I get dressed?" she asked.

"Do you have to?"

"I'll make your favorite midnight snack, even if midnight was a long time ago." She pulled a shirt over her head. "Tell me about *Johnny Appleseed*," she continued, walking into the kitchen. But she didn't want to hear about it. She didn't want to hear about what he was going to do in Europe—bringing their joint work and leaving her here. She was snubbed. She could shout at him, for taking their partnership for granted—and at herself, for continuing to tolerate it. But what was her choice? Dance was the marrow in her bones. She was immobilized without him.

She started a pot of tea and put two slices of seeded rye in the toaster. "Butter or cream cheese?"

"Butter," he said. "You?"

"It's too late to eat." She looked at her watch. "Too early, actually. Lemon in your tea?"

He nodded, handing her one from the wire basket by the toaster. "The farm girl has to be the main attraction in *Johnny Appleseed*," he said, growing increasingly animated. "The piece hinges on her."

"You should have a backdrop like a Rodgers and Hammerstein set. Make it real theater," she said, speaking in spite of herself.

"Great idea. We'll have to find a farm girl over there."

"Where?"

"So far it's Brussels and Stuttgart. I'm not sure where else."

The trip had been in the offing for a long time. "Boris?" Katya looked up from the cutting board, where she had quartered a lemon.

"There, was that so difficult? You give my name a nice spin."

"Shall I come with you?"

"Not this time, precious," he said.

Would he ever see her as separate from him? She was carrying a clipping in her purse as if it were a talisman of truth. She knew it by heart. "Yanakov is an alchemist. The magic is in the selection of the ballerina. Yanakov elicits rare emotional depth and technical prowess from Symanova. Our guess is that he hasn't begun to tap her potential."

The great privilege of Katya's position was joining Mr. Y's

creation, his mind twisting and turning, churning. To dazzle him not just with technique, but with ideas; to see him jumping off her choreographic suggestions like a pole-vaulter scaling new heights. On the good days, their collaboration was as seamless as two birds in flight. Maybe it was unreasonable to want an acknowledgment of herself and her art as apart from him. The subject was closed anyway.

She accidentally woke Maya when she tiptoed in at dawn. "What the hell time is it?" Maya propped herself up and rubbed her eyes. "Don't you ever get tired of him?"

Katya sat down on the edge of her narrow bed and took off her boots. "I've never been so tired in my life."

"I'm moving out of this rathole," Maya said. "I can't believe I'm telling you at this ungodly hour, but you're never around."

Katya felt desolate. "I'll miss you."

"Yeah, right."

"I mean it. Where are you moving?"

"A two-bedroom on West Seventy-Third. With Fiona."

Katya pictured Maya and Fiona coming back from a performance, laughing about a missed cue or a boy who had almost dropped one of them. She felt absurdly jealous. She longed for the old times, when Maya had dispensed her acerbic commentary as they peered through the window watching company rehearsals; brunch with Maya's parents.

"It'll be a step up in the world," Maya said. "At least we'll have a living room."

"That is a step up!" Katya said, trying to sound upbeat. "I'll have to find something," she added, lying down in her clothes. "Mr. Yanakov will be happy I'm on my own."

"Jesus, will you get a life?" Maya pulled up the blanket.

"It'll help him pretend no one knows about us, like a little kid on a beach who closes his eyes so no one will see him changing," Katya said.

"You realize how warped that is?"

Katya put her hands behind her head and stared at the

ceiling. "Sometimes I feel like I'm holding up a house of cards."

"You said it, not me."

"I wouldn't want the whole thing to collapse," Katya said.

"How many times do I have to tell you? You're not in charge of him."

"I don't feel in charge of him," she said. "Not exactly." Sometimes his place felt almost like home; the smell of rye toast filling his kitchen during the small hours, tea steeping on his table—one leaf folded down so it fit against the wall. Occasionally he preferred honey instead of lemon. While on tour, Katya had bought him a selection of honeys that lined his kitchen counter. "My choice of honeypots," he said. She didn't love the pun—disturbingly apt for his jaunt across Europe this summer.

"He's a big boy," Maya said.

"He's not a happy man," Katya said.

"No kidding! Why you fawn over him I'll never know," Maya said, yawning.

"I'm good for him."

"Will you get real?"

"Seriously, he likes being around me."

"So do I, or I did when I used to actually see you."

"Okay, knock it off." Katya felt terrible. Maya was the only simple pleasure in her life. Her offbeat humor and blunt cynicism were saving graces. Maya was the one who got Katya to laugh, who took her into her family—another pleasure—no matter how much Maya complained about them.

"I'm giving it another year or two, with Fiona and me finally getting to live somewhere other than this tenement, and then I'm doing something else."

"Seriously?" Katya was shocked, despite Maya's having expressed this desire over the years. "Are you wedded to that time frame?"

"I'm not wedded to anything else, am I?"

"Why?"

"You know why! Do you see me getting any solo roles other

than a few vampy parts here and there? Do you see Mr. Yanakov fawning over me? That's your job, baby."

"C'mon." There were things Katya couldn't tell anyone—about Mr. Y's sexual attentions and the way he looked at her. But most of all, working with him. That feeling of elation when they coalesced over a new piece of choreography, when he saw—once again—how completely she understood his process. The sense that together they had created something neither could have done alone. "What're you going to do?"

"I'm embarrassed to tell you. My mother wants to start a jewelry business. No gold and diamonds, mind you. She wants to be a trendsetter. She's been obsessed with this idea since she and my dad came back from London. You know…sell fat yellow plastic bracelets and giant hot pink necklaces you could use for lassoes. Says it's the next big thing. Sounds like a great idea."

"It does sound like a great idea! Is she excited you're going into business with her?"

"She has no clue. I haven't mentioned it; if I did, she'd tell me to quit right now."

"How could she tell you to quit?" Quitting was giving up.

"You would say that," Maya said. "When the time comes, my mom will find a place for me." For once, Maya seemed dead serious. "You must think I'm a loser."

"No, not in the least. I'm envious."

"Of what? You're the one with the talent."

"No, it's not that," Katya said, close to tears. "It's your certainty. And parents like yours."

"Ah. Except when they drive me crazy, which is often."

Katya smiled wistfully. Maya couldn't see it. Her home was as water to a fish; too familiar to appreciate.

"You've got everything going for you," Maya said. "You're the one with the big career."

"I don't know about the big career. But he's a genius," Katya said, without naming Mr. Yanakov. She didn't need to. "Ideas come bursting out of his brain. He can access every step he's ever choreographed."

"Please. Don't try to impress me at this ridiculous hour."

"I'm not. It's just that he never writes anything down," she said, trying to focus on what was going well—at least before to-night—their joint creation, more concrete than whatever their relationship was. "Who's going to remember it?"

"Wait, where's he going?"

"I worry about losing his work. There's no record of it other than in his memory."

"Do you have news? I'm all ears."

Katya laughed. "Funny you should ask. He's going back to Europe this summer."

"Hallelujah!" Maya said.

"He didn't invite me."

"He didn't invite me either! Count your blessings, get some perspective."

"I don't seem to be able to see it that way," Katya said. "I'm pretty upset, actually." She looked at Maya. "I must sound awful. I'm sorry. It's just that…" Was it unreasonable to expect him to take her along? She felt diminished, as if she were back in Variations Class worshipping the great man, instead of serving as his prima ballerina, his lover, and his collaborator. He was at the center of everything she did, but the reverse wasn't true.

She thought of the man at the stage door—a psychiatrist—and wondered if he would come to the theater again. The last few performances she'd opened the stage door half wishing he were there, half fearing that if she came out with Mr. Yanakov, Dr. Curtin would run away.

"I can't help it," Katya said to Maya. "Mr. Y is a great artist. It bothers me that there's no means to remember his work," she added, trying to pick up a different strand of conversation. "Anyway, he has a softer side."

"You're an idiot to bet your future on that maniac."

There was no trying to convince Maya of the random tenderness Mr. Yanakov displayed in his bedroom. Why try? Katya closed her eyes, desperate to sleep. "It's like being inside a balloon that bounces between the studio and his apartment."

Apparently, those were the two defining points of her existence—to one she went in stealth, to the other as prima ballerina.

"There's more to life than that," Maya said. "If you're nice,
Fiona and I will invite you over."

25

1963

"We've reached that point, Dr. Curtin." Dr. Roth closed his notebook and looked at John.

"What is that?"

"The time to ask you to sing."

"Please!" John groaned.

"I understand it's a challenging request," Dr. Roth said.

John wouldn't subject his worst enemies to this treatment. "I've forgotten how." He should forswear song. He could spend the rest of his life in silence.

"Is that true, Dr. Curtin?"

Dr. Roth sat quietly.

"I can't," John said.

"Take the time you need, Dr. Curtin."

Time was the enemy. He would be stuck in an agony of memory forever.

Dr. Roth cleared his throat. "Dr. Curtin?"

The pit of John's stomach burned—hot, fiery rage. He hated Dr. Roth. He was crippled with fear. The officers tossed back beer and screamed for more, while Herr Kommandant waited for Janko to choose his next selection. The place reeked of cigar smoke. Janko would forget the words; Herr Kommandant would banish him outside.

"Shall I turn off the lights?" Dr. Roth asked.

"Maybe."

When had John hesitated to sing for the kommandant? How was he going to treat his patients if he couldn't treat himself?

Inflamed and distended in his throat, his voice surged; abraded machinery, rasping. He croaked and stumbled and started into *"Hänschen Klein,"* about how little Hans went out in the world, but his mother missed him so much that he came back.

Haltingly, John reached the end and buried his head in his hands.

"That was an accomplishment, Dr. Curtin," Dr. Roth said. "I appreciate the difficulty."

Nothing was any better.

26

1963

"Room 914," the nurse said. Katya tapped on the door. Daddy was lying with a plaster cast from his ankle to his upper thigh, hung from a chained contraption worthy of a horror film.

"Katherine!"

"Dad, I came as soon as I heard. Aunt Mary said it was a bad break, but geez! I'm only sorry she didn't reach me sooner." So much for staying out until all hours at Mr. Yanakov's. Katya felt terrible; it had taken her aunt two days to find her. Holding yellow carnations, Katya walked over to Daddy's bed and kissed him.

"Nice to see you whenever you get here," he said. He looked much older, his chest bones prominent above the drooping neckline of a hospital gown.

"How are you? Tell me the details."

"I tripped picking up the morning paper," he said. "Not quite the dancer you are."

"Katherine!" Aunt Mary came through the door. "I'll take those," she said, reaching for the carnations.

"Seriously, what happened, Dad?"

"Curb's uneven; it was too early, too dark," he said. "I got twisted like a pretzel. Mrs. O'Connor saw me crawling up to the front door and called an ambulance. See what I mean about not paying attention? How many times have I told you to pay attention? I should follow my own advice."

"It must hurt like all get-out," Katya said, recalling her spill during *Seasonal Colors*.

"They have me pretty doped up; I'm okay," he said. "You should have seen how colorful my leg got. Swollen like an elephant."

Katya sat on the edge of the bed and took Daddy's hand. "Sounds awful. How long are they keeping you?"

"That depends," Aunt Mary said, filling a glass for the carnations, "on what kind of help we can get. Right now, he can't make his way across the room. Honestly, I think we're better off taking care of him ourselves."

"I have Sundays," Katya offered.

"Good," Aunt Mary said.

"And I can free up more time," Katya said, turning to him. She would have all the time in the world with Mr. Yanakov leaving. "Don't worry, Dad, we'll get you back into fighting shape."

He smiled. "Not sure I ever was." Something in his face had relaxed. "Can't keep my eyes open," he said, drifting off.

Aunt Mary set the carnations on the window ledge and put on her coat. "I'm going home to sleep now that you're here." She tiptoed out.

The hospital cafeteria was an underground hive, buzzing with worried relatives from across the city. At the table next to Katya, an extended family whispered anxiously in Spanish. Several Black families were lined up to buy a meal before heading back upstairs. Katya sipped a cup of burnt coffee and chastised herself for being out of touch, although she still invited Daddy to her performances. She winced remembering that first invitation from Mr. Y, when turning him down in favor of Daddy felt like a matter of life or death. How wrong she was, although she wasn't turning down Mr. Y anymore, was she?

She tried to get to Queens to see Daddy every month or so, but had she tried hard enough? There wasn't a lot of conversation. He was usually reading the Sunday paper, or listening to a ball game. It occurred to her that she hardly knew him. She pictured him frying cube steaks with ketchup or making scrambled eggs—his two specialties. Over the years, he'd worked up a decent chicken chow mein as well. He used to keep a bowl of Jell-O and some cheese in the fridge for all those late nights Katya got home from class. Other than that, he went to his accounting office Monday through Friday, and on Saturdays too, especially during tax season. She thought of the box of crayons he used to keep in his desk drawer, for when he took her along. That was before ballet school consumed her Saturdays.

She was a long way from that little girl. She was living on her own for the first time, having moved to a tiny one-bedroom on the West Side. She liked having her own place; it was a refuge from Mr. Yanakov's passion and energy, despite the grinding of early morning garbage trucks and the occasional knife fights down the block. But she missed Maya, snoring noisily when Katya tiptoed in at night, standing with one hand on her hip, a towel wrapped around her head, pronouncing something or other "absurd."

Katya checked the wall clock by the cashier. She would peek in on Daddy before visiting hours ended. At least he was in good spirits. She was glad she had no other plans. When she'd told Mr. Yanakov about Daddy's accident, he said she should take as much time as needed. That was what Katya wanted, but Mr. Yanakov's tone had made her feel discharged. He'd promised to be in touch once he got overseas, but she was doubtful.

Was Mr. Yanakov leaving her? God help her if that was true. She needed him to dance, and she needed dance to live. It was that simple. The thought of Mr. Y being away was disorienting; the coming weeks stretched out in a vacuum. He was an organizing principle, boiling day and night. She did not receive public acknowledgment for their work together. Would she disappear further with him gone? He could find another collaborator in Brussels, or Stuttgart. He'd certainly find plenty of accomplished dancers, including plenty of women. Although it was only a few short months ago, it felt like eons since Mr. Y lay on top of her as the two of them sketched out *Present Tense*, his eyes shining as he drank in her suggestions.

How dare she think of Mr. Yanakov—or herself—with Daddy injured? She was grateful to be at the hospital; Aunt Mary's phone call had been alarming. She stirred her coffee, idly watching doctors and nurses pass through the cafeteria. A group of orderlies got in line and loaded their trays. Whatever was for dinner smelled like overcooked onions.

She yawned and stretched. She was being unreasonable; it was stress that was making her so negative. Hadn't she wished for Mr. Yanakov her whole life—this beguiling and enthralling man—and hadn't he given her his attentions? She must be worried about Daddy. He looked weak and depleted, chained up like that. He was facing a long recovery.

"Excuse me." The doctor standing next to her table cleared his throat.

Katya looked up.

"Aren't you...?" he started.

Where had she seen him? Those caring eyes. "Dr. John Curtin" was embroidered in blue above the pocket of his white coat. The man with the white roses.

She put down her coffee and stood up. "Katherine," she said, extending her hand. "I mean Katya," she said, blushing. "I must be tired."

He looked baffled.

"That's my given name," she said. She felt as if she had just run into a long-lost friend.

"What are you doing here?" he said. "Please, sit down." He was beaming. "Is everything all right?"

"Not really," she said. "Well, yes, fine. Actually, no... My father's in the hospital. He had a bad leg break."

"I'm sorry to hear that. May I?" he asked, pulling out the chair next to her.

"He's in traction," she said.

"That's horrible," he said. "But you're here! Is he okay?" he added quickly.

"He seems pretty beat up," she said. "At least I'll be able to spend some time with him; we're not in season. I'm off for the summer." So was her choreographer, off to Europe. For the first time, she felt a sliver of relief at his absence. "We've been performing more than usual. We were in Paris, then had a short run after we got back." She looked at John. "Of course," she said, concerned that he might think she'd forgotten his two bouquets of white roses. "You've been in both places. It's… remarkable in a way, isn't it?"

"Yes! It is."

John had come to *Three Muses* in Paris and seen her in New York, in *Present Tense*, which she had cocreated with Boris Yanakov, no matter that no one else knew that. John had seen her exposed in *Charged Particles*, which was like seeing Mr. Yanakov's bedroom on stage. She could be embarrassed by that, but instead felt a surge of pleasure. John's being there rendered her dancing immediate, intimate, as if he were the only person who understood her performances, despite full houses in Paris and New York.

Did he even know who Boris Yanakov was? Lots of people came to a ballet and paid no attention to the choreographer. (Mr. Yanakov would hate hearing that, but it was true.)

"What's your dad's name?"

Right, Daddy. "He looks wan. Whatever they're giving him for pain must not be enough."

"Oh, dear. The underestimation of pain," he said. "Unfortunately, it's a frequent problem. How can I help?"

"Gosh, no need to do anything, but thank you!" He was so thoughtful. "My dad will be fine. I'll check with the nurse when I go back up. Patrick," Katya said. "My dad's name is Patrick Sillman."

John looked puzzled. "I thought you were Russian. Or at least your parents were."

She laughed. "The illusion of ballet. Katya Symanova's a stage name," she added. "To my father I'll always be Katherine Sillman."

"Ah." He was gazing at her with unfettered joy. "I don't use my real name either," he said.

"Really?"

"I was born Janko Stein. When I came to America I thought I was choosing an ordinary name. There was a man on the boat…" He trailed off. "It turns out I didn't even spell it correctly."

"I didn't choose," Katya said. "My choreographer did. Boris Yanakov. He…We…" Now was the time to tell John about him. Mr. Yanakov didn't feel like a partner right now—whatever that was supposed to feel like—he felt like he was a world away. Why would John care? She didn't even know him.

"Apparently the critics don't pay attention to ballerinas with American names," she said.

She sipped her coffee. "May I ask where you're from?"

"Yonkers." His expression clouded. "Mainz," he added. "Germany." His face went vacant, as though there had been an erasure. He remained silent while Katya registered the dinging and chinking of dishes and the hushed conversations of worried hospital visitors. She should not have asked.

"Excuse me," he said, after an interval. "Where I come from, there's nothing left."

"That's so sad." She was surprised to feel heartbroken. He was a refugee.

"Where were we?" he asked, his expressiveness returning, his face alight with concern. He exuded benevolence. "Oh yes. Your dad. I am sorry he's laid up, and I'm happy to help in any way I can, but running into you…" He leaned toward her. "Is a miracle."

"Katherine, you are a sight for sore eyes!" Daddy said when she arrived the next afternoon. He tried unsuccessfully to sit up; his leg was still suspended from chains.

"How're you feeling?" She bent over to kiss him. He looked less worn out than yesterday.

"Nice of you to check in on your old man."

"C'mon, Dad, you're not old." He was younger than Mr. Yanakov.

"I told that headshrinker not to worry."

Was Daddy in such bad shape? Before her white roses, Katya had never thought about headshrinkers, much less met one. She'd found herself talking to John Curtin last night in the hospital cafeteria and, for some reason, had agreed to meet him when he got off work today. Maya and Fiona were having a party; Katya could kill some time between visiting Daddy and heading uptown. "What headshrinker?"

"He stopped by this morning," Daddy said. "Nosy fellow. Asked too many personal questions. His name was Curtin, I think."

What an extraordinary man, showing that kind of concern for a perfect stranger! Katya hoped she hadn't said anything to make him go out of his way. She felt doubly glad she was meeting him later; he could tell her how Daddy was doing.

"How generous of him," she said.

"Waste of time," Daddy said. "What's new at the ballet?"

"Not much, with Mr. Yanakov overseas."

John stepped into the hospital elevator trying to manage his agitation—fearfully, exuberantly awaiting another glimpse of his ballerina. (She wasn't "his," he reminded himself.) He was pinching himself for his astonishing good fortune, brimming with the reality that she wasn't some mythical goddess who would vaporize with the dawn but was, in fact, a girl from Queens. Katherine Sillman.

"Katya!" She was sitting on a bench in the lobby, her long legs crossed, wearing a light-blue cotton shift and sandals. He strode over and kissed her hand as she stood. "Where to?"

"The uptown subway. West Side," she said. "If that's all right. I'm on my way to some friends."

"Anything!"

"Do you always work Saturdays?" she asked.

"I have to; I'm just getting started." He held open the glass door to the outside. It was warm, but not oppressive. "How's your father?"

"Doing okay, considering. Making jokes about his fall—not the ballet dancer I am. Stuff like that."

"A great sign."

"But then"—she looked concerned—"it's crazy. He joked about you, and now I'm wondering whether there's something I should know."

"He told you we met?"

She nodded.

"I'm glad," he said. The sky was turning orange-pink, Manhattan offering a sensational sunset. Uneven rooftops were delineated in backlight. "That means I can tell you about my visit with him. We take confidentiality seriously in our profession." Puffy clouds—tinged in pastels—sailed overhead. "What a nice guy."

Her smile was so fleeting, he wondered if he had said something to upset her. "Headshrinkers tend to be embarrassing," he said, pushing on. "Did your father say the usual?" They waited for the light to change at Fourteenth Street. Most of the shops had closed for the night, but the sidewalks were teeming with people.

"Headshrinker. That was it," she said. "Is he okay?"

John smiled. "With you taking care of him?" He shouldn't belittle her concerns. "Don't worry. I just asked a series of routine questions. Sometimes with a major injury like his, the patient can feel kind of low. He seems fine."

"That's good."

He was glad to have provided her that. "May I ask about your mother?" Did he sound too much like a psychiatrist, swooping in while the subject was ajar?

"She died when I was seven."

The light turned green. "I'm so sorry." They headed west on Fourteenth, jammed with people jostling each other for a piece of sidewalk. He shouldn't have asked.

"It was a long time ago. I hardly remember her."

"That's so difficult!" John said as they crossed Third Avenue. He could see the Union Square subway stop, which meant Katya was about to leave him. He tried slowing his pace. "Terrible for you," he said. "And heartbreaking that she never got to see you become a dancer." If only he had the rest of the night to continue this conversation, but he couldn't go any slower; they had reached Union Square.

"I was Katherine then," she said wistfully. "I didn't become Katya until I was seventeen."

She was lovely, standing with the park behind her, the sky transforming from orange to a deeper shade of dusk. Parents were gathering the children chasing each other around the trees to come home for bed. "What do you prefer to be called?"

She looked at him. "At this point," she said, hesitating, "everyone calls me Katya. Except my father and my aunt Mary, his sister."

The streetlights came on. "I guess your new name helped move you forward."

"Why do you say that?"

"It opened a new chapter," he said. "I know mine did. Grief is nothing if not twisted and uneven." Where was he going with this? She was trying to catch a train, while he felt his life depended on their encounter. "I was desperate to leave my old self behind," he continued. "My training psychiatrist thinks I abandoned too much with the name change. He's determined to dredge up everything associated with Janko Stein."

She nodded thoughtfully.

It was the second time that John had pronounced his old name for her. Other than Dr. Roth, no one other than Barney and Selma knew it. Katya wasn't Jewish, but he felt she understood. Barney and Selma wouldn't dwell on her religious background; they would judge her by her character. That was who they were.

"I guess Dr. Roth is right," John said. "There are happy memories lost in the rubble." It felt imperative to continue on the subject of grief. His or hers? Hers, he thought—her lost mother. "We need a concept of emotional stamina, just as we have one for physical stamina."

"Physical stamina I understand," Katya said, removing a subway token from her wallet.

She was about to descend into the subway and disappear.

"The Circle Line?" he stammered, desperate to see her again. "How about it? We could go next weekend!"

She looked at him, eyes wide, like she was trying to solve a problem.

"I'd really like that," she said.

It occurred to him that he could do something other than stand stupefied, as if Katya had been carried away on a gust of wind rather than entering the subway.

He started to walk north, past the Flatiron Building, past the shoe repair shops and the dry cleaners and the office buildings that would be teeming with activity come Monday morning. He could grab a bite near Times Square at his regular coffee shop. He continued uptown, streams of taxis rushed by, hustling on a Saturday evening.

"How ya doing, doc?" The host at the Broadway All-Nighter grabbed a menu and limped toward a table in the back. He must be past seventy. "The usual?"

John nodded. Pastrami and rye—his missed lunch and over-due dinner. He flipped absentmindedly through the pages of the jukebox, embarrassed to recall his anxiety slithering across the table on that first awkward date with Ann. Riven with desire for the office secretary, focused (shamefully, he now thought) on a pair of hips and a set of shapely, nylon-sheathed legs.

And now Katya.

He imagined her bursting from the wings of the Peter Stuyvesant Theater, leaping and spinning, twirling on air, while he sat on the edge of his seat, breathless with anticipation. Well, not quite. Music was difficult; it was intolerable at times. There were experiences to be borne without the possibility of appeasement. He wasn't cured and wasn't curable.

He needed a better outcome for the people in his care. A strange banker, he was, dealing in the peculiar coinage of patients' memories. There was both burden and benefit in managing that depository. And what about his own memories? It wasn't getting any easier with Dr. Roth, but John had come to accept that their sessions textured the painful regularity of living.

Buttering his toast, John wondered idly how Ann was doing. She must have found somebody else by now.

There was tomorrow night. And the next and the next. And four more until Sunday, and the possibility of Katya.

෨

Candles flickered around Maya and Fiona's apartment. They had shoved the furniture against the walls to make room for dancing. The whole company was jammed in, pulsating to Elvis Presley. For a drink you could wedge into the skinny railroad kitchen and scoop ice cubes from the sink. There were two bottles of Jack Daniels and a jug of orange juice on the counter for whiskey sours.

"Big enough to party, don't you think?" Maya said as Katya slid sideways out of the kitchen with a glass of orange juice. The record player was so loud the floor was vibrating. "We couldn't have done this in that shoebox of a squat."

Katya laughed. "What a great place."

"Cat's away," Maya said, leering. "Is the mouse playing?"

"Please!" Katya. It was too warm to blush. "I've been busy with my dad," she said over the din.

"How is he?"

"Coming home soon. They're going to teach him to use crutches. Let's hope he doesn't push himself."

"You should follow your own advice."

"Very funny." Katya took a sip of orange juice. "He seems pretty cheerful. At least when I visit."

"What'd you expect? He's your dad. Mine's ridiculous that way."

Someone switched the record. "Connie Francis!" Maya said. "You dancing to *Stupid Cupid*?"

Katya gyrated toward the kitchen to put down her glass. Hands overhead, Katya mouthed the words and bopped back to the living room.

She couldn't believe her luck. Practice all day, dance all night.

Burn up the stage at the Peter Stuyvesant Theater, *grand jeté* at the *Opéra*. Boogie at your best friend's. What a life. Partner with the boss—in more ways than one.

Connie Francis crooned over a sax that was going nuts. "Katya!" Paolo shimmied toward her, a whiskey and a cigarette balanced in one hand.

"Ciao, Paolo!" She didn't want to think about Mr. Yanakov right now. He wasn't thinking about her. She tossed one arm in front of her and then the other.

"It's been a while since I've seen you on the floor." This was dancing—it really was, Katya thought as she shimmied toward Paolo—even if Mr. Yanakov would curse the notion.

Feeling lighter than she had in months, Katya threw her hips from side to side. She couldn't fathom why she'd talked so much to John Curtin. She'd said more about Mama in the space of a few blocks than she ever had to anyone else. It must be something about his being a headshrinker; he was trained to make people talk. He had been nice to visit Daddy.

Paolo put his hands around Katya's waist. "Crying shame that you're in love?" he asked, pretending he was singing the song. "Woo woo woo, it'll set you free," he said, spinning her twice.

27

1963

"I've never seen it like this!" Katya said over the boat's chug-ging. The Hudson was mottled with sunlight, buildings orga-nized like a futurist doll's house.

"Manhattan without dirt or grime. Or heartache," John said. "Isn't it a wonderful illusion?"

Katya nodded. A voice on the loudspeaker called out land-marks. Tourists' cameras clicked like castanets. "You'd never know I'd lived in the city my whole life."

"I'm delighted to take the girl out of Queens," John said, smiling.

"I think we'll get a better view if we go over to the rail," she said. "Is that okay?"

"Of course!" He was on his feet before she finished asking. "May I get you a Coca-Cola?" No less chivalrous than when he handed her white roses.

"Thank you." Something in his eyes felt intimate and in-viting. She hurried toward the railing, brushing back her blue chiffon scarf. It was refreshing, the wind coming across the deck, blowing away everything except John.

Was it all right to go with him on the Circle Line? Contrary to expectations, Mr. Yanakov was sending telegrams on a reg-ular basis. One arrived this morning, telling her it was gray and rainy in Brussels. Katya had no interest in the Belgian weather; she was focused on the sunshine illuminating New York Har-bor. Water splashed up from the sides, washing her with a light spray.

"There she is!" Katya said, pointing excitedly to the Statue of Liberty as John returned with drinks. "So majestic."

"It's something to sail into the city," John said. "You feel as if Lady Liberty were welcoming you personally."

She looked at him. "Tell me more."

"It was like sailing through a magic curtain and leaving the darkness behind."

"Really?"

"There was some of that, but also plenty of wonder and fear about what we were sailing into."

He was so earnest. She wondered what he had left behind but was afraid to probe further. "What happened when you landed?"

"I was taken in by the most loving couple in the world, Barney and Selma Katz." He looked like he was going to cry. She felt terrible. "Their son was killed in action in Sicily. They gave me everything they would have given him."

"Oh, John, that's beautiful."

"It was as if the gods were looking after me."

She wanted to distract him. "Do you really know how to read people's minds?"

He smiled. "I try to quell people's demons."

"Are you successful?"

He looked puzzled.

"At quelling their demons?"

"I try," he said. "You can imagine it's not easy. Demons come in all shapes and sizes... How did you come to ballet?"

"I've been studying since I was a child."

"Your father got you lessons?"

"Actually." She paused. "It was Aunt Mary. My father helped. But Aunt Mary lit the spark."

"Lucky."

"Yes, it was. She was trying to give me a way forward after my mother died."

"Ah. I was thinking lucky for me, and for all of us who've seen you dance."

"That's nice of you."

"What about Aunt Mary?"

"She was the first career woman I knew," Katya said. "Never married. At the time I was impressed she could afford her own wardrobe." Why was she talking inanities about Aunt Mary's clothing? Why would he care?

"That is impressive!" John said, smiling.

But he did care, or at least welcomed her to say what she wanted. She took a sip of Coke and looked back across the water to the Statue of Liberty. "I didn't know she was so big."

"She's got a big job."

"Here you see Wall Street and the financial district," the voice on the loudspeaker said. "The center of the nation's banking industry."

Katya leaned over the railing, squinting at Lower Manhattan. John put his arm around her—gently, as if he didn't want to be too forward. His hand on her waist felt warm and protective. If only he would kiss her, just pick up her chin and kiss her. "I know it's not very nice," she said, moving closer to him. "But banking sounds numbingly boring."

"Compared with being a prima ballerina?" he asked.

"Think of all those men in their gray suits and matching briefcases, holed up in an office on the top floor of a skyscraper, day in and day out, like mice in a cage."

"Beg to differ, Miss Symanova," John said.

Had she offended him?

"Not today, they're not holed up," he said. "Today's Sunday."

"Oh," she said, relieved. "A day of rest."

"Too bad every day can't be Sunday," he said.

"Yeah, too bad," she said, giddy as he drew her in tighter.

28

1963

"What're you doing?" John asked when he called a few days later.

"You don't want to know," Katya said, giggling.

"But I do."

Something about their ride on the Circle Line had made her homesick—for what, she wasn't sure. "Rinsing out a few pairs of tights before I go to bed."

"How often do you do that?"

Was she really talking about dirty tights? "Nightly ritual."

"Ah. What about tomorrow?"

"What?"

"What're you doing tomorrow?"

"Visiting my dad," she said, endeavoring to sound less silly.

"May I take you to dinner afterward?"

She agreed without hesitation.

Katya stocked Daddy's refrigerator and helped him practice using crutches around the living room, then up and down the front path, and finally on the sidewalk.

"Listen to that, it's a golden oldie!" Daddy said as she stowed a few cans of tomato soup in the kitchen cabinet. "Turn the radio up, will you, Katherine? The Andrews Sisters!" He grinned. "I can just hear your mother—'Patrick, make it louder!' She loved those gals." *When they begin…* Syrupy harmonies wafted out of the radio. "You can't believe the memories this brings back. Mama would snap her fingers like a big-band conductor, spinning between the refrigerator and the sink, waving a table-spoon." Daddy closed his eyes to *Begin the Beguine* and rocked back and forth. And Katya remembered, too, Mama swinging her around the kitchen, mouthing the words. It was twenty years ago, but Katya knew the music, felt Mama's arms around her. The memory was bright and immediate, as if a fresh rain had scrubbed off the haze.

Katya opened a package of hamburger and began browning the meat. "You don't tell stories about Mama," she said, tapping her spatula to the beat.

Daddy looked wounded. "Guess I'm not a raconteur." He leaned on a crutch to shift his position. "Hear anything from the choreographer?"

Katya jiggled the pan. "He's been sending daily telegrams," she said. The smell of hamburger fat was making her queasy. Yesterday, Mr. Yanakov sent one that said how much people in Brussels admired him. This morning, he wrote that he was heading to Stuttgart and that Simon Worthington of the Stuttgart Dance Troupe wanted new choreography. *Will write from Germany. Next time, we go together.* She wondered what prompted that one. She had thrown both telegrams out on the way to Daddy's, as if by doing so, she could relieve herself of trying to decode them. Mr. Yanakov must be compensating for his indiscretions, which was a nice way to put it. She should be glad to be hearing from him but was instead savoring her boat trip with John like a favorite song, turning it around to imagine the accompanying dance steps.

"I wasn't paying attention," Daddy said.

Katya shut off the flame and sat down next to him.

"Mama had so much going for her." He sighed. "We don't speak ill of the dead."

"I remember her laugh," Katya said. It was raucous. And another thing she remembered—egg-encrusted dishes stacked in the kitchen sink and a greasy frying pan on the stove, but who cared? Daddy was a cleanliness nut, so there hadn't been a dirty dish lying around since Mama died. Overall, Katya would rather have Mama than have clean dishes.

"What's for dinner?" Daddy asked.

Le Ballon Français was muraled in splashes of yellow and red
and blue, hot air balloons floating across the walls, the scent
of warm bread and seafood drifting from the kitchen. Katya
was in sky blue—silk, John thought, though he wasn't sure—a
dress of dazzling fit and style. The maître d' showed them to
the center of the room. Katya angled through the crowd like a
rippling wave; diners stopped talking and paused to admire her.
John pulled out her chair and took his seat across from her. She
sat forward, lengthening her neck like a swan.

A waiter delivered bread to the table. "How's your father?"
John asked. He felt the slightest press of her leg against his. Was
he imagining it?

"Fine," Katya said. "More mobile."

"Good! What do ballerinas do over the summer?"

"Company class, no matter how hot."

"Every day?" he asked, passing her the bread.

She nodded. "We're not even in rehearsal for the fall season
yet. Mr. Yanakov's away," she added.

Yes, John could feel her leg, like a passing butterfly's wing.
"Mr. Yanakov?"

She seemed to color. "Boris Yanakov. Our choreographer. I
spend a lot of time with him… But he's away for the summer.
It's more relaxed with him gone."

"He's taking a long vacation, eh?"

"Not quite," she said, breaking off a piece of bread. "He's
in Europe, working in Belgium and Germany." She spoke so
quietly, John could hardly hear her.

"I know nothing about ballet," he said. "I had no idea what
I was getting into."

"You make it sound like a medical procedure!"

He laughed. "My colleague's wife handed me a ticket to *Three
Muses*, and I just went."

"Boris Yanakov's breakout work, the one that established his
reputation."

"You were sensational. I don't understand how you do it. I

feel like dancers could provide some additions to med school anatomy… You have to have discipline in your profession."

She smiled. "Once I started lessons, there was nowhere else I wanted to be. I'll grant you it's hard work," she added. "*Three Muses* is a strenuous ballet. The ending is the hardest."

"You're exhausted by that point."

"It's not that. It's that the ending doesn't always come together the way you want it to."

"It was so moving."

"The night you were there…" She trailed off, puzzling over something. "That night I felt…emptied, like I had nothing inside except music streaming through." She looked at him. "I'm glad you got that ticket," she said dreamily. "And that you came to see us in New York too. I hope you enjoyed it." He recalled the terror that *Charged Particles* stoked, his cowering in the Peter Stuyvesant Theater like a burn victim smelling smoke. "Enjoy" was not an accurate descriptor. What should he say to this mesmerizing woman, who possessed the stage like a winged goddess—half earthly, half celestial? To witness Katya Symanova dance was to collide with a vital essence. Enjoyment was beside the point.

"You were amazing," he said.

"Tell me about you," she said lightly, after the waiter took their orders.

"I had an idyllic childhood," he said. "Two parents, a little brother named Max." He stopped.

She waited, her head to one side, exposing her long neck, her elegant throat.

He stretched his legs. Should he go on? He would rather run his index finger along the inside of her forearm.

"John," she said quietly. "You left off with your parents and your brother."

"Oh. One by one, they were taken by the Nazis." He couldn't contain himself. His story gushed out—Herr Glitzenstein, dressed like he was headed to the bank where he used to work, drilling vocabulary in the makeshift school in their dining room;

Mutti singing by Janko's bed—music from an earlier, unsullied
time.

Katya was rapt.

"It's funny; I've never recounted this with a beginning, a
middle, and an end." Years of silence welled up in him. He
didn't want to cry in front of her. "The mind is a complex
organism. Memory is full of tricks."

Katya leaned forward, the shawl collar of her dress shimmering in candlelight. "This must be horribly painful."

Maybe he did want to cry in front of her.

"One night, my father didn't come home," he said. He
picked up his glass and took a few sips of water. "He was shot
two blocks from our house for violating curfew."

Katya gasped, crossing her hands over her heart. John had
seen her do that before! Seen her Muse of Discipline, quiver-
ing and graceful. Now she was across the table giving him that
same, prized gesture.

"You are…" He had no idea how to finish the sentence.
He couldn't shake the feeling that she was a spirit come by
enchantment. He folded his hands under his chin and gazed at
her. Finally, he said, "I think Papa was at secret meetings to try
to overthrow the Nazis."

"He was brave to stand up like that."

"It seems insane."

The waiter delivered bowls of cold strawberry soup.

"Your father was trying to protect his family," Katya said, a
tear rolling down her cheek.

"I really don't mean to upset you," John whispered. He
reached across the table and wiped her tear with his finger.

"Please," she said, brushing her hand across the back of his,
pausing for a moment before picking up a spoon.

"Your compassion…means so much," he said. Years in Dr.
Roth's office hadn't bestowed this kind of serenity. The feeling
of her hand against his. "I'm so lucky," he added, rapturous in
the pink shadows of Le Ballon Français.

"How so?"

Her lips caressed the spoon, her tongue finding the last bits of strawberry.

"In this country, I had Barney and Selma. They gave me everything."

"I see why," she said. "I've never met anyone like you."

"This is perfect for a warm night," he said, spooning some soup. "What about you?" He was in a fever. "Your growing up?"

"Oh, just dancing. Every year, more training," she said. "They add classes until you have to drop out of high school or get permission to leave school early every day. Don't worry, I finished high school," she said, smiling. "Moved downtown with my friend Maya as soon as I could. I didn't realize joining the company meant so much work. But it's what I love most in the world... I worry about my dad."

"Yes, it was a serious fracture."

"He did his best to raise me. He and Aunt Mary gave me my ballet lessons. All I've done is leave him. I don't mean to sound harsh, but the good thing about his accident is that I'm spending more time with him." She had something more to say. "He's never said much. We've never said much to each other." She looked at John. "I used to expect it to get easier. It turns out, it's just the opposite."

"I know what you mean," he said.

At the entrance to her building, she stood with the calmness of a reflecting pool. John stepped toward her and laid his hands on her arms. The scent of her perfume felt like a private message. He brought her to him, his palm on her back. Her lips parted slightly. He leaned forward to accept her invitation.

A kiss—at once a homecoming and the stirring of a passion that had waited a lifetime to awaken. Her body against his, live with possibility, relaxed and fluid. He wanted to stand pressed against her forever, sinking into whirlpools of kisses. Or sweep her up and carry her home. Start with the arch of her foot and kiss every inch of her, toe by toe, calf by calf, thigh by thigh.

And yet. The lightness she had displayed over dinner was dissipating.

"May I call you again?"

She nodded.

Blissfully hopeful, he whispered goodnight and headed north to his one-bedroom on West Sixty-Sixth.

Katya walked upstairs to her apartment.

John was a symphony, capturing the whole of her in that kiss, his warm lips on hers, his tongue discovering what mattered most. He understood—understood everything, it seemed. As if he had known her all her life, yet arrived with the freshness of a budding flower.

He was warm, he was tender. Against him she felt luminescent and beloved.

John unlocked his door, wondering if he had been too open.

On the other hand, Katya's reaction to his riptide of information had lent spine to John's flimsy memories of Papa. Maybe he should have completed his disclosures—talked about Mutti and Max—ignored the risk that Katya could float away just as she vanished into the wings.

He took off his jacket and loosened his tie, amused to consider psychiatry's treatment modality: harnessing talk to tackle pain. Physician, heal thyself. But his experience had a density that talking couldn't dispel.

Sitting down in the stuffed brown armchair rescued from Selma's basement, he closed his eyes to relive the texture of Katya's glossy blue dress and his palm gliding down her silky back, cautiously bringing her closer. Her arms cool against the evening's warmth, their kiss momentous.

She lay down in peace.

His eyes brimmed with kindness; his hands set her body alight.

His kiss.

Mr. Yanakov was shorter than Katya. When he kissed her, she experienced the fire and brimstone that were creativity's underbelly. In the studio he pushed her to her limits and beyond, stretching her legs, bending her torso, hovering over her on the floor. It wasn't often that he kissed her. It was rare, in fact.

Whereas John.

He was tall but not imposing. So natural, as if they fit.

With Mr. Yanakov, she tested steps that might cohere, but might just as easily be the fleeting offspring of their charged partnership. On good days, they were a flowing, dancing stream. When Katya and Mr. Y were fully synchronized, the mirrors bounced two reflections: Katya's, and a second that was her outline, waiting to be sketched in. Was it Katherine Sillman? Or whatever her choreographer discerned before arranging bits of motion into a whole, like a tile worker laying mosaic?

Whereas John.

He asked questions aimed at the heart of things. He wanted to know her—including Katherine Sillman—not an object of his invention.

Mr. Yanakov's mind catapulted ahead and simultaneously reversed, scooping up—what? His past? She knew so little about it, and she didn't share hers. He didn't inquire, as if she hadn't existed before he named her.

Whereas John.

All they'd done was talk—about her, about him. About their families—skirting over pain, while acknowledging it too. For he gave off an immensity of caring. In an Olympian feat, he had converted the horrors of his experience into a fountain of goodness. He had checked in on Daddy and endeavored to ensure his comfort; he had taken her on the Circle Line, water slapping against the boat while they enjoyed Manhattan's skyline together. He'd smiled at her delight and leaned across the table at Le Ballon Français, his attentiveness like light.

Mr. Yanakov's furious energy ignited his couplings with

Katya, which were not preceded by tender kisses or idle banter but by the relentlessness that characterized their art.

Then again. There was something more between John and Katya than talk, and it wasn't only their kiss. (That glorious kiss, as if he had found all of her!) It was also her certainty that someone had been in the hall in Paris. She had felt him there, and he had materialized. John Curtin, who had not just watched but *seen Three Muses.* He had received the message she transmitted. And come again to see her in New York. It was her dancing, her work, no matter what the critics said, no matter Mr. Yanakov's opinion.

And yet. Mr. Yanakov's ballets were emblazoned on her limbs. (Why didn't he memorialize anything? She couldn't stand that he didn't record his work.) He had spurred her to excellence, summoned her inside his creative process, insisted on a dedication to their art that matched his. Even if she couldn't trust him, she owed him fealty.

Every day, he telegrammed.

He had trained her body, made his ballets on her, and given her the stage. Together they innovated movement.

Sweet Jesus. Boris Yanakov was that much to her.

29

1963

Katya detoured to St. Patrick's Cathedral before company class on Saturday afternoon. Not to attend Mass—she didn't need to mouth words and hymns that were second nature—but for sanctuary and anonymity.

Genuflecting before she started down the great center aisle, Katya took a pew on the left toward the altar, where she could avoid the street noise and bathe in the rainbow of colors refracted through rows of stained-glass windows. She felt alone in the cavernous space, less a child of her parents than an autonomous woman. St. Patrick's bore no resemblance to the small parish church where Daddy had taken her on Sundays. It was not Mama whom Katya recalled from church but Mama's persistent absence, as much a part of the Sunday scenery as the colorless windows over the pews.

Jolting Katya awake, sound burst from the cathedral organ, as if the gate to paradise had just been flung open. Massive chords streamed from above, filling the cathedral as surely as light from the stained-glass windows. The organist began practicing the same few phrases, the nave sufficiently empty that Katya could hear him turning his sheet music back to start a certain section over again and again; not so different from the discipline of barre work, Katya thought.

She leaned against the wooden pew. What was she doing with John? Kissing him! What was she playing at? How could she not have disclosed her relationship with Mr. Yanakov?

The organist paused, pulled out all the stops, and struck a titanic chord. His pedaling reverberated throughout the cathedral. Katya was surrounded by music, joyous and celebratory. She and John had had conversations different from any she'd

experienced, as if she were part of a couple like ones she'd
jealously observed, who shared a friendship, who confided in
each other with the regularity of morning dew. Conversation
as pleasurable as melting into a *penché*, as exciting as a *grand jeté*
knifing the stage. John was affectionate and serious. He had
journeyed through hell and back again.

Arpeggios from the organ spilled over the balcony, looping
and intertwining, traveling the keyboard; music aimed toward
God. If only Katya had more time with John. She gazed at the
gilded sanctuary before her—fluted stone columns fanning out
like the *corps* extending *developés* in unison; the windows above
such a deep blue, she was convinced they contained an essential
truth. Here was one she understood: she could pretend to linger
over dinner, or at the door to her apartment building, but Boris
Yanakov—not her grueling schedule or the exigent demands
she placed on her body—rendered any contact with John a lie.

The thought of meeting Mr. Yanakov in the studio at the
end of the summer shot a peppery streak of fear through her.
She was in a vaunted position with the great man, but he owned
her career and her future and her name. To see John was injudi-
cious and wrong. She could not square how she felt about John
with her need for Mr. Yanakov. Mr. Yanakov was her means to
dance. She needed dance in order to be. How could she imagine
that she could date John with the insouciance of an ingenue?

She bent down on the red kneeler, her head pressed against
folded hands. In John's arms, there was a belonging.

After class, Katya peeled off her leg warmers and stuffed them
into her bag. "You look like the cat that ate the canary," Maya
said, throwing a dress over her leotard.

"Shh."

"You're a blushing teenager."

"Don't tease me. He's too special for that." They picked up
their bags and walked outside. "We're meeting for a picnic dinner in Central Park."

"Cute. Will you please unload Borrrrris the Dictator?"

"Maya!"

"Now's your chance to hotfoot it out of here."

"I'd never dance again," Katya said.

"Are you insane?" They crossed the street and headed north on Sixth Avenue. "You could work anywhere."

Work was sitting at a typewriter in an office, like Aunt Mary. Or Daddy's dreary accounting practice—days proceeding like drips from a rusty tap. (Katya needed to call him.) The studio, on the other hand, was sacred space. Sinking into *pliés* was reciting a favorite prayer. Katya's calling was to channel heat during floor combinations, to irradiate patterns from invisible ink—generating movement that only she and Mr. Y could see. If the fiery surge Katya felt when she leapt onstage was work, then she wanted to work forever.

"They'd hire you in London or Paris in a heartbeat," Maya said.

"I don't want to go to London or Paris."

"Fine, how about Copenhagen? Or San Francisco? They have a company."

"Too far from my dad."

Maya stopped at the corner of Fifty-Ninth and Columbus and faced Katya. "What is the matter with you? It's this guy, isn't it?"

"I don't even know him."

"I can see it in your face. You're head over heels."

Katya couldn't bear to hear her say it. What was she going to do? "I have to be able to make ballets."

"Oh, for heavens' sake. The amount of fourteen-carat ding-dongs I've gone out with—you haven't heard the half of it. I'd kill for a good man. If this guy is for real, you're crazy to let him go. What about love?"

Katya shrugged her shoulders. "I can't think about it."

Wasn't love as fluffy as pink cotton candy? What about trust and reliability? (She couldn't trust Mr. Yanakov.) What about the reliability of her own body? She would age—it would age—and then what?

"Aunt Mary says you can only trust yourself," Katya said, without much conviction.

"Don't get all romantic on me or anything. We wouldn't want that. My parents can't shut up about me finding a husband. They act like two lovebirds who found their perfect mate," Maya said. "God knows, they're not perfect. But still. There's so much drudgery in what we do. Wouldn't you rather settle down? Let yourself go, eat what and when you want? Stop hurting? Sleep in or go to the movies?"

"Not really," Katya said. What if Maya was right? What if Katya was head over heels?

Maya sighed. "See you tomorrow." She turned west on Fifty-Ninth. "Do me a favor and don't be stupid," she said, calling to Katya over her shoulder.

❧

The evening was balmy. Katya lay next to John on a blanket. "Is it too early to see a star?"

"Let's stay until we do," John said.

"We'll see one even in New York?"

"With you here? I think so." He reached over and held her hand.

He felt warm and cool at the same time.

"I brought a bottle of wine," he said. "Shall I open it?"

"No," she said, too firmly. "I mean no, thank you, not for me. I don't drink."

"Not good for your profession?"

"No. Well, yes, that's true."

"I've upset you," he said, propping himself up on his elbow and looking at her tenderly. "I'm sorry."

No one spoke with such caring. "It's a beautiful evening," she said.

He brushed the back of his hand down her cheek.

She touched her cheek where his hand had been, feeling soothed even though she hadn't known she needed soothing. "I avoid alcohol," she said. "There's no reason you would know," she added. "My mother drank." She couldn't—didn't want to—leave it unsaid.

"Ah. No wonder. I should have been more thoughtful."

"I've never met anyone as thoughtful as you." He was haloed in compassion. "My mother was drunk when she was killed." It felt suddenly urgent to share her deepest confidences, as if intimacy with John were preordained. "She was hit by a truck crossing Northern Boulevard. I was a little girl on the jungle gym when Aunt Mary came running across the playground at recess. I knew something was wrong." She rubbed her stomach to dissipate the sick, twisty feeling at the recollection.

"How awful," John said, gazing at her as if she were all that mattered. "That's an abandonment in more ways than one."

"An abandonment." How did he know? "It makes everything worse, doesn't it? Much less benign than a regular accident, not that that's benign. When Daddy first told me Mama drank, it was like she died a second time. As if she'd left me on purpose."

"No one would leave you on purpose," John said gently.

Boris Yanakov had just done so. "I don't think that's true," Katya said, anguished over the searing reality of her choreographer. What about the man beside her? What was she going to do?

"Heartbreaking," John said, wrapping her in a full embrace.

"It changed me when I found out," Katya said, her face in his chest, clutching his shirtsleeve as if it were a life preserver. "Made me feel like I couldn't rely on anyone."

"I can't stand that," he said, holding her tighter.

"Daddy blames himself. He says if he'd been paying attention, he could have stopped her."

"It's an illness," John said. "Drinking."

She looked up at him.

"That's the latest science. Illnesses are not something we can control," he said.

Was he sent to deliver mercy? Understanding? "That would put it in a different light. Very different."

She turned toward the sky. "Look!" she said. "A star!"

"What did I tell you?" he said, leaning over to kiss her.

30

1963

Katya's *tendus* and *jetés* were as dependable as the leather tackle in a riding stable; barre work as measured as spokes on a wheel: to the front, to the side, to the back, to the side. Lars was teaching, more dispassionate than Mr. Yanakov, rarely raising his voice. *Frappés, rondes de jambes, grands battements.*

Time for center work. The mirrors were a wall of admonishments. There could be no letting up, no slacking off. Katya needed to be in her best shape when Mr. Yanakov came bounding back, bursting with ideas for the fall season, engorged on a raft of choice ballerinas. Katya felt ill thinking about his European exploits. But she sensed that even as Mr. Yanakov leapt from conquest to conquest, he would want her more—not less—when he returned. Together, they would sweat through choreography that she would inhabit so thoroughly that next rehearsal she would predict what would spring from his head—privy to his virtuosity, vessel of his imagination. Their pattern was as familiar as first position; it was her life's architecture.

Was this what she wanted?

Anchor the leg, pull up from the diaphragm, as instinctive as breathing.

The hall outside was cooler than the studio. She threw on some clothes in the dressing room and headed out, peering out the window over the stairwell. It was drizzling.

He was there, standing under a black umbrella.

She couldn't believe her luck—John had appeared, like an answer to a prayer. "How did—?"

"How did I know when company class lets out?" he said excitedly. "I called. Where to?" he asked, brushing her lips.

"I wonder," Katya said. He was standing here—so

close—looking at her in his trusting, kind way. "Could we may-be…? Would it be okay to stop at my place? I'd love to shower and change."

"Of course." He folded his arm around her.

The drizzle steadied to rain. They headed west. Leaning against him, she noticed the shabbiness of her neighborhood—windows barred, rusted fire escapes hanging like so many paths to nowhere. John felt calm and reassuring. Against him, she felt treasured.

"I'll be down in a minute," Katya said when they reached her walk-up. She ran upstairs, the rain beating harder. It was pour-ing. John would be soaked by the time she finished her shower. She checked to see if her apartment was presentable. At least she had made the bed this morning. She hurried back down the steps, her heart pounding. He was a lone figure on the sidewalk. Water droplets covered his wavy hair despite the umbrella.

"Maybe it's drier inside," Katya suggested, holding open her front door. Rivulets of rain slid down his face. He was smiling.

"I'll wait here," he said, pausing at the foot of the steps to close his dripping umbrella.

"It's cramped at my place, but at least I can give you a chair," she said. "If you don't mind."

"I don't mind at all," he said.

Luxuriating in hot water, she took a bar of grapefruit-scented soap and lathered her breasts, rehearsing a plan for her future. She would dance her hardest and her best but would get to know John, who was now sitting by her little table on the other side of the shower wall. She washed between her legs, suds running down, surprised by a pinprick of regret that John had never known—and would never know—Katherine Sillman. Not the house in Queens where Katherine had grown up, nor Mama, who had left so early. He would never know Katherine as a student.

Katya kneaded shampoo into her hair, grapefruit whiffs filling the bathroom. No one came to her apartment. Except

John, blown in with the rain. A warm stream massaged her back. Terrified to open the door and find him there, she was more terrified to find him gone.

She towel-dried her head, put on black slacks and a print blouse, and rubbed the steam off the mirror so she could see to brush her hair.

Marshalling her courage, she opened the door.

"Katya." John stood up. He took in the sweep of her body and laughed.

Katya looked down. "Oh." Her blouse was askew, several buttons undone at the bottom. She started to cry. All the things that hadn't aligned. She should have done things differently—not succumbed to Mr. Yanakov, not wanted him so badly. She should not be hiding this glaring reality from John.

"My sweet Katya," John said, running his hand down the back of her head. "Don't get upset over buttons. It's pouring. We don't have to go out."

She looked up and nodded, tracing the shape of his cheekbones and the lines of his mustache with her index finger, as if he had just been found.

She was afraid he was already lost to her.

He scooped her up and placed her on the bed. Moving aside her wet hair, he bent over. Slowly, carefully, he unbuttoned her cockeyed blouse.

Naked, she reached inside the shoulders of his jacket and slid it off. She loosened his tie and pulled it through his shirt collar, her assertiveness both a choice and an affirmation, just for today. Leaning on her elbow, she watched him undress. His body hair matched the swath of dark brown across his forehead. He picked up his clothes and put them on the chair next to her little table, then surprised her by walking around the bed to settle along her back. He ran his palm slowly down her front and felt the outline of each rib. He turned her over to kiss her open mouth. Rolling between her thighs, he licked her shoulders, wet from her hair, and kissed each of her nipples, erect and hard. To the left, to the right, to the left again.

Through months and years she had practiced, tethered to an unbending schedule, relentlessly thrusting higher, farther, longer. She had pushed past endurance—her profession's essence. She had relied on discipline to deliver heart-stopping performances every night, a soloist atop a company of dancers who lived the way she did, who shared her ambition to exploit every muscle. She wrapped one, then the other leg around him. In them was the measure of her experience. She closed her eyes and let him take her over and through herself, dancing better than she ever had. Somewhere during the night, she glimpsed what it might mean to be whole.

31

1963

John waited outside Dr. Roth's office. Finally, he would complete this lamentable process.

"Where did we leave off?"

How could Dr. Roth not remember? "You had me sing," John said. "It was more like tortured groaning."

Dr. Roth raised his eyebrows. "We weren't going for an audition at the Metropolitan Opera, Dr. Curtin. It's our job to probe the burden of memory and try to alleviate what pain can be alleviated."

Why did Dr. Roth insist on saying "we" and "our"? The burden was John's alone. Katya had given him more in the space of a few days than Dr. Roth had in years. "I believe I'm ready to terminate my treatment, Dr. Roth."

"Is that so?"

"I think I've gotten what I can from this process."

Dr. Roth looked at him. "The best termination is one in which the psychiatrist and the patient arrive at that decision jointly." Maybe that was why Dr. Roth had a habit of speaking in the first-person plural; John and Dr. Roth were meant to be working together. "I don't see any reason to depart from that standard, do you, Dr. Curtin?"

John could think of a reason: a ballerina had been sent to him by a mysterious fairy godmother. Katya's insights across a bowl of strawberry soup were infinitely more valuable than Dr. Roth's across decades of practice. "Can't I make that decision alone?"

"It is my job to train you to the level of the gold standard of our profession. Our relationship is a good place to model it. Let's review the process of transference," Dr. Roth said.

"I don't think that will be necessary," John said. "I'm familiar."

"In that case, I need to counsel patience. Let's pick up where we left off last time."

It was frustrating, but John could tolerate anything if he could spend time with his ballerina. What was Dr. Roth but a persistent itch?

❧

Katya turned and brought the covers over her right shoulder as she settled into him. "Mmmm." It was getting light. "Tell me about your mother and brother," she said.

To wake up next to Katya was to dance in the Elysian fields. Her skin was pliant, her back smooth. Her calves were warm and supple. John had seen her mounted like a statue on a plinth— bent forward with one leg nailed to the floor, the other pointed away from earth, away from gravity. She was athletic. She was strong. He had watched her spun like a pinwheel, tossed into flight, her jumps suspended on air. In his embrace, she was an impassioned woman whom he had traveled across time and oceans to partner. He should herald his love. He should take a great, heaving breath and sing for all the world to hear.

"We don't have to talk," he said, kissing her black hair. He slid his palm down her back to her hips and leaned over to graze his lips across her face. "I have a better idea." He pulled her toward him.

"No," she said, gently pushing back.

"There are so many things I'd rather do." He stroked the inside of her thigh with the back of his hand.

"No," she said again, moving his hand away.

"We were forced to leave Mainz," he said hesitantly. "Aunt Ella's family had moved in a while before. Everything was sold. Mutti threw a few things into a valise, begging Aunt Ella to do the same or risk being killed." He stopped. "Everyone in Aunt Ella's family was murdered, but that was later."

"Oh my God." Katya held his face in her hands.

"You don't need to hear this."

"I do."

"She told me—"

"Who?"

"Mutti. Mutti told me to carry the valise with the valuables. Suitcase, I think you call it. Photographs, jewelry. She said I was the man of the family now."

"You were so young!"

"True. But it eats away at me that I let Mutti down." He looked at Katya. "I've never shared that with anyone before," he said quietly.

"Only you could interpret that as letting Mutti down," she said, gently palming his forehead. "No one else could."

"That's kind of you," he said. "You feel heavenly."

"I wish I could provide absolution like a priest. Jewish people don't do that, do they?"

He smiled and shook his head, leaning forward to kiss her. "Are you sure we can't find something more enjoyable right now?"

She shook her head, insistent.

"We were hauled away in a truck," he said, with a sigh. "People died with their eyes open, corpses frozen in sitting position, urine and feces and vomit covering the floor."

"I can't do this to you," he said. "My memories are staining your sheets."

"Please," she said.

"Mutti asked me to sing for the SS man and he took me away." He covered his eyes. "Mutti and Max were gassed while I sang for the kommandant," he mumbled.

"Good God," Katya said. She held him, his cheek on her breast.

"Certain music brings back unbearable memories," John said, running his index finger gently down her cheek. "All kinds of music, actually. And then someone handed me a ticket to *Three Muses*. The music was hard. I wanted to leave the theater." He paused. "Your arms feel luxurious…"

"Imagine, leaving before the Muse of Discipline danced

onstage," he said. She held him tighter. "I don't deserve such beauty," he said.

"You were so young!" Katya said, repeating the phrase like a refrain.

John looked up, his face wet with tears. "'Singing is embedded in our tradition,' Papa used to say. 'It's a way to keep our memory.' I guess Janko was dealing with something larger than himself."

"I guess he was," Katya echoed.

"Papa said, 'Memory holds us together.'... It occurs to me Papa might be pleased. He assigned me a job, and not just any job but the one I have: to husband people's memories." John was sobbing. "My darling, look where you've brought me. You have taken me somewhere new."

Katya stroked his hair. "I heard the first report," she said quietly. "My father canceled my birthday party because FDR died—it's ridiculous to talk about a birthday party, but Edward R. Murrow was reporting from Buchenwald that day, the same day I got my ballet lessons. I'm trivializing the worst experience," she added.

"Not at all! You've honored it with your ballet lessons. You're a ray of sunshine, Katherine Sillman. How marvelous."

She kissed his forehead. "Of course you deserve the music. I want to invite you in."

"Dance with me." He fingered her nipple and brushed his lips along the side of her neck. He tasted her breasts, gliding his right hand down her belly, finding her pleasure, moving over her with the grace of an unfurling song.

Afterward they dressed and sat on her bed. Quiet and still, holding hands. As if, if they remained that way, the day would decline to start.

"I'm not sure what there is to eat, but at least there's coffee." Katya got up.

"Let me make it," he said. "I'm sure you have things to do." He filled the kettle and sat back on the bed, watching her open a dresser drawer and examine old leotards. "How do you choose?" John asked.

He looked so sincere and kind. Katya hated to leave him for class.

She shrugged her shoulders. "Depends on my mood." Mr. Yanakov would prefer the navy blue one. She didn't know how she knew that. "I like varying the colors," she said. She selected a clean pair of tights and sat down on the floor next to her ballet bag, pulling out dirty clothes and piling them on the floor. "Excuse me," she said, embarrassed.

"I love the behind-the-scenes view of the ballet," he said, smiling.

32

1963

The summer collapsed like thawing ice: June melted into July, July into August, August into September.

Boris Yanakov was on his way back. If only Katya could halt the flow of days. Too often she tried broaching the subject of her choreographer with John, and too often she failed; either John didn't hear her, or she gave up. She didn't want to talk about Mr. Yanakov. She wanted to experience John.

But still the time came, inevitable and unavoidable: Sunday morning in the studio with Boris Yanakov.

"Is there anything to eat?" Katya said as she sat on the floor, sorting things for morning rehearsal.

"I brought over some bagels last night. Do you want one?" John said.

"No, thanks."

"I'll start the coffee."

The smell of coffee meant wrenching away from John, toward rehearsals and Mr. Yanakov. What good was self-pity?

"Needs another minute," John said, sitting down to watch her.

She had to do it. "There's more to ballet than what you've seen," she said, swiveling around, the bag in her lap. "Much more." She stood up.

"I'm not my own," she said as bravely as she dared. She brought her bag to the door and returned to the edge of the bed.

"Who's ever 'their own'?" John asked. "Coffee, Miss Symanova?" He walked into the kitchen.

She couldn't believe he was waiting on her. "I'm serious,"

she said more firmly. "I'm really not my own. I won't be around much from now on."

"Disciplined by your art," he said, handing her a cup of coffee.

"I work for a very demanding man," she said, trying again. She checked her watch. She couldn't be late. "Boris Yanakov," Katya said. The name filled the room like smoke from a fire. He was trespassing here.

"Ah," John said. "The moody artist." He sat down next to her. "Isn't that the stereotype?"

Katya took a sip of coffee. "I don't know. He's always struck me as unique." She put her cup on the little table and squeezed between it and the bed to check herself in the small mirror on the wall. "He's created dozens and dozens of ballets. They pour out of him. It's something he and I work on together, actually. I love that part—helping him choreograph. He doesn't record any of them. He doesn't need to; he remembers every step."

"Must be a real taskmaster."

She turned around. "That's one way to put it," she said. She looked in the mirror and removed a few bobby pins from her bun.

John watched her fuss in front of the mirror.

"The time went so quickly with him away," she said between the pins in her mouth. She tucked in a strand of loose hair. "He'll want to get busy right away with his ideas for the fall season."

"Looking forward to it?"

She couldn't think how to respond. "I've been with him since my student days. It's like I've known him all my life."

"Then I'd love to hear more about him," John said.

"He renamed me for my first performance—the *pas de deux* from *Don Quixote*. I danced with Fernando Sanchez."

"I'm green with envy."

"Don't be," Katya said. "Fernando left the company years ago. He's a principal in London now, doing well." She recalled her shyness in Variations Class when she was first paired with him. "I don't think Fernando pays much attention to girls," she added. She sat back down.

"Poor guy," John said, kissing the top of her head. "Doesn't know what he's missing."

"That was the first performance Mama didn't come to."

"How painful." He picked up her hand. "That's so hard for a child. For you, I mean."

"It's best not to think about it," she said.

"Why shouldn't you? How can it not—?"

He was so earnest. "You don't have to," Katya said, taking his hands. She couldn't begin to comprehend how he lived with his ghastly memories. "You really don't."

"What?"

"You don't have to talk to me about this stuff."

"I do," he said, wrapping his arm around her. "What am I, if not a believer in talking it through, retrieving our past selves? Memory works in mysterious ways," he added.

It was a sin, what she had kept from him. "If I hadn't been so taken with ballet," Katya said, edging closer, "I might be a housewife now." She would rather dance. She would rather be with John.

"What a loss to the world that would be," he said.

33

1963

Mr. Yanakov was spinning in front of the mirrors, humming to himself. "Katya!" He hurried toward her. "I missed you." He clasped her buttocks, pulling her into a tight embrace. What had she done? "It's not the same," he said. Locked in his arms, facing the mirror, she hardly recognized herself. "It's not the same being away."

He was assimilated into her every fiber, but she had never felt farther away. She was alone with him in the studio, a place that held the promise of ascendancy. "Liftoff," Cape Canaveral called it. Together she and Mr. Yanakov would create new, bigger, better work. Always better. What if she'd jeopardized everything? Recklessly thrown it away?

"Welcome, Mr. Y," she whispered. "Boris. How was your trip back?"

"Exhausting. It's good to be home."

Where was home? She thought of Daddy, hopping around the living room in Queens. That wasn't home. Mr. Yanakov's living room was crammed with records. The ones he was considering for ballets lay randomly on top of their jackets on the sofa. No one ever sat there. His bathrobe was flung over the wicker chair next to his bed. (Sometimes he preferred to walk around naked.) On his kitchen counter was a loaf of rye in the breadbox and not much in the fridge besides butter for toast, and lemons, and the occasional jar of caviar from an adoring patron. She didn't sleep at Mr. Yanakov's. It wasn't home.

Her apartment, Katya thought, had become home. John had climbed the steps, dripping with rain, and shared her bed. He had watched her sort through dirty tights and fussed over coffee as if he belonged there; he brought bagels. He infused Katya's place with his love and transfigured Katya's apartment from a stopover to swap leotards into a place that was sacrosanct. He exuded the warmth she imagined in a mother's embrace. How crushing; how impossible.

Mr. Yanakov tipped Katya's head and scanned her torso, her navy-blue leotard thoroughly worn. Could he see John painted on her, brushstrokes visible beneath her clothing? "Recognize the physique?" she asked nervously. He angled her left and continued his gaze down her thighs and knees and calves and feet turned out in old *pointe* shoes. She was nicked with fear, and with longing and regret and confusion.

"Katya, I'm telling you, it's not the same," Mr. Y repeated, shaking his head. As if he had traversed Europe against his will. Surely arranging the legs of a bevy of ballerinas wasn't his only activity. There had to be one or two or four whom he took to bed to help inspirit his creation, embody his dreams. After a lifetime of trying to curry his favor and seal his affections, after years of wondering about his wives in Paris and the women strewn across the globe, Katya seemed to be craving his infidelity—anything for a little patch in which to negotiate her autonomy. "We don't have to rehearse," he said. He sounded pleading. "We could go to my place."

Not now. She felt a spreading dread. She had gone off with John as if Mr. Yanakov were doing the same, as if their relationship meant nothing to him. What if she had been drastically mistaken, her assumptions wrong? Maybe he intended to stay true to her. He had certainly sent enough telegrams. Mr. Y took her face in his hands, inches away, unconcerned. He was tired, and happy to see her.

Mr. Yanakov was integral to her daily routine, like the *pointe* shoes on her feet or this old blue leotard. No matter what he had done, it was indisputable that she'd betrayed him. "We're here, we may as well work," she said, gently putting her palm on his chest to separate them. Their home was the studio, she realized; that was something she understood. She didn't want to be someone who behaved as she was behaving. But there was John, who was his own constellation—and wondrous.

"You'll have to come back to Europe with me."

She got up from the floor.

"We're starting with the Stuttgart Dance Troupe after the New Year," Mr. Yanakov said. "Simon Worthington loves my work. He's an up-and-comer in Europe." He paused. "He's a bit of an *enfant terrible*—British, but they threw him out for being homosexual. What a ridiculous bunch of prudes. London's loss is Stuttgart's gain."

John was a flare's sparking whoosh. With him she was what she had not been—a spontaneous woman. "Worthington wants to introduce his company to American choreography," Mr. Y was saying. She had more to say to John, more to hear. Talking with him was not the means to the next dance step but the key to the music.

Katya shook out each of her feet and then her wrists.

It was irrelevant. She would have to tell John she'd made a grievous mistake, that she'd wronged not one man, but two.

"We're in conversations about reviving *Three Muses*," Mr. Y went on. "Stuttgart's a great town, and Worthington's a great talent. You'll like it there." His presumption seemed to be that she was hand luggage. No, she had yearned for this—to be by Mr. Yanakov's side, dancing and creating.

Wait a minute! Stuttgart? She couldn't go to Germany. What about John? She couldn't go anywhere. "Tell me about the fall lineup," Katya said, trying to divert Mr. Y as well as herself. "I'd love to see what you're thinking about."

"I have it," he said. He headed toward the turntable. "*Veiled Road*, *Rain Song*, and *Madison Avenue*. Warhol's doing the sets for *Madison Avenue*." She could not help but marvel; Mr. Yanakov had returned with the season envisaged, sets and artists included. "As to *Veiled Road*, the theme is what we can't explain. The mystery in everything. Lovers we can't live without, for example." Was he spouting brilliance, or did he suspect her? "*Veiled Road* looks at contradictions that separately ring true.

Irreconcilable conflicts. In other words, human nature." He leaned over the turntable. "You know who's the master?"

Herself?

"You?" she said.

He laughed. "Not bad, Katya. I was thinking of Beethoven. He captures mystery better than the best. He's the epitome." Mr. Yanakov dropped the needle on the turntable. "You're dancing to the slow movement of Opus 127. The string quartet will be in the pit. The first bars are really quiet," he said over the music. "But you'll need to find the beat as soon as the players start." He thought for a moment. "Remind me to check acoustics. If the beginning isn't audible, it's a missed opportunity. It's pointless, to miss the beginning," he added meditatively.

She would miss the rest of the beginning with John, which was not a beginning but merely the harbinger of an inexorable end, entangled as she was with her choreographer. And because of her art, which was nourishment.

Taking Katya from behind by the shoulders, Mr. Yanakov stood on tiptoe and nudged her toward the center of the studio. "Paolo pushes you forward," he said. "Like this." They fell in: Mr. Y, directive and sure; she, poised to imbibe his ideas. A muffled, pulsating throb passed among the four stringed instruments. The beat was not quite a heartbeat in repose, more like one in expectation. Or was it reflection? "Paolo will guide you, because you'll have no peripheral vision out of the hood of your cloak. He'll leave you so still, we can't tell you're alive. It's a loss of identity for you."

Mr. Y let go of her shoulders. "What I haven't figured out yet," he said pensively, "is the *corps*."

Katya listened to the music accreting color and texture. She decided it was elegiac. "The *corps* is in a line," she said, turning to Mr. Yanakov. "Two lines, actually, each cutting a diagonal. The boys are bisecting me." Her pattern with Mr. Y: together, they worked as one.

"Good," Mr. Yanakov said. He got behind her again. "Step step stop, up *en pointe*, fingers on the boy in front, right leg out, left leg out. *Piqué* turn, repeat. That's how the girls enter. The boys walk steadily forward, oblivious to the agitation in the girls behind them."

Katya closed her eyes and pictured herself center stage, divided by the boys. She saw John in the audience, holding white roses, then tried to dismiss the image. "The *corps* should dance in concentric circles," she said, listening to the music. "The boys surrounding the girls. I don't know how to choreograph that," she added. "But you do, Mr. Y."

"I suppose I do," he said, planning a series of jumps around the stage. She could tell because his hands were making leaping motions. He spun and dove, eyes up, eyes toward the floor.

"Good work, Katya," he said, stopping for breath. "You're coming into your own."

"I've asked him to read it," Mr. Yanakov said, later that week.

"Who?"

He didn't answer. When Mr. Y was in process, he kept everything to himself. If something happened to him, his work would be lost. Dance was ephemeral. Life was ephemeral. It would be devastating to lose Mr. Yanakov's body of work. Katya was the only one paying attention (she smiled thinking of Daddy's admonition to pay attention), Mr. Yanakov's steps imprinted on her like ritual scarification.

He put on a succession of records and listened for a few minutes before turning off the record player. "Never mind." He eyed Katya. "This one's for you to dance alone. *Let the rain kiss you,*" he whispered, walking toward her, snapping his fingers. "We'll put the music underneath," he said. "*Let the rain beat upon your head with silver liquid drops.* Great poetry, isn't it?" He paused, lost in thought. "The poem is 'April Rain Song.' Wouldn't it be something to have Langston Hughes read it during performance?"

If only she could splice herself in two so she could deliver Mr. Yanakov to the public and say yes to John.

"I think of running," Katya said, moving to the corner.

"Good," Mr. Y said. "We'll put the poet stage left. Do the circumference." He closed his eyes. *"Let the rain sing you a lullaby."* He thought for a moment, then pointed imperiously. "Center."

She crumpled to the floor, rolling with her arms overhead. *"The rain makes still pools on the sidewalk."*

She stood and bent sideways, stretching left and right, extending back and forth.

"The rain makes running pools in the gutter. Go on," he said.

She reached in front, palms parallel to the floor.

"Nice," Mr. Yanakov said. He trotted around the perimeter of the studio, waving his right hand in circles above his head: *"The rain plays a little sleep song on our roof at night/ And I love the rain."*

Their joint creation had never been better. Mr. Yanakov's work was her inspiration. Her inspiration was his work. Maybe she could ignore everything else.

"I'm still stumped about the score," he said.

"I have an idea!" Katya uncurled herself from a ball on the floor. "Why don't we skip the music?" John could watch unfettered. He would not have to hear music; he would not have to suffer.

Mr. Yanakov looked puzzled.

"We'll have a recording of an afternoon shower," Katya said. "The rain will be the score."

"Interesting," Mr. Yanakov said thoughtfully. "A ballet without music."

"It would feel different," Katya said. "I'm used to taking my cues from the music."

"Right," Mr. Yanakov said slowly.

"But I could do it," she said.

"You'll access the rhythm from the poetry. I like that," Mr. Yanakov said.

34

1963

Langston Hughes stood with Katya in the wings and scanned the program. He was elegant, gracious, and intimidating. His voice would saturate the well of the Peter Stuyvesant Theater. It was Katya's job to animate his every syllable. She was in charge of the stage.

"I expect you and Mr. Hughes to do well together," Mr. Yanakov said, coming from behind and whispering in Katya's ear. "Nice rapport." He smoothed his hand down her derrière and disappeared into the shadows.

Katya and Mr. Hughes had rehearsed together only once. She was concerned about properly synchronizing; she needed to dance his every beat. She felt supremely accountable.

She was dancing on cracking ice. If she jumped, she would land with each foot on a separating floe. She was afraid of losing Mr. Yanakov's esteem; she was afraid of slipping and taking John down. How dreadful. John had suffered enough.

Next to her, Mr. Hughes let out a full, throaty laugh. "'*Rain Song*, a ballet without music,'" he said, waving his program as he read aloud. "They don't seem to get that the poetry is the music," Mr. Hughes said.

Katya nodded in agreement.

"Two minutes," the stage manager called.

John adjusted the bouquet of white roses in his lap. An expectant hush blanketed the hall. Langston Hughes, dressed in tails, walked to the microphone. A rain screen formed the backdrop, the sound not a drip, drip nor a driving shower, but the swish of light rain.

Katya stepped out, quiet as breath, robed in a floor-length gray tunic. Her hair was loose, her arms bare. John could see her face, her eyes cast down as she took her position center stage. He couldn't believe he knew her.

Let the rain kiss you. The poet's voice, mellifluous. *Let the rain beat upon your head with silver liquid drops.*

Undulating and rippling. Flowing. Katya was lighter than silence, deeper than memory, her body fluid.

Let the rain sing you a lullaby.

Langston Hughes stood before the microphone, his words luxuriant. Underneath them, the rain rushed and sang.

The rain makes still pools on the sidewalk.

Over the past couple of weeks, John had experienced Katya's commitment to her art. He missed her with an ache that felt like sorrow.

The rain makes running pools in the gutter.

Katya streamed from one diagonal to another, flooding the stage with movement.

The rain plays a little sleep song on our roof at night.

And I love the rain.

Katya rose and sank, leaping higher, tilting lower—a cascading waterfall.

Let the rain.

She floated and swirled, returning to her starting place like spume from a breaking wave.

The poet paused.

Sing you a lullaby. Langston Hughes stepped back from the microphone.

John was overcome; he understood Katya's gift. She had danced a ballet without music, like an answer to grief.

Over the applause, Katya walked toward Mr. Hughes and brought him center stage. Mr. Yanakov strode energetically out—his patent leather shoes gleaming—and bowed. He put Katya between himself and Langston Hughes, and the three stepped forward together.

Backstage, Katya passed Maya, who was twisting her pink satin sheath to get ready for *Madison Avenue*. She had a fox stole around her neck. "Damn," Maya said, banging her heel into the floor. "I never thought I'd miss *pointe* shoes." Pulling a tuft out of her fur stole, she said, "Can't have this falling off when I fling it offstage, can we?"

"I wish I could watch," Katya said.

"No, you don't." Katya had never seen Maya this nervous. "It'll be a miracle if I don't twist an ankle in these things," Maya said.

"*Merde*," said Katya. "You'll ace it." She headed for the dressing room and sat down in front of the mirror to freshen her makeup. It was a relief to be alone. She needed silence to get in character for *Veiled Road*.

She finished her face and lifted a long white cloak off the hook marked "Miss Symanova." Not until the end of *Veiled Road* would Paolo push the hood from her head. She adjusted the cloak on her arm. It was heavy. She had talked with the costume shop about using lighter fabric, but Mr. Yanakov had been insistent. "You'll carry the weight like a yoke, Miss Symanova; it's part of the choreography." No matter. For much of the ballet Katya would remain stationary while the other dancers moved around her.

She headed toward the wings and laid the cloak over a chair. She could feel that John was here.

The applause for *Madison Avenue* died down. Maya came offstage.

"Tell the truth," Katya said. "How was it?"

"Could've been worse," Maya said, bending to unbuckle her heels. "I hate these things. *Merde*, Katya!" She headed toward the dressing room, dangling her heels by the straps.

Katya lay on the floor, warm-ups to calm her roiling core. Mr. Yanakov paced at the far side of the stage. *Click, click, click* turn. And again. He was always anxious opening night.

What would happen when the curtain came down? Katya was longing for John, was dancing for him but, too, felt an icy fear. "Five minutes," the stage manager called. She stood up and went for the cloak.

Paolo came over, dressed in white tights and a pale blue jacket. "Let me help you." He draped the cape over her shoulders. From the pit came the faint sound of the string quartet tuning. The *corps* filed into position, dipping their feet in rosin, squeaking and shuffling to get the right consistency on their shoes. Paolo shook each leg, and his wrists and arms. "I'm no better than he is," Paolo said, pointing to Mr. Y, whose rhythm was unbroken. "I hate nerves."

Mr. Yanakov was too distracting; Katya couldn't look. Why couldn't life follow the predictable discipline of a ballet class? The same daily order, week after week, year after year. The rest was pandemonium.

Against the punctuation of Mr. Yanakov's patent leather shoes, the stage manager called, "Two minutes."

Katya adjusted the shoulders of her thick cloak. She had to give up John. She had to tell him the truth.

"Places!"

She pulled the hood for *Veiled Road* over her head. It extended a few inches beyond her face, causing temporary blindness. Balance would be an extra challenge. Paolo came behind and placed his hands over her shoulders. Her job was to embody Boris Yanakov's quintessence, to reveal his work and ensure its fullest rendering. The curtain lifted. One by one, four instruments laid down the opening rhythm.

There was music; of course there was. A string quartet played sorrow and loss, as if summoning the end, suggesting that hope was illusory. John tried to call up what he could from Dr. Roth and, most of all, from Katya. Her smile, her words that opened a path away from desolation. Her touch. He must be mistaken to sense such hopelessness.

She looked like a hooded wanderer. Or maybe she was a religious celebrant, arms outstretched, edged forward by the man in blue. Lines of dancers came on, their hands over the shoulders of the next, spinning and kicking in formation. Katya's partner turned her toward the audience and left.

Katya faced forward, her eyes on the back of the hall. The sets behind her—clouds and a blue sky—were meant to suggest heaven; that's what Mr. Y had said. Only he didn't believe in heaven. He believed in the primacy of his own creation, from which Katya had emerged as an accomplice—and, she knew, inspiration.

She straightened up and opened her arms. She was to remain in that position, still as prayer, steady as discipline.

The boys lifted off in a series of measured, circular leaps around her. She could hear Mr. Yanakov shouting, "Boys, take your time. Stay suspended longer. This is slow, serious music."

Katya waited as the *corps* exited. She would dance for herself tonight, unpartnered until the last segment, hooded until Paolo uncovered her head at the end.

The music's inward, contemplative turn was her cue to move. Mr. Y stopped pacing. She could feel him eyeing her with the precision of a sniper.

Couldn't she work beside him and save something for herself? His work was nothing without her execution. Absent Katya Symanova, Boris Yanakov's choreography was no more than two hands flailing in air. She could, she would assert herself. He would see that she had needs too. He would adapt. Katya might be his creative partner, but she wasn't the first or likely the only woman in his life. She would stay with John, and Mr. Yanakov would understand.

Readying herself to move, Katya thought of Mama, as if John had returned Mama to Katya by pronouncing her ill instead of blameworthy. In a rush of compassion, Katya regretted that her arms couldn't spread wide enough to embrace the dead, and simultaneously recognized that in that embrace lay courage. Flooded with optimism—jubilant—she lowered her arms and stepped forward to dance.

35

1963

Katya dabbed cold cream to remove the last of her stage make-up and zipped the skirt to her rose-colored suit. The opening night party was in the ballroom of the Hotel Marquis, a few blocks away. She slipped on black patent leather heels and hurried from the dressing room, closing the single button to her cropped silk jacket on the way.

"Not bad, Miss Symanova," Mr. Y said, momentarily breaking off with Lars as she tried to tiptoe past. She halted, adjusting a bobby pin in her bun. "They liked it, don't you think?" She gave them a nod and smiled.

"You're on your leg, Katya," Lars said. "Nice work."

"That's very kind of you," Katya said. "Will you gentlemen excuse me for a minute?" she added, as lightly as she could manage. "Be right back."

"Katya!" It was hot and muggy. The air felt like a dirty blanket. Aside from the bulb over the steps at the stage door, the Peter Stuyvesant back lot was dark. Heat lightning arced across the sky, the rumble of thunder following. John ran through the shadows. "For you," he said, handing Katya the flowers and extending his right foot to take a deep bow. "For the gift you have given me."

"John, these are lovely!" She turned and squinted toward the stage door.

"You were magnificent," John said, wrapping his arm around her.

"Did you like *Rain Song*?"

He put his hands over his heart. "I loved it."

"It was for you."

He stepped back, eyes welling. "Incredible. Thank you."

Embracing the bouquet with the tenderness of a lover, she twisted toward the stage door again. "I have to…" She turned back to John.

"I can't wait to celebrate you!" he said. "I need to know how you've been. You've been working so hard! I missed you," he said, leaning over to kiss her.

Behind her, the stage door clicked open. Katya jerked with surprising violence. A distinguished-looking man in a tuxedo bounded down the steps. John recognized him; he was the choreographer Katya had brought out at curtain calls. Boris Yanakov.

"Ready, Miss Symanova?" Yanakov strode toward them, then halted, as if bewildered. After a moment, he adjusted his cummerbund and came up next to them. "Very nice flowers, Miss Symanova." He kissed her slowly on the lips and then slid his arm around her waist. "You were lovely tonight, darling."

"May I introduce you?" Katya said, her voice shaking. She edged away, eyes darting between the two men. "John, this is Boris Yanakov."

John was stopped.

So, it was a fantasy. He never should have… Why hadn't she?

"Boris," Katya said, her inflection rising, "this is Dr. John Curtin."

Why had she?

Yanakov stepped forward and extended his hand. "How do you do, Dr. Curtin?"

Katya's publicity photo flashed through John's mind. Eyes cast down, an unnamed burden across her face. A taxonomy for that burden cried out as John mindlessly shook Yanakov's hand. With his densely packed physique and graying hair, Yanakov was a stone monument.

"What kind of doctor are you, Dr. Curtin?"

John was in Herr Kommandant's living room, suffocating

in cigar smoke. It was stuffy and hot, and he had forgotten the words to the songs.

"John is a psychiatrist," Katya cut in.

Another flash of heat lightning, another grumble of thunder.

"Dr. Curtin works at Mercy Hospital and has a private practice," Katya said to Yanakov.

"Miss Symanova does a brilliant job interpreting my work, don't you think?" Yanakov said, running his hand down Katya's back.

John looked at Katya and nodded. Where was his voice?

"It's all new," Mr. Yanakov said.

John nodded again.

A few fat raindrops began to fall.

Katya stepped to the side—just a few inches—beyond Mr. Yanakov's reach.

"We're off to Stuttgart after the season is over," Yanakov said. "To collaborate with Simon Worthington. We'll bring my work there—to Germany, that is."

"Yes," John managed. The officers were closing in, stomping and shouting. He would not be able to exit through their chairs. "I'm familiar."

Yanakov turned to Katya. "Miss Symanova will help teach the Germans my work so they can take it into repertoire, get it into their bones."

"Ah."

Katya had turned pale, her expression vacant. It was raining harder.

"And she'll perform my pieces," Yanakov said, grinning. "She'll show them how it's done."

"Of course," John said. "Show them how it's done."

"The Germans are anxious for new ideas," Yanakov said.

"Ah." John tried starting again. "The choice of poetry as music in *Rain Song*." He was squeaking. "It was…" He looked at Katya. "Extremely affecting." Not five minutes earlier, he had believed with all his heart that that piece was her gift to him. "What was the other one called?" If he could come up with

more words, he could keep talking, and if he kept talking, he
might escape what was in front of him.

"You mean *Veiled Road*," Yanakov said.

"Yes, that's it. *Veiled Road*," John said. "I'm no judge of ballet."

"You aren't, are you?" Yanakov said with mock lightness.

"But it seems to have some profound themes."

"Nice that you noticed, Dr. Curtin." Yanakov unbuttoned
and rebuttoned his jacket. "*Veiled Road* is a ballet about unrav-
eling mysteries." He shook himself to adjust the shoulders.
"We're often blind to what's in front of us, aren't we?"

John nodded stupidly. An arc of lightning flashed before
them, illuminating the whole lot before it went dark again.

"Blind to the consequences of our choices," Yanakov added,
eyeing Katya's flowers.

"Yes," John said, looking miserably from Yanakov to Katya.

Yanakov turned to Katya and placed his hand on the small
of her back. "Miss Symanova, shall we?" He nudged her forward.

"We have a party," Katya said to John, standing her ground.
Her eyes combed John's ashen face. "Over at the Hotel Marquis." She waved her bouquet of white roses in that direction.

I am not my own. Katya had told him, but John hadn't listened.

"For major donors and the board. Critics too," Katya added.
"It's standard for opening night."

"I see," John said, nodding slowly. He hadn't wanted to hear.
No wonder he'd hardly seen her since her choreographer returned from Europe. The storybook version was vastly more
palatable than the truth. "It was a beautiful evening," he said
quietly, looking at Katya. "It was a beautiful time." How often
had he reminded himself that he knew better than to plunge
headlong into a fairy tale?

"I'm glad you enjoyed it," Yanakov said. "Shall we, dear?" he
repeated. He pressed his hand into Katya's back.

Katya broke away. "Just a minute!" she said.

"What are we waiting for, Miss Symanova?"

Raising his right hand as he confronted grim reality, John said, "I don't want to hold you up." Katya Symanova was the consort of the man who controlled her career. That man was brusque and impatient. He was harsh. He was old.

"We're not in a rush," Katya said, wincing as Yanakov squeezed her arm. It was beginning to pour.

Why had she given herself to John with such openness? Danced in his arms with the assurance of the beloved?

She was leaving for Germany.

"No rush," she said again, with a tormented expression that was excruciating to witness. She brought the white roses to her heart. "The party goes late into the night."

She was so vulnerable. "A lovely performance, Miss Symanova," John said, anguish knifing him like an assailant. "Good night, Miss Symanova," he said quietly, tipping his head toward her. He picked up her hand and kissed it tenderly, then extended his to Yanakov—whose face was a thunderous sky—and left.

Katya was in agony. "Mr. Yanakov," she said, pulling away. The rain had progressed to a full-on storm. "Boris, please." She hurried across the now empty lot, searching the block.

"I see Dr. Curtin had other things to do," Mr. Yanakov said, coming by her side. He took her elbow. "I was just thinking about *Charged Particles*." He spoke slowly, as if he were planning to sink into a lengthy conversation. They were both soaked.

Wasn't there a chance Mr. Yanakov would see what she needed? After all, he had noticed her as a young girl peering through the studio window, watching him arrange dancers like a general ordering troop formations. He had placed his muscular hand on her torso, steadying her as she kicked her first part-nered *grands battements*; he had collaborated with her as prima ballerina, the two of them alone in the studio. They worked so well together, shared a common choreographic vision: Katya Symanova, the repository for his brilliance; the master's chosen one. She needed Boris Yanakov the way a drunk needs a bottle.

Damnation. Damn damn damn.

"About *Charged Particles*," Mr. Yanakov repeated.

"*Charged Particles* was a ballet with a clear message," Mr. Yanakov said, choosing his words with care. He was unnaturally calm.

He had said in rehearsal that mankind was never meant to split atoms. Was he going to annihilate John? Had he already done so?

If there was anything that could worsen the impact on John than her concealed relationship, it was Mr. Yanakov's proclamation that she was headed to Germany. Shame on her for entertaining the idea that Boris Yanakov would countenance John in her life. She shuddered at what she had inflicted.

Continuing in the same deliberate tone as if he were about to impart hallowed wisdom, Mr. Yanakov said, over a crack of thunder, "The apocalypse comes from fracturing atoms into particles that were meant to be fused together."

Was he announcing that Boris Yanakov and Katya Symanova were fused?

"*Charged Particles* was last season," Katya said, attempting to gather her thoughts. "It's history."

Mr. Yanakov stared through her as if she hadn't spoken. "It is an awe-inspiring, deadly energy that comes from the split."

"Is that how you feel?"

Mr. Yanakov gave half a nod.

She waited to hear more.

Since he remained silent, she stepped to the curb and knelt to lay down her roses, rain dripping from her hair. Maybe a little girl coming from the Peter Stuyvesant Theater would find them.

"Miss Symanova." He gave her his hand to help her up and faced her head on, poised for a pronouncement. Wiping the rain off his face, he cleared his throat. "You don't think I missed you flirting with your young swain at the *Opéra*, do you?" he said.

"What?"

"Your friend the psychiatrist."

"I didn't know him then. I don't understand."

"No, perhaps you don't," he said passing his index finger under her chin, as he had done in front of Luigi's that first night. If she wasn't certain he was enraged, she might have thought he was being affectionate. "I saw him present those lovely roses," he said. "There's nothing out of the ordinary in that. After all, you gave an excellent performance." He straightened his posture, an instructor trying to ensure his student was sufficiently chastened. "But I couldn't help noticing that when I inquired about the flowers later that evening, you declined to tell the truth."

She stared at him, aghast. She had forgotten that Mr. Yanakov asked about the roses. But now that he mentioned it, it was true; she had lied to him. She recalled telling him that some crazy Frenchmen had thrown them at her. She was astonished—and, in the instant, pleased—at her perceptiveness. Somehow, she had already known John was more than an enthusiastic balletomane. She had never hidden anything from Mr. Yanakov before because she had never needed to. She felt vindicated; she had understood John's import from the start.

Mr. Yanakov cleared his throat again. "You have too big a talent to waste on a civilian, Katya," he said. "Our work together is too significant. Apparently, you fail to recognize that yourself."

She was stupefied, her mind racing back to Paris—*Three Muses* (she had sensed John in the audience) and Mr. Yanakov's post-performance mania—reeling from Mr. Yanakov's reconfiguring of events. It was earth-shattering; her version had been upended. She was speechless. The rain had soaked through her rose-colored suit. It clung to her, soggy and shapeless.

Oblivious to the downpour, Mr. Yanakov paced the back lot, as if he were thinking up new combinations in the studio. Katya looked at him, his expression less victorious than penitent. He seemed almost contrite, as if he was relieved to have owned up to his role in matters of deepest consequence to her. It was surprising. Surprising, too, were his powers of observation. In a few short moments, Boris Yanakov had recognized the threat that John posed because he had ascertained the measure of John's worth. Before Katya and John had had a chance to discover what was between them, Mr. Yanakov had punctured it with an arrow aimed directly at her heart. He was complicit in John and Katya's demise.

Katya was completely disordered, wrestling to make a shred of sense out of these revelations. This was the man to whom she had devoted her life and her art. He was teacher, mentor, lover, and artistic partner.

Where was she?

Her personal life was apparently beside the point; or more accurately, he was her personal and her public life, he was her career. He had put art above all else, forgetting—or denying—that great art is the triumph of the human spirit, and that the human spirit depends on love. He looked deflated, walking rather than pacing the back lot, lacking his usual, purposeful stride. It dawned on her that she had the capacity to hurt him, and that perhaps she already had. There might even be a fissure in his iron resolve and a glimmer of distress—or was it neediness?—that hadn't been there before.

Against the night's wreckage, she took dim, bitter solace in that.

"Katya," he said quietly. "Perhaps we should head over to the Hotel Marquis."

He watched her struggle to collect herself.

"You were born to dance," he said, as if he were atoning for something. She saw that he could not express what he felt. She saw, too, that if he had ever been a man who aspired to love, love was now inseparable from his art. In his heart and mind—maybe even in his memory—art and love were fused. "Time to go," he said.

She stepped toward him. She would not jeopardize his reputation, or hers, or the company's; she was a professional.

Beleaguered with something closer to grief than despair,

Katya Symanova placed her right hand in the crook of Boris Yanakov's elbow and, with a ballerina's grace, set out for the party.

VEILED ROAD

36

1963

The telephone sounded like an air-raid siren. John rolled over and looked at the clock. Three thirty in the morning. He hadn't been sleeping. The storm had not abated; thunder was exploding outside like gunfire.

"John, I know it's obscenely early."

"Katya!"

"I'm just back from the party." She was Yanakov's, his crown jewel. John felt belittled by that man, shamed. Instead of bringing rationality to bear, John had immersed himself in a fantasy. "I'm sorry," Katya was saying. "But I didn't want to wait." Was Yanakov in her bed? "I owe you an apology. Several, actually."

John rubbed his eyes. Coming awake, he was reentering the nightmare. That magnificent performance. Was it just last night? *Rain Song* was a ballet without music, a false promise. "Katya?" he said again, more question than statement. Who was she?

"I'm wondering if I could see you." Her voice was breaking. "It would be better to talk in person."

Better for whom? His present had evaporated; his future was a curl of smoke. Would he be forever entrapped in his own memory—the good parts scooped out? Only bits of rotting rind would remain.

"No," he said. His memory had congealed into fetid clumps littered across time: the night Papa failed to come home; Mutti, kissing Max's head when Janko was taken away; a foot protruding from the ashes, five toes intact. And now, the horrendous scene on the back lot.

"I can understand why you might not want to," she said.

The look on Katya's face last night. John had felt her floating away, as if she were a nymph receding into a myth.

He sat up in bed. He wanted to see her at any time of day or night. Of course.

"I've been horrible to you," she said. Was she weeping?

Her choreographer. She had been enmeshed with that man since she was a young girl.

"I think I might be able to help clear things up."

How? Her name was Katherine Sillman. She gave John himself.

"Is it possible to get together just for a little while?" They had met in the most improbable circumstances. It defied logic that it was over, but then it defied logic that it had ever begun. Logic had nothing to do with it. John was mistaken; he had been shockingly oblivious. He'd missed Boris Yanakov and conflated Katya Symanova the ballerina with Katherine Sillman the woman.

"I don't think that's a good idea," John said. "In fact, I'm sure it's not." There was no point; she was shackled to her choreographer.

"Please?"

If shackling it was. Boris Yanakov could have been her choice. She could be a willing and eager partner.

"No, I don't think so," John said, more firmly.

Was he giving up this easily? He had found healing and joy with Katya Symanova. Their bodies entwined like song and dance.

There was nothing to give up. She had been spoken for since childhood.

"Katya, I wish you well," he said, hanging up.

The telephone rang a second time. He couldn't endure hearing her voice again. He had no more to say.

And then a third. Did she mean to torture him? Knocking several psychiatric journals off his nightstand, he picked up the phone again.

"Barney's in the hospital." Selma sounded hoarse. "We came by ambulance."

"Oh my Lord." John squinted at the clock. Four o'clock. "What happened?"

"Collapsed at the dinner table. They took him to Beaumont."

"Are they saying anything?"

"The nurse whispered something about a stroke."

"Coming," John said, getting out of bed. If he could find a cab, he would be there in half an hour. With luck, maybe twenty minutes. But he suspected his luck had run out.

The triage nurse pointed to a cluster of doctors and nurses huddled outside the room.

Selma was leaning over the gurney, her head on Barney's chest. "We've lost him, dear," she said through tears. "He's gone." She stood up and hugged John. "The last thing he said was, 'Tell him I love him.'"

Was he referring to Buddy?

"You've been a wonderful son," Selma said. "Say goodbye."

"I'm so sorry, Selma," John said, wrapping his arm around her. He couldn't bear to think of Selma soldiering on by herself. He gazed at Barney, who looked wise and kind as always. In death, his face had relaxed. "What a good man he was," John said.

They stood by the bed and watched him—peaceful and still—half of a loving whole, now forever split. Barney and Selma were comfort and warmth. They were selfless. They gave John the new world.

37

1963

A black limousine pulled up to Barney's gravesite, gaping ready for his coffin. Dirt was piled to one side. "They've covered Buddy," Selma said, holding John's arm as she looked around. "I asked them not to." She took a crumpled tissue from her pocket and wiped her eyes.

"This is our family plot," Selma said, bending down to pick up a few stones from the roadside. She clung to John's elbow as they walked across the grass. "My parents." She placed a stone on each marker. "Aunt Mabel and Uncle Saul. Buddy." She shook her head. "I can't get near that poor boy," she said, eyeing the mound of dirt dug for Barney's coffin that blocked Buddy's headstone.

"Let me do it." John took the stone from her hand and climbed around to Buddy's grave. Buddy, who had given John his room and his clothing and his parents. "Thank you," John murmured, running his hand over the uneven granite surface. He set the stone on the right side.

"Very kind of you, dear," Selma said. She turned to the line of cars pulling in behind the hearse. "Family means more than family." She smiled sadly, watching the people walking toward them. John wondered at her composure in the face of this kind of loss. "Family is who you love and who loves you," Selma said. He was humbled before her simple generosity. "That was one of Barney's favorite expressions."

The rabbi put his arm around her. "Over here, Mrs. Katz." He seated her in a folding chair. "For you, son," he said, seating John next to her. Rachel and David stood next to them, the other mourners behind.

"Friends," the rabbi said. "We are here to bury Barney Katz, cherished husband, father, and friend." He paused for a few stragglers to arrive.

May his soul be bound up in the bond of life eternal, and grant that the memories of our husband, father, and friend's life inspire us to noble and consecrated living.

Amen, the crowd murmured.

"Selma asked for this next prayer, which Barney liked to recite when he visited his beloved son's grave," the rabbi said.

John teared up; crushed that he hadn't come before.

At the rising of the sun and at its going down, the rabbi chanted.

We remember them, the mourners intoned.

...At the rustling of the leaves and in the beauty of autumn

We remember them. John hadn't been able to bury his family.

At the beginning of the year and when it ends

We remember them. Barney.

As long as we live, they too will live; for they are now a part of us,

As we remember them. John's memory bridged an ocean.

When we are weary and in need of strength

We remember them. All the unburied.

When we are lost and sick at heart

We remember them. Papa.

When we have joy we crave to share

We remember them. Max.

When we have decisions that are difficult to make

We remember them. Mutti. John gasped, in thrall to his mother's pain, as if by sucking in his breath, he could take the measure of the impossible, unbearable decision that was thrust on her. If only he had died with his family.

When we have achievements that are based on theirs

We remember them. No. John would rather live. He would rather sail into Barney and Selma's open arms, floating in their swelling, billowing embrace. He had survived to fill the empty spaces—his own and his patients'—with something beyond negativity and despair. Katya was alive; she was well and dancing. There was that.

As long as we live, they too will live; for they are now a part of us...

He should fall on his knees in unspeakable gratitude to his mother, who, in a moment of daunting, fearsome perspicacity, had faced down the enemy and saved the life of her firstborn. Mutti was victorious. Mutti had won.

As we remember them. Papa, Mutti, Max. John remembered his family; he would always remember them. He was the guardian of their memory. The agonizing past; the crowded, aching present; the vast uncertain proliferating future; the collapsing, imploding, chaotic spectrum of time unleashed by tragedy. Without John—son and brother, brother and son—his family were dust motes swirling in history's cyclone.

He would remember.

Amen.

38

1963

Katya sat in front of the mirror, finishing her makeup for *Veiled Road*. She was alone in her dressing room, looking at the shadows under her eyes, her skin drawn and pale. She had danced *Rain Song* as an elegy to opening night, when John had been in the audience.

It was quiet. The whole theater was quiet, as if the audience had been privy to that wretched scene on the back lot three nights ago (it may as well have been three years), followed by Katya's wretched middle-of-the-night call to John.

Could she make it better if she spoke to him in person? She could find him at the hospital and admit there had been no justification for her behavior other than the straightforward: She was attracted to him, and—unlike whatever she felt for her choreographer—her attraction was unencumbered, elemental. His touch ignited an urgency; she couldn't extinguish the searing memory of his palm running from her hip to her thigh. She craved being wrapped in his arms.

But he was gone, sacrificed at Boris Yanakov's altar. She couldn't see how to reconcile herself to that sequence of events, much less Mr. Yanakov's role in it.

What about her choreographer, pacing in the wings? In a confounding twist, it appeared he was more committed to her than she'd understood.

The stage manager called, "Five minutes." Katya rose, put on her heavy white cloak, and headed out from her dressing room. Her years of *pliés* had been premised on rock-solid belief: backbreaking discipline was not just one answer for how to live; it was the sole answer.

Paolo was waiting for her, shaking his legs. He was jittery. "Nerves don't get any easier," he said under his breath.

"You're right," she said, adjusting her cloak. Rock-solid belief turned out to be malleable. At some point her body would fail, and what would be left to Katya?

"Two minutes," the stage manager called.

For now, Katya had to step slowly onstage, hooded and guided by Paolo, her charge to remain still as death.

Death chewed up time with the zeal of a famished vulture; no allowance for sleep or anything else. John didn't want to leave Selma, whose modest row house was overrun with company. Barney's neighbors, friends, customers, even people whose only connection had been the infrequent prescription, came bearing lox and bagels, honey cakes and babkas, and above all, kindness.

Out came the photo albums, guests huddled around them with tissues and commentary. They admired Barney and Selma's wedding pictures and the one with Barney standing in front of his newly opened pharmacy. "We had just finished painting the inside," Selma recalled. "Cleaning out that cellar would have tested Cinderella. That's what happens when you lease an old tailor's shop. Spools of thread, broken irons, bolts of dusty cloth." ("Never let anything go to waste," Selma had said. Her friend Ida knew somebody who knew somebody who knew somebody who ended up using that cloth.)

Barney in his pharmacist's shirt, grinning behind the counter, proud of never having turned down a customer. John heard him: *I was about to close up, but let me help you. Dinner can wait. Tell your Minnie to get plenty of rest and call me if you need anything. Pay me when it's convenient; just make sure little Benny gets better.*

Pictures of Buddy—his first day of kindergarten, wearing shorts and new shoes, holding his schoolbag like an offensive weapon. "He was a troublemaker, but you couldn't help but love that boy," Selma said. "Between making us *meshugenah*, he was always there to carry a bag of groceries or help an old lady across the street." Buddy in his high school graduation gown.

"You can see he's lost his mortarboard," she added. Buddy in uniform, the same photo that hung over the sofa.

Barney and Selma on their twenty-fifth wedding anniversary. (John had taken that one.) "He bought me a corsage," Selma said, blowing her nose. Barney on marriage: "Whatever your wife asks of you, the answer is yes."

Rachel turned to David. "What did I tell you, dear?"

"That's the spirit," Selma said, getting up to check a pot on the stove. "He always took the trash out right away, and came home at lunch to shovel the walk, even though Buddy shoveled at twice his speed."

Barney's legendary carving skills, perfectly suited to Selma's capon, which was never short of luscious, so juicy and tender. How did she roast it so it never dried out? As a matter of fact, Selma's cooking in general was a marvel. Even now, during *shiva*, when she was supposed to sit still and let everyone do it for her.

Memories meant to bring Selma comfort lent John some as well.

❧

Katya finished company class and ran for the subway. She had a few spare hours to get to Mercy Hospital. "Just running out to Queens," she said to Mr. Yanakov. "Checking on my father."

She stopped at the lobby information desk to ask where the office of psychiatry was, trying to ignore the looks she received. Maybe she was in need of a headshrinker. She needed to calm down, that was sure. Was she going to apologize? Beg forgiveness? Try to explain?

What was there to explain?

"Who're you here to see?" asked the volunteer at the desk. Katya recalled Daddy upstairs with his leg chained to the ceiling, tired and gaunt in his hospital gown. She had been worried about him. But look what his hospitalization had delivered: Dr. John Curtin, appearing in his white doctor coat like a good angel, while she was sipping burnt coffee in the basement cafeteria.

"Dr. Curtin, John Curtin," Katya said. This was worse than

stage fright. She had been wobbly during last night's performance of *Veiled Road*. Tonight, she'd better anchor herself. She straightened a bobby pin. (What did it matter what her appearance was?)

The volunteer leafed through the directory. Katya trembled, hoping some hidden reservoir of confidence would supply her a few words when she found John.

"Dr. Curtin, was it?"

She nodded.

The volunteer checked a piece of paper.

Katya tried to reassure herself that you couldn't rehearse for this.

"I'm sorry, ma'am. He's out for the week."

"The week?"

"That's right, ma'am."

Katya hadn't prepared for that. The week? Because of her? She headed uptown in a fog of disappointment.

At Luigi's, Katya Symanova and Boris Yanakov were greeted like movie stars. The season was an unprecedented success. Once again, Mr. Yanakov was wowing New York.

"Simon Worthington's coming over to meet with me," Mr. Yanakov said. "You'll be there too, naturally. It'll give us a jump on the season over there."

Was there nothing to discuss besides Stuttgart? Worthington was at the cutting edge of European choreography, Stuttgart a fresh opportunity. But she didn't want to go to Germany. She didn't want to leave New York.

39

1963

"*Three Muses* was a triumph in Paris," Mr. Yanakov said to Simon Worthington. Katya started her stretches. "Play us the opening."

Lydia put down her paperback and started in. The beat was somber and purposeful.

"You'll find the ballet has hidden complexities, Simon," Katya said, getting up from the floor. All her core assumptions were wrong. Why was John away for a week? Where had he gone? She had to find a way to communicate with him.

Mr. Yanakov waved at Lydia to stop.

"The *Requiem* was unfinished at Mozart's death," Worthington said. "Which makes it an elegy to the composer himself."

"The world was moving on without Mozart, wasn't it?" Katya said, struggling to understand what she'd lost. She had everything she wanted and was bereft. "The ballet needs a fresher, younger look," she added, pulling up her right leg warmer. "Wouldn't it be great to dance it barefoot, in tunics—homage to modern dance?"

"Barefoot?" Mr. Yanakov said, his legs apart like a sentry roused by hostile fire. The wrinkle lines going down his cheek had deepened since Europe. He was shorter than John.

"Great art should never go stale," Worthington said.

"Tunics and bare legs are for crazy women like Isadora Duncan," Mr. Yanakov said. "She was utterly undisciplined."

"I love Isadora's freedom," Worthington said.

"Freedom is bunk," Mr. Yanakov said.

Katya pulled up her left leg warmer, quite certain of her loss. It had to be love.

৩

It was dark outside and dark in the dimly lit corridor leading to
Dr. Roth's office. John steeled himself.

"Now that your career is underway," Dr. Roth said, "we'll
finish wrapping up." When John most needed him, Dr. Roth
was terminating therapy.

"How can I serve my patients when adulthood is so elusive?
Even the things that should be instinctive," John added. "Like
finding a wife and starting a family."

"The dating game is never trouble free, if that's what you're
saying," Dr. Roth said.

"I'm not asking for trouble free. I'm just trying to avoid
calamity," John said, in a storm of self-reproach.

"Better to call it the mating game," Dr. Roth added, with an
uncharacteristic chuckle.

"I've never felt more at sea," John said. Katya belonged
to someone else. "Belong" was a level of possession beyond
John's ken. Was he jealous? It wasn't that simple. Why had he
visited such a glorious place with her if not to touch the impossible? He'd been as delusional as when he fought his way back
to Mainz.

"You'll find a nice girl," Dr. Roth said, smiling kindly. "You'll
know when it's the right one. Remember that when you encounter obstacles. You will, of course. We all do."

"That's true about obstacles," John said, vertiginous from
severed connections. It wasn't enough to be unmoored from
family and home, and that whatever he'd had with Katya had
sunk—or, more accurately, never launched. Or that Barney was
gone. (Selma would be saying *Kaddish* daily.) Dr. Roth was having him set sail as well.

"Good to recognize what's normal," Dr. Roth said blithely.
"It means you've profited here."

"It's hard to see the profit," John said.

"You recreated the line at the camp as part of our work
together. You left your mother and brother a second time." Dr.
Roth pushed up his glasses. "You spoke German, you addressed
your captors and your family; you grieved your father."

Katya, not Dr. Roth, had returned Papa to John. She had led John to the edge of self-forgiveness and showed his profession to be worthy of Papa. But Katya had left on the arm of her choreographer.

"Don't forget, you also sang here," Dr. Roth said.

"Remembering isn't a problem. Unfortunately. But did any of it do any good? Music, for example." John had thought Katya understood; she gave him a ballet without music. Nothing made sense. She was liquid in *Rain Song*, fluid and graceful against the poetry.

"I had you sing to confront trauma," Dr. Roth said. "Because in my judgment, you not only lost music, music *became* the trauma."

Was it music that had been missing on the dark, murderous street that swallowed John's father? If so, it was Katya who helped recapture it. John had watched her inhabit the Muse of Discipline, dancing to melodies from Mutti and Papa's living room, the chorus singing a lament to John's missing childhood. Katya was the reason he had withstood the terror of *Charged Particles*. He had stayed to see her dance and witnessed his ability to climb through fear.

"Singing saved you," Dr. Roth said quietly. "Against all odds."

What about John's singing, dogging him like a rabid mongrel? He'd never considered it music; quite the opposite. "I suppose it's true," John said, reflecting on Dr. Roth's stubborn paradox. Yes, it was in the music; it was in the singing. Amidst the tatters of John's ruptured childhood, maybe the loss of the music was not forever. Maybe, without quite naming it, he'd been seeking the music all along, searching behind for its echo. Or maybe the music was part of some inexplicable luminosity that danced ahead, impelling him forward.

"You've given yourself access," Dr. Roth said. "Never shut that window into yourself, no matter how deep the pain."

"So, it's about access to pain," John repeated.

"That's it."

"Then I should be in great shape."

"Part of what we did together was learn how to manage that pain," Dr. Roth said.

"Ah." John was left to nurse Katya's absence—no less mysterious than her appearance—abloom with insoluble questions; pain as sweet and precious as a single, salty tear.

"You've done the work," Dr. Roth said. "Should you need me, I'm here." He stood up and shook John's hand. "Trust what you know."

People were ten deep on the subway platform. John felt no release, only the disorientation that he'd been detached from something on which—apparently—he'd relied.

He pushed through the throngs, late for his patients at Mercy, turning over Dr. Roth's parting words: "Trust what you know." What did he know? He'd pursued Katya Symanova like a magnet that found its opposite pole. Their chance meeting in the basement of Mercy Hospital had struck him as providential. He had trusted himself and been wrong. There must be something more than trust.

Memories crowded in like passengers jammed into his subway car. Frau Koch, screaming, "He's not one of us, he's one of them!" Mrs. Leventhal, thrusting a ballet ticket at him. Katya Symanova, wafting across the stage, delicate and powerful. They had come in from the rain together. She'd wept in his arms when she stepped out of the shower. They'd made love that afternoon.

The way Papa looked at Mutti. It was more than trust; it was love.

Was there something more than love?

The subway screeched to a halt. No. There was nothing more than love. John had had love. Not just from Mutti and Papa, but from little Max too. And in America—from Selma and Barney. John had been showered with love, he thought, running up the subway steps. He just had a habit of losing it.

And Katya? he wondered, hurrying toward his office. What were they together? Something as ephemeral and necessary as breath, gone as surely as Katya leapt offstage at the end of a number.

☙

"May I hear more about these three mythological ladies, Boris?" Worthington asked, leaning against the barre as Katya stretched.

"*Aoede* is Song, and *Mneme* is Memory," Mr. Yanakov said. "My favorite is *Melete*, Muse of Discipline. In Greek, the word has multiple meanings—the practice to gain mastery of a subject, but also the discipline to prepare for prayer, as in, a priest making ready."

"Memory is the most powerful," Katya said.

"You must have thought about casting," Mr. Yanakov said to Worthington. "You need great sensitivity in the scene we marked this morning—the one where Memory puts a spell on Song, defiling her singing."

Worthington nodded.

"The second spell is simpler," Mr. Yanakov said. "That's the one that ties Discipline to the Old Faun. Any decent boy can play that part. The faun makes terrible demands, but my choreography takes care of that," he added, looking satisfied.

"The third spell," Mr. Yanakov said, "separates Song and Discipline."

"They're grieved to be apart," Katya said, kneading a cramp in her left calf. "Because they fit together like music and dance."

Mr. Yanakov started pacing. "For Song and Discipline, you need two dancers who are really attuned to each other."

"Yes, very well matched," Katya said, afraid she would cry. She was oddly reassured that Mr. Yanakov had clarified her point; she couldn't communicate its importance right now, through either speech or movement. For she had come to inhabit a pervasive sorrow, as if her body—her instrument—had been re-formed so that it was no longer composed of muscle and bone and tissue, but of loss itself.

"It's an education watching you two," Worthington said. Lydia stood up to stretch.

"Are we on a break?" Mr. Y asked.

"Good idea, Mr. Yanakov," Lydia said, shutting her music. "Back soon."

"You two have quite a collaboration," Worthington repeated.

"Is that what it is?" Mr. Yanakov said, glancing at Katya.

"How do you do it?"

"It's rather organic," Mr. Y said. "She's my memory."

"I don't have a choice," Katya said. "He refuses notation."

"She'll carry on my work after me," Mr. Yanakov said airily. "After all, no one's immortal."

Katya started. "Mr. Yanakov..." Did he just say she would carry on his work? "It is true," she said slowly, "that Boris's work has to be preserved."

"You make me feel like pickled relish, Katya." He sounded almost melancholy.

Was she his collaborator or life raft? She looked at Worthington. "Boris's ballets are like blood running through my veins," she said, trying to take in her new assignment—guardian of her choreographer's work.

"So that's the legacy plan, eh?" Worthington said.

She felt a weight bearing down, a burden from which she would never be freed: forever saddled with Boris Yanakov's memory.

"It seems so," Mr. Y said. His tone had a poignancy she hadn't heard, as if he were considering his mortality for the first time. He looked spent, a lock of hair falling over his forehead.

"Then Katya's the one we really need in Stuttgart," Worthington said.

Before Katya could respond, she registered Mr. Y's expression. Was it shock, or distress?

She had a flashing sense it might be defeat.

40

1963

"You're too tall for these," Selma said, laying Barney's suits out on the bed. "I'll give them away. But go through his ties, dear, will you?"

"It isn't easy, is it?" John said, sliding the ties across the hanger.

"No, sir. It's awfully quiet around here. Good thing Rachel drops the baby off when she runs errands." She sat down next to the pile of suits. "They say it's good Barney went fast. I guess it was. For him. But we sure miss him, don't we?"

"He was a wonderful man," John said, picking out a blue paisley and a brown wool tie. He recalled the patience with which Barney had listened to his customers' woes. They all received the same respectful treatment. "I learned so much from him." John was lucky to have had not one but two fathers, each of whom was high minded and admirable in his own way. Papa more formal, Barney more down to earth.

"You can't take only two. He'd love to know they were getting some use."

"How about these?" John asked, holding two more. They were striped.

"Very debonair."

"That's not a term I associate with Barney," John teased.

"You never knew him as a young man," Selma said.

"What was it like when you first met?" They had to have been flirty and romantic at some point. It was hard to imagine. John had always seen them as a unit of strength and understanding. They were made to be parents.

"He was so serious," Selma said. "He needed me to loosen

him up. Fortunately, he was a quick study," she added, lighting up. "He was a good man. A very good man."

"Yes, he was."

"That's the main thing," Selma said. "We need more like him."

"We do," John said, handing Selma the hanger with the rest of the ties. It was excruciating to think of Katya spending the rest of her life with that man. "I'll enjoy wearing these. They'll make me think of Barney. Thanks, Selma. It's an honor."

"Coffee?" Selma laid the rest of the ties on the suit pile.

"Sure."

"I can't get used to saying President Johnson," Selma said as they walked downstairs.

"So sad, isn't it?"

"I loved President Kennedy," Selma said, putting up the water to boil. "He had energy and glamour. And that Jackie. What a lady."

"A national tragedy," John said. It wasn't supposed to happen that way—that one man with a gun could submerge the country into grief.

"I should ask how you're doing," Selma said, putting out cups and saucers.

"I'm fine."

"I have to say, you look like hell."

"Gee, thanks, Selma." He took out the milk and sugar and sat down.

"I have a feeling it's not just the assassination," she said, opening a tin of rugelach.

John looked at her.

"Or Barney. Although I know it's hard for all of us." How did she soldier through, as generous and selfless as always? She must be terribly lonely.

"I'm okay," John said.

"Son, it's written all over your face."

"Eagle-eye Selma. Who's the psychiatrist here anyway?"

She laughed. "It's about a girl, isn't it?"

He nodded, choked up over a ballerina of mythic talent and beauty, whose discipline derived from a calling as compelling as prayer: to dance.

She'd sent a note he kept in the breast pocket of his jacket, guarding it like a talisman, as if it were too sacred to leave on his bureau at home and too prized to leave on his desk at work. A card that defied response, enclosing a single white rose petal from his Paris bouquet. *I want you to have this*, she wrote. *Because only you know what it means to me.*

"Well?" Selma said, pouring the coffee.

"It was fated not to be," he said, a single tear falling down his cheek.

Katya lay on the floor to warm up.

"We'll have Katya dance Discipline in Stuttgart," Mr. Yanakov said to Worthington.

"Actually," she said, sitting up, "I'd like to try Memory."

"Why bring that up now?"

"I'm game," Worthington said.

"You've mastered Discipline," Mr. Yanakov said. "You did a fine job in Paris."

"Time for a new challenge." Katya stood, picked up her left foot, and squeezed it behind her knee. "How about…I dance Discipline in the first act, and Memory in the second."

A smile spread across Mr. Y's face. "She comes up with some good ideas, doesn't she?" He started laps around the studio, waving his arms and talking to himself.

"Memory lifts the three spells," Mr. Yanakov said. "But not completely. So Song has her melodies restored, but she tends to impart melancholy. Discipline is separated from the Old Faun," he went on. "But not exactly. The Old Faun needs Discipline, so she's elevated from supplicant to partner."

He slowed his pacing.

"Song and Discipline are allowed to reconnect." He stood still and looked at Katya. "But only briefly and at a high price—they must each take part of Memory's burden and carry it for the rest of time." He fell silent.

"About the ending," Worthington said. "I did some research and couldn't find a thing about three muses."

Mr. Yanakov laughed. "That's because there's nothing to find."

"What?" Katya said.

"Well, we have three muses," Mr. Y said. "They come to us through history from Boeotia in ancient Greece." He gave a mischievous grin. "But there's no story attached."

"Are you serious?" Katya asked.

"Someone had to make it up, didn't they?" Mr. Yanakov said.

THREE MUSES

...or music heard so deeply
That it is not heard at all, but you are the music
While the music lasts. These are only hints and guesses,
Hints followed by guesses; and the rest
Is prayer, observance, discipline, thought and action.

—T.S. Eliot, "The Dry Salvages," from *Four Quartets*

1973

The curtain dropped, and the audience rose to their feet, clapping and cheering.

"What did you think?" her grandmother asked.

"I liked it!" She stood on tiptoe so she could see through the people in front of her.

"Wasn't it a little sad at the end?"

She wiggled her loose tooth and shrugged her shoulders. "Maybe. I liked them dancing in bare feet. Grandma, here they come!"

"Yes, that's the curtain call."

She tried bowing and curtsying like the dancers onstage.

"Watch you don't bump the person next to you," her grandmother said.

The lights came up, and they started down the steps from the balcony. "Remember, company manners when we go to the stage door. You have to be very polite."

"You already told me that. So did Mommy."

"That shows it's important."

They walked around the edge of the theater and waited in the back lot.

"Will we get to see the people in the ballet?"

"Probably, but that's not who we're waiting for. We're looking for the lady who came out at the end for a bow, the one in the long black dress. This was a very special occasion for her. She put on this matinee as a memorial."

"You told me."

"Ready with your program?"

She nodded.

"Got your pen?"

"No, Grandma, you do."

They watched and waited. A few dancers came out, carrying their bags.

"Remember what you're supposed to say?"

The girl nodded again.

"Okay, here she is." Her grandmother pulled the single white rose that was sticking out of her purse and handed it to her. "Go ahead, dear. I'll be standing right here."

Katya Symanova came down the steps. She was very tall. The little girl skipped over and said, "Excuse me?" thrusting the white rose toward the ballerina.

Katya paused.

"My daddy said to give this to you."

Katya stopped and looked from the girl to the rose and back again. "That was very nice of you," she said. She brought it to her face and smelled it. "And very nice of him too."

"Would you mind signing my program?" She remembered that she was supposed to be polite. "Please?"

"Of course." Katya smiled and took the pen from her. "What's your name?"

"Maxine. Maxine Levin Curtin. Levin used to be my mom's last name. Know how to spell that?"

Katya's eyes widened. "Yes. I believe I do." She started to write something and stopped. "Who brought you to the ballet?"

"My grandmother," Maxine said, pointing across the lot.

"Do you think you could introduce me?"

"Grandma!" Maxine shouted.

"Shhh." Her grandmother put a finger to her lips and walked toward them. "How do you do," she said. "I'm Selma Katz." She extended her hand. "I'm so sorry for your loss."

Katya paused. "That's very kind of you."

"Can you sign my program now?" Maxine asked again, jumping up and down.

"Patience, dear! And say please." Selma put her hand on Maxine's head. "Her motor runs day and night, but she's my best little girl, aren't you?"

"That's only because Barney's a boy." Maxine looked at

Katya. "Grandma can say that because he's my little brother. Otherwise, you're not allowed to play favorites."

"I see."

"Maxine," Selma said. "Please give Miss Symanova a minute."

Katya took a tissue from her pocket and dabbed her eyes. "I'm so glad your grandmother brought you today," she said to Maxine.

"Me too!"

Katya opened the program and thought for a minute before signing it: "To Maxine, with love from K.S. Remember to sing and dance."

Katya watched Maxine skipping away, Selma calling after her to slow down. Maxine was clearly a happy little girl.

John was the father of two children. He must be well.

How generous to have sent his daughter. Maxine was a peek into his current life. Perhaps the injury Katya had caused had been subsumed into something greater. She took it as an intimation of grace.

The memory of him was an ache that had been smoothed out by time, but more so by her acknowledgement that his feelings for her were life-sustaining—a wellspring—and that her feelings for him were akin—an affirmation that she had the capacity to love and be loved.

She wished he had come today. But she understood that he could not. For what was between Katya and John had no place to land.

She considered this afternoon's performance. *Three Muses*. It had gone off all right, even well. There was liberation in her choice of bare feet and tunics, a quiver of satisfaction in overruling what she knew would have been Mr. Y's strenuous objections.

Boris Yanakov had been cut down seven months earlier by a heart attack. Consistent with his impassioned nature, his ending was abrupt and dramatic. It was closing night in Moscow; the

New York State Ballet was on tour. In the midst of proclaiming himself a victim, President Nixon had discovered that cultural détente earned him positive press. The tour was a distraction from Watergate's tightening grip.

Katya had just finished a solo when she registered a thud she took to be falling scenery. She swept into her curtsies and hurried offstage to change.

It was apparent that something was horribly wrong. Soviet medical personnel were pushing their way through a crowd in the back corner stage right. Lars threw on his coat and plunged through, Katya just behind, standing *en pointe* for a clearer view.

Good God! They were setting up a human barricade around Boris Yanakov. A police officer barked orders in Russian as several burly men gathered around to pick him up. "Let me go with him!" Katya shouted, trying to elbow in.

Lars shouted over the heads of the surrounding dancers—"Mark, you're on!" He ran after Mr. Yanakov and disappeared through the stage door, trailed by a line of police.

Katya was frozen. For a moment, the world went silent, as if the theater had abruptly emptied.

"Miss Symanova, you have to change," the wardrobe mistress said. She wrapped her arm around Katya and rushed her to the dressing room.

Katya twisted around. "I need to go to the hospital," she said, pleading.

"Dance for him," the wardrobe mistress said. "He would insist."

The last *pas de deux*, the end of the program. The audience was delirious.

Dropping her head for a final curtsy, Katya felt a streak of pain—her muscles on fire, her joints swollen to bursting—and knew that Boris Yanakov was dead.

What did it mean to live without him? Katya had been his other half for most of her life. They were conjoined, congruent. He was synonymous with ballet. She felt like a character in a story of his making, a story that was folding into itself. She had not been with him at the end; she had not said goodbye.

What remained were the rote, physical demands of her profession. She went to class; she worked out. The studio was an airless cube, her body stripped of emotion. Despite the kindness of company members, she was acutely sensitive to the conflicts Boris Yanakov had aroused, as well as her own ambiguous, privileged position.

Occasionally she remembered she was responsible for Mr. Yanakov's work. She wondered just what that meant, other than an arduous duty to wear him for the rest of her days—the difficult, along with the wondrous—whether she wanted to or not.

She was not alone in recognizing her responsibility. The New York State Ballet's board of directors did as well, and insisted she plan a memorial.

As she stood outside the Peter Stuyvesant Theater contemplating the events of the day, Katya realized she felt uplifted for the first time since Mr. Yanakov's death. Was it because the obligation to serve as his memory would slowly disperse her anger? At him? Maybe the obligation to serve as his memory could diffuse sorrow, so that it was spread to nothingness by wind and time.

And yet.

This afternoon, she'd glimpsed a path forward.

In life, Mr. Yanakov's ability to express himself was limited to the colors he mixed in the studio. He was not a man who trusted other people, and he was not a man to be trusted.

In death, his palette covered a broader spectrum.

Katya was starting to see the significance of his legacy. Her body was aging, and her appearances would dwindle. In summoning the means to express what he felt for Katherine Sillman, Boris Yanakov had left Katya Symanova the fulfillment of her calling. Her chain of performances—stretching back to her teens—felt like one grand rehearsal for this afternoon, her debut. Mr. Yanakov had bequeathed the certainty that dance would anchor her life, and the chance to share her artistic vision with the world.

The opportunity felt boundless.

Finally, to become herself.

Katya twirled the white rose between her thumb and forefinger—its velvet petals, tips edged in pale pink; its pleasing form, balanced and poised on its stem. She brought it first to her heart and then to her lips. Then she took a deep, slow breath, and luxuriated in its exquisite scent.

The partially opened bud would bloom and flower in full before it, too, floated away.

PERMISSIONS

AUTHOR'S NOTE

Two people of blessed memory helped inspire *Three Muses*: Henri Parens and Ellen Boucher.

It was a stroke of grace that at age fourteen, I entered the orbit of Dr. Henri Parens (1928-2022), who became a prized mentor and friend. His extraordinary life—his flight to France from his childhood home in Belgium; his mother's insistence that he run away at age twelve to save his life; her murder in Auschwitz when he was thirteen; his journey to America as a young teenager; his talent and love for singing; his creation of a warm and loving family; and his career as a world-renowned psychoanalyst, scholar, teacher, and healer, helped inspire *Three Muses*. And yet. The story of *Three Muses* is fiction and bears virtually no resemblance to his. Dr. Parens wrote a powerful memoir, *Renewal of Life: Healing from the Holocaust*, Schreiber Publishing, 2004, as well as a companion volume, *Meditations While Healing: Further Thoughts on Renewal of Life*, Shengold Publishers, 2020.

My treasured cousin, Ellen Kaufmann Boucher (1920-2014), grew up in Mainz, Germany and escaped to America in 1937 with her grandmother (my great-grandmother). The rest of her immediate family was gassed at Auschwitz. Ellen wrote a wonderful memoir for her children and grandchildren that she generously shared with my family, called *Granny's Memories*. Many of Janko's childhood memories of Mainz come from Ellen's fond recounting of growing up there. So too, Mutti's *gugelhupf* was inspired by Ellen's delicious baking. After her death, Ellen's children donated her papers to the U.S. Holocaust Memorial Museum.

Having served in Europe and been wounded in the early days of the Battle of the Bulge, my father, Seymour ("Spence") Toll, described to me the sleeping conditions on troop ships used for transatlantic crossings in the 1940s. I borrowed from his description for Janko/John's transatlantic crossing. Any errors are mine.

The story of Janko's first encounter with an orange was adapted from an experience of the late Congressman Tom Lantos of California as recounted in: *Against All Odds: Holocaust Survivors and the Successful Lives They Made in America* by William B. Helmreich, Transaction Publishers, 1996.

Portions of *Three Muses* were published as excerpts in: *Poetica E Magazine*, *Slush Pile Magazine*, *Vol. 1 Brooklyn*, and Yale's *Letters Journal*.

ACKNOWLEDGMENTS

Three Muses is dedicated to my amazing parents, Jean and Spence Toll, who were passionate lovers of the written word; and daunting, unstinting critics of my writing by the time I reached seventh grade. They made their vast curiosity and passion for language core family values.

My mother was a professional editor and copyeditor whose skills were formidable. In addition to completing a steady stream of book editing assignments, she compiled and edited two brilliant encyclopedias of voluntary organizations in Montgomery County, Pennsylvania, and Philadelphia. She was a poet with a delightful ear for doggerel, and a reader of wide-ranging taste and depth. Most of all, she was the spectacularly competent chief executive and manager of a busy family of six. She was tireless in seeing to her four daughters' cultural education. To that end, she introduced me to ballet at age four. When I became smitten, she entered me into the School of the Pennsylvania Ballet (I have no idea how she knew to do that) and lovingly ensured that I saw as many ballet performances as came to my hometown of Philadelphia. Although my enthusiasm far outstripped my talent, it was at that school that I received my ballet education and experienced the thrill of watching professional dancers rehearse.

My father was a superb writer, with a combination of wit, pith, and clarity that will always command my respect and envy. He was a voracious reader and polymath, as well as a captivating speaker, who deployed these sumptuous talents in a career as a trial lawyer and author.

I am thankful beyond the telling of it that both my parents encouraged me to write. Their belief in me is a sustaining, priceless gift. Other than legal writing, however, my mother did not live to see anything of mine in print. In the last decades of his life, I was extraordinarily blessed with my father's insistence to keep at it despite (the typical) mountains of rejections. There are no adequate words to acknowledge what this fountain of love has meant to me.

It doesn't take a village to write a book, it takes a metropolis. I started working on *Three Muses* in 2010 and am the grateful recipient of guidance, mentoring, and support from a wide and loving community.

Boundless thanks to—

Regal House Publishing for awarding the 2020 Petrichor Prize for Finely Crafted Fiction to *Three Muses*; Jaynie Royal for welcoming me into the Regal House family under her impressive leadership; Pam Van Dyck for her help, patience, skill, wisdom, and generous editorial guidance;

The terrific team who helped launch *Three Muses*: Dan Blank and Beth Parker;

The Virginia Center for the Creative Arts for nourishing me during two major revisions of *Three Muses* in 2017 and 2018;

Anne Morin, Eve Wildrick, Alan Morrison, and the board and staff of the Butler Family Fund, as well as the extended Butler family, who gave me a deeply meaningful career in social justice, and just may have seen where my writing life was going before I did;

Ellen Silva for opening the door to book reviewing;

David Stewart and Holly Smith for providing early book reviewing opportunities at the *Washington Independent Review of Books*;

Paul Harding and my Tin House Summer Workshop classmates who not only gave me invaluable feedback, but also a joyous first experience in an immersive writer's workshop;

Brian Hall and my Colgate Writers' Conference classmates;

The March 2019 Monson Arts Residents;

The editors and other professionals whose wise counsel made *Three Muses* a stronger book: Susanna Einstein, Gràinne Fox, David Groff, Jane Rosenman, Pauls Toutonghi;

The extended Toll-Barth-Grossberg family for their

encouragement and interest, including and especially, my elders of blessed memory;

My sisters, whose support means so much: Emily Toll, Elizabeth Toll, Connie Toll;

Readers and commenters on early fragments of *Three Muses*: Dave Beckwith, Cary Bricker, Marni Graff, Lauren Deimling Johns, Hugo Quené, Molly Rauch;

Emily Hauser (then a graduate student in classics at Yale) and Hugo Quené for helping to suss out information about the "historical" three muses (there wasn't much!);

Jonathan Huston for help with German (any errors are mine);

Readers who generously read the full manuscript and made it better: Frances Bennett, Jan Charone-Sossin, Ruth Goldway, Elizabeth Grinston, Jessica Krash, Anthony Pipa, Rima Sirota, Alice Stephens, Ericka Taylor, Annet Westhoek;

Dr. Nathan Kravis who read *Three Muses* in manuscript not once, but twice, to check for accuracy in John's psychiatric training (any errors are mine);

Cherished couples circling the globe for their continuous and generous interest: Elizabeth Grinston and Simon Rice, AnnJ Gumbinner and David Lauter, Hugo Quené and Karin Wagenaar, Marjolein Quené and Henk Westhoek, Rima Sirota and Tom Rosenstiel;

Three fantastic groups of women I have been so fortunate to be part of: Sunday's Readers, Michelle Brafman's Glen Echo writers, Jean Graubart's summer writers retreat;

The constellation of remarkable women who have been by my side during this long journey which also includes: Peg Romanick Allen, Dawn-Michelle Baude, Debra Benator, Helena Campbell, Sharon Charde, Sue Chinn, Tanya Coke, Rubie Coles, Nadia Ghent, Amy Gottlieb, Lisa Hochstein, Ruth ("Tiny") Hoffman, Lynn Kanter, Aliza Kaplan, Jessica Krash, Lisa Lang, Kirsten Levingston, Laura McBride, Gwendolyn Mok, Randon Billings Noble, Martha Plotkin, Sejal Shah, Kathy Sommer, Ericka Taylor, Johanna Wald, Mary Kay Zuravleff; and three women of blessed memory: Allison Ranelle Brown, Virginia Rutledge, Deborah Visser;

Jane Stewart whose musical expertise, copyediting skills, and caring heart combine to make her my ideal reader, trusted editor, and beloved friend;

Cary Bricker whom I was lucky to find in law school, Rachel Cavell whom I was lucky to find when we worked together as paralegals, Naomi Goldstein whom I was lucky to find in college, and Julie Langenberg whom I was lucky to find at age four;

Liz Kislik and Nancy Liebermann for more than they know;

The deeply valued people not named here who have so greatly enriched my life; and

My daughters Lila Becker and Naomi Becker and my husband Dan Becker—without whom, nothing.